Kawaihae Killer
A Barefoot Sleuth Cozy Mystery

Christine Wellert

DreamLifeBooks Publishing

Also by

Barefoot Sleuth Cozy Mystery Series:

Beach Club Bloodshed
https://a.co/d/exE7kOG

Waikoloa Warfare
https://a.co/d/0533MzrY

Contents

Chapter One

SUMMER

"MY HAND IS SLIPPING; I can't get a hold of him!"

"Just hold on a little longer, I almost have it." I tried to smother my irritation as I threw a tight smile in Elliot's direction.

He glared back at me. "Hurry, otherwise, we're going to have guts spraying everywhere!"

Bright red sticky blood started oozing out around Elliot's hand, forming a web-like pattern as we both stared down at it in horror.

"Shit! We're losing him!" Elliot's panicked eyes bored into mine.

My heart was running an Usain Bolt race inside my chest.

"I'm trying!" I yelled as I used the last of my strength to slide my hand underneath the body and drag it the last few feet to the dumpster.

Elliot held steady pressure over the gaping hole while I dropped legs that were heavier than they looked, and I hunched over, my hands on my knees while I caught my breath.

"We are going to be in so much trouble for this." Elliot's voice trembled.

Nodding in agreement, I sighed and looked down at the body in front of us. Just over five-foot tall, smooth skin, naked as the day he was made. My eyes caught on his nether regions. Jesus. Maybe it was better to end it for him.

"On the count of three you're going to reach both hands underneath, and we're going to heave him in, okay?"

"Blood's going to spray all over the place if I let go," he whined.

"Do you have any better ideas? Besides, this is all your fault. If you hadn't stabbed him, we wouldn't be in this mess!"

"It was an accident. How was I supposed to know this would happen?"

"Grrr," I growled, still winded from dragging the body all the way from our condo to the dumpster. "Let's just get this done already. If you get covered in blood, it's your fault." I blew out a frustrated breath. "Ready?"

He glared at me but nodded and reached underneath the torso, curling his right hand up and around in order to keep pressure on the carotid artery.

"One, two, three!" We tried to lift him up, but the sucker was heavier than he looked. I should've guessed that from the effort it took to drag him over to the dumpster. We had him at about waist height when Elliot's hand slipped off the artery and the bright red, viscous, corn syrupy-like blood started spraying everywhere. My hands started to slip, and Elliot's side dipped low as he tried to avoid the spray.

"Lift!" I hollered.

Somehow, we managed to get the body up and over the lip of the dumpster; it made a loud thunk as it hit the bottom. We could hear the faint sizzle of blood spray hitting the inside walls.

"That's going to be fun when the sanitation guys pick it up on Thursday. Wonder how many reports will get made," Elliot mused, his glasses covered in blood, his Nico Santos-inspired hairstyle destroyed. Ever since a guest at his work commented how much he looked like the character Oliver T'sien from *Crazy Rich Asians* he'd worn his hair that way, although right now he looked like a bloody Chinese rooster.

"Hey, Summer!" a voice called from behind us.

We both turned, our eyes wide. *Busted.*

Our neighbor Harry stood in his red bathrobe, clutching a black and white kitten to his chest.

"This isn't what it looks like, Harry," I began.

He scratched his chin, the silver stubble on it patchy and thin, then lifted bushy eyebrows that reminded me of Santa Claus.

"It looks like you just threw a body into the dumpster and you got covered in blood in the process."

"Well, technically, yes, that is true." I shared a look with Elliot.

"He was a dummy though!" Elliot chimed in.

Harry's eyebrows rose even higher. "So you killed someone because they were dumb?"

I sighed, scrubbing my face with my hand. This day was not going as planned.

"No, what he means is that it's a mannequin. It's one of the practice dummies we use during lifeguard training." Sticky red fake blood dripped from my head onto my temples, making little rivulets down the side of my face. I swiped at it with my sleeve instinctively, then grimaced. The 'blood' used in the dummy was made of a substance that was virtually impossible to wash out of clothing.

"Hmm." Harry looked skeptical, and frankly, I couldn't blame him.

"It's true!" Elliot tried to smile charmingly at Harry, but the effect was ruined by the fact that his face was painted with red streaks, making him look like a serial killer ala *Dexter*.

Another neighbor came around the corner of the building carrying a bag of trash and humming. She looked up, staring at us in horror before dropping her bag and running back the way she'd come.

"Why don't we go back to your place and talk about this?" I suggested, mentally performing the countdown until I heard police sirens.

"Oh, no. You're not coming into my house dripping blood. No siree Bob. I've seen how those movies end," Harry said. He sniffed self-righteously. "And here I thought I might join your detective firm. If this is how you operate, I don't want any part of it." He tsked. "Of all people, I would think you would be above faking a crime scene just to get some attention."

With that, he flounced away, the kitten bobbing against his chest, his little paw sticking out and pointing at us accusingly. Yikes. Harry's feelings appeared to be a little raw still. When I asked him for some help on my last case, he proved to be more helpful than I anticipated. But since then, I'd let the ball drop on keeping in contact with him. I made a mental note to have coffee with him sometime in the coming weeks.

After coming on board to work at my dad's PI firm a little over a month ago, I'd fought to learn the ropes and gain some credibility. I watched as some of the credibility blew up in smoke as Harry hightailed it back to his condo, no doubt jumping on the old coconut telegraph to announce my latest screw up to whomever would listen. I blew out a breath as Harry disappeared into his condo after a last accusing look thrown in our direction. *I should've handled this situation differently.*

Murder, real murder this time, came to mind as I swung back towards Elliot. "This is all your fault. If you hadn't decided to mess with the dummy, we wouldn't be in this mess."

"My fault?" he retorted, his eyebrows scrunching together, his eyes narrow. "You're the one who brought the thing home in the first place. You're the one who said it was okay if I checked it out. How was I supposed to know it was so easy to puncture?"

"Easy? You stabbed it with an ice pick while gleefully yelling '"Take that, McClatchy!"' and laughing maniacally."

He puckered his lips into a pout. "I still can't believe they stopped publishing *In Touch*. How else am I going to get all the tea on Beyonce?"

A growl rose up in my throat, and I stared at the sky, hoping to find a measure of patience before I choked my best friend and roommate right there in the parking lot.

Sirens wailed in the distance. *Hmm...that didn't take long.*

An HPD squad car roared into the back parking lot and skidded to a stop right in front of us. An officer jumped out of the passenger side, his weapon drawn. "Freeze! Put your hands up!"

Elliot and I looked at each other. "Which is it? Freeze? Or put our hands up?"

It took everything in me not to reach over and pinch Elliot. His mouth was going to get us killed one day.

"It's okay, Lenny, you can lower your weapon. I know these two."

My eyes tracked over to the driver. "Cole! What on earth are you doing on patrol?" I sauntered over, letting my hips sway a little extra as he watched me with those turquoise blue bedroom eyes, a little smirk on his face, the brown hair curling at the collar of his uniform just begging for me to run my hands through it.

"That's it, Summer. Use your feminine wiles to keep us from wearing prison orange. I look terrible in orange," Elliot said, cheering me on.

I spared him a glance and threw him stink eye before turning back to Cole. Barely contained amusement played over his features, eyes twinkling and lips trembling from suppressed laughter.

When I was close enough to hug him, he stepped back. I frowned. Not exactly the response I was hoping for from my yummy detective boyfriend.

I wrinkled my nose at him and narrowed my eyes. "What?"

He cleared his throat. "Uhh, Summer, honey, have you looked in a mirror?"

Leaning forward to look at myself in the squad car side view mirror I let out a strangled squeal.

"Uh, boss, what should we do with the perps?"

Three heads swung over toward the officer, the peach fuzz on his upper lip glistening from sweat and pimples standing out against the flush on his face. He still held his service weapon, albeit now pointing down at the ground.

"You can stand down. Whatever these two are up to, I can just about guarantee it isn't illegal. Hairbrained probably, but not illegal."

"Hey!" I spun my head around.

"Yeah, hey! I take offense to that. Can't a person take out the trash without being accosted by The Man?"

I shot Elliot a glare. Really, that mouth of his...

Chapter Two

SUMMER

"Okay, so describe the exact look on Cole's face when he got out and saw the two of you covered in fake blood," Lani demanded.

She tucked her feet underneath her on the couch, looking like a tiny Hawaiian fairy with her big, almond-shaped brown eyes and halo of long curly brown hair framing her face.

Elliot handed her a cocktail, his latest creation. He'd been pumping both Lani and I full of different recipes over the last few weeks in preparation for a cocktail contest being held at the Fairmont Orchid.

Lani held up her glass, examining the cloudy blue liquid with skepticism. She raised her perfectly shaped eyebrow at Elliot.

"It's called an Ocean Cosmos. It has Blue Caracao, coconut cream, macadamia nut liquor, and a little bit of pineapple juice," he told us, holding up each bottle as he listed the ingredients.

Dutifully I took a sip, letting the liquid sit on my tongue for a minute before swallowing. Sweet, maybe too sweet, but with a luscious nutty, creamy finish.

Elliot watched both Lani and me expectantly, a look of nervous anticipation on his face.

Lani held her glass up after taking a drink, staring into it deeply before setting it down. "It's pretty good," she said.

"Pretty good? That's it? Not, best drink I've ever had, blew my mind?" Elliot started pacing. "Pretty good is fine when it's just you guys." I wrinkled my nose at him as he marched back and forth across our living room. "But the drink I create has to be a complete original, unequaled by anyone throughout the history of drink making." His pacing increased, and he started tapping his fingers together.

"Why does it matter to you so much, Elliot?" My question stopped his pacing, and he threw a vulnerable look in my direction.

"Because the prize is $5000, and I want to use the money to take TJ on a romantic vacation."

"Don't you think it's too soon for that? I mean, you guys just started dating like, what, a month and a half ago or something?" Lani said, voicing the same question rolling around in my head.

"You guys think it's too soon?" Elliot sounded genuinely worried as his brows knitted together, his hands clutched together in front of him. He'd waited a long time to find love, and I knew he and TJ were being very careful with each other.

"Have you talked to TJ about going on a trip? Maybe try asking him theoretically if he'd be interested and see what he says."

Elliot seemed to take my suggestion into consideration as he quirked his lips in thought. "You're probably right. It's just that he's so perfect, with that Lance Bass body and perfect hair and teeth. We'd make the most beautiful babies." He sighed and fanned himself.

"Umm, Elliot, I hate to break it to you but—"

He threw a kitchen towel at Lani. "Yeah, yeah, I know. But with future advances in modern science and the splicing of genes, who knows? Just let me have my little fantasy, okay?"

We were interrupted when the doorbell rang, just as my phone also chimed. I looked down at the Ring app on my phone, my eyes lighting up when I saw who was standing out front. I sprinted to the door and swung it open, then leaned casually against the doorframe, trying to hide the fact that I'd just sprinted for the door like the gate was closing on my flight to Heaven or something.

Cole grinned at me from the threshold then leaned in for a kiss, a heart-stopping, mind-melting kiss. I wrapped myself around him as he pulled me into his body. When we finally came up for air, I smiled up at him.

"Hello."

"I see you managed to get all of the blood off of you," he replied.

I narrowed my eyes at him. "That's your response after a kiss like that?"

He smirked down at me. That was another thing—he was tall, 6'3" of gorgeous muscle, tousled, collar-length, silky chocolate-colored hair with golden highlights from the sun. And I would be remiss if I didn't mention his perfectly shaped ass, which I now found myself caressing.

Where was I again?

"Once we don't have an audience, I'd be happy to show you in great, focused detail *exactly* what I think of our kiss," he answered back, his voice low and gravelly.

I spun around. Elliot stood watching, hands on his hips, his lips pursed like a disapproving auntie. Lani, on the other hand, was clapping and whistling enthusiastically.

"Yeah, yeah," I said, making shooing motions with my hands at them.

Cole snaked his arm around my shoulders and snuck in another quick kiss before following me into the living room. He took in the half-finished glasses and raised an eyebrow.

"Another candidate for the drink contest?"

Elliot nodded enthusiastically. "Yeah. You wanna try it? The girls aren't very good judges of what's good versus what's a masterpiece."

"Uhhh!" Lani and I both protested.

Sensing a war, Cole tried to diffuse the situation. "Sure, I'd love to try one. But Summer and Lani both have pretty good palettes for cocktails, so I'm sure they also have good feedback for you," he said diplomatically.

Rather than respond, Elliot just sniffed and disappeared into the kitchen.

"So, Summer told me all about her adventures today. I would've loved to have seen your face when you pulled up." Lani said.

His face lit up, a devilish twinkle in his eye. "It was something, alright. When the call came in I rushed over, worried that maybe something had happened to Summer, but as soon as I saw them, I knew." He turned his head toward Elliot, who had just walked in and handed Cole a glass. "You stabbed it, dude?"

Elliot shrugged. "It seemed like a good idea at the time."

Lani and I both rolled our eyes and Cole snorted.

"What on earth were you doing with the training mannequin in the first place?" Cole asked.

"Chief Kalepa has me doing the CPR certifications for all of our new recruits. The mannequin was malfunctioning during training, so I volunteered to take a look and see if I could fix it. Meanwhile, he got a replacement from the company, and since we didn't need the broken one right away, I decided to incorporate it into my Halloween decorations."

He quirked his lips and squinted an eye at me.

"I know, I know. Not the smartest decision. But how was I supposed to know old slasher here would go all Michael Myers on it?"

Cole smirked and Lani outright laughed at my naivete.

"Yeah, yeah." I fanned a hand at them before turning my attention toward Cole. "Why were you in a patrol car today? Is this some new torture Takada's thought up for you?"

Cole shifted in his seat and blew out a long sigh. "Yep," he said, his face pinched.

"What was his excuse for assigning you to a patrol car?" Lani wanted to know.

Silence blanketed the room for so long I thought he might not answer. Eventually he inhaled slowly and then exhaled. "He says he thinks maybe I forgot how to do basic police work. So, he's making me ride with rookies once a week and have them teach me how it's done."

My mouth dropped open in shock. "You can't be serious."

"Unfortunately, I am very serious." The set of his shoulders told me he'd rather talk about anything but this.

"Holy crap. Dude, that sucks. I'm so sorry." Elliot said.

Cole lifted his shoulders. "Honestly, I really don't mind that much. Someone needs to train these newbies and at least start them out on the right foot." He clinked the ice cubes in his glass and tightened his lips.

"So it's a good thing, then?" Elliot wondered.

"Let's just put it this way. I'm doing my best to make it a good thing. Jonah's had to pick up the slack on our cases when I go on my weekly patrol ride, though. It's not fair to him." Regret filled his face when he looked at me. "I might need to spend a little more time in the coming weeks at work trying to keep our cases moving in the right direction." His knee bounced, his expression tight. He didn't add anything more on the subject, so I let it go for now, promising I would circle back when we were alone.

Unsure how to navigate the minefield of Takada's continued torture of Cole, I changed the subject. "Looks like we might get a little window of good conditions if Hurricane Luisa stays south. The last I saw, the forecast said there'd be some intermittent wind and swells, but that's about it. I'm hoping since Dad doesn't have any new clients on the schedule I'll be able to get some diving in, especially since the next class I need to teach isn't for two more weeks. Since Chief Kalepa decided Brody needs to do all of the on-beach training at Beach Club I'm off the hook from having to run that, too."

Mauna Lani Beach, otherwise known as Beach Club Beach, is where I worked as a lifeguard intermittently. I'd reduced my schedule from full-time down to just shy of part-time once I started working for my dad at his investigation firm, TS Jenkins Investigations. I'd been able to navigate both pretty well so far, but it had only been a little over a month since the big change. A ribbon of worry wound its way through my brain about managing both though.

Currently, I was working under my dad's P.I. license as an investigative assistant, but when business picked up, I knew I might have to choose between lifeguarding and investigative work. Especially because the online classes required by the state for my P.I. license were only going to get harder. I was managing fine, but I knew that couldn't last. Not to mention, if I didn't get in the water at least a few times a week, I got really cranky, so balance was key.

At the moment my dad didn't have any new clients, so I had more free time than I was used to. Scuba diving was a passion of mine, but I hadn't been able to get out much recently between work and dismal ocean conditions. The forecast looked great for the next few days though, and I hoped to take advantage of it as much as possible.

"Actually, that was why I stopped by. My Navy buddy, Jeff, flew over from Oregon yesterday to run his friend's fishing charter for a little while. He wants the boat ready to go out by this weekend. Since he's new to this area, he had questions about the dive sites, and I thought you might be able to help. He asked if we could all have dinner together—he's hoping to meet the 'woman who snipped them and put them in her purse' as he likes to say."

Elliot snorted and Lani smirked. I narrowed my eyes.

Cole held his hands up. "Hey, his words, not mine."

"Hmm. I'm not sure if I even want to meet this douchenozzle now." I crossed my arms over my chest and lifted my nose in the air. The effect was ruined by Cole grabbing my waist and tickling me until I squealed.

"Don't worry, he's not all that bad. He just likes to give me a hard time. It's what we do." He paused for a second. "But don't go falling in love with him or anything, okay?"

I crinkled my nose and lifted an eyebrow in question.

"When we were stationed in San Diego girls always seemed to fall all over him. Any time a girl tried to get close to me, it was only to get close to him," he explained.

Elliot hooted. "Ahh, so you mean you weren't always the stud? Oh dear, how did your ego handle it?"

Cole shot Elliot an injured look. "I don't have a big ego."

We all snorted in unison, and he gave us all stink eye, one by one before sitting back in the couch.

"Well, not when it comes to my looks anyway."

He turned back toward me. "Will you go with me?"

Something about the way he asked, the glint of insecurity in his gaze gave me pause, but I answered, "Sure, I'll go. It'll be nice to meet some of your friends." I rubbed the back of his hand, sensing he needed reassurance.

Relief flashed across his face, and he smiled, a great big happy smile. My heart pitter pattered, and I answered his smile with one of my own.

Gagging noises from Lani interrupted our little lovefest, and I reached over to pinch her, but she easily evaded my reach, her little ninja moves carrying her across the couch and over to the kitchen.

"Who wants pizza? I'm starving!" she called, picking up the menu for Blackrock Pizza that we'd left posted on the fridge.

Later that evening, after everyone had gone home, I lay in bed and replayed my conversation with Cole. Something about it felt off; I just couldn't put my finger on why.

Chapter Three

SUMMER

BUTTERFLIES TICKLED MY STOMACH when the doorbell rang; I blew out a breath, saying a silent prayer that I wouldn't embarrass myself at dinner tonight. I'd never met any of Cole's friends before and I wanted to make a good impression, despite that whole 'having Cole's balls in my purse' thing. I smoothed the front of my dress one more time before opening the door.

Cole stood in the entrance, the scent of his aftershave tickling my nose, the ocean and pine scent calling to me like a nice juicy steak to a hungry dog.

"Did you just smell me?" he asked, his lips twitching at the corners, his eyes filled with laughter.

I wrinkled my nose at him and pivoted back toward the living room, but he grabbed my arm and pulled me in close.

"Uh uh, you can't escape that easily." He nuzzled my neck and ran his hands from just below my hips upwards, pausing with his thumbs just below my breasts. His eyes turned black, and I rose on my tip toes to give him better access. His interest became apparent as it pressed into my stomach, and I shimmied in even closer.

Just as things started to get really interesting, my phone started buzzing in my little silver purse, breaking the spell. We slowly stopped our exploration, his hands still cupping my ass as he pressed me against him. He gazed into my eyes, deep turquoise rimming the black pupils.

"Elliot's not home," I whispered, ignoring my phone and any rational thought that tried to penetrate my lust-fueled brain.

His grin was sinfully wicked, and we raced each other to my room, barely shutting the door before clothes started flying through the air.

Later, as we both lay snuggled into each other, laughing like loons, I heard a ding from the vicinity of Cole's dark green khaki shorts that lay strewn over my dress on the floor.

He grinned at me, but then his eyes shifted over to his shorts, and he grimaced.

"We should probably get going, huh?"

He nodded, then grimaced again, clearly reluctant to get out of bed. I kissed him and slithered out, grabbing my clothes, aware of Cole's eyes on me. When I turned to look at him, his eyes drank me in. My gaze traveled from his face down the length of his body, pausing mid-way through. My eyes widened in surprise.

"Already? How is that possible?"

He smirked.

I threw his clothes at him and scampered off to the bathroom to try to repair all the hard work Elliot had done before he left, but it was useless; my hair was a bird's nest with fine hairs flying all over my face. Eventually I gave up and just brushed it out as best as I could and threw it into a bun.

Cole was waiting downstairs for me, and his eyes flashed appreciatively as I made my way over to him.

"That color looks nice on you."

"Mmmhmm. You sure it's not the fact that my dress looks like it's practically painted on?"

"That too," he said with a twinkle in his eye, his grin wolfish.

On the drive to meet his friend, Cole seemed a little tense. He responded with one-word answers, his attention obviously elsewhere. I tried to draw him into the conversation. "Tell me more about your friend Jeff." Cole didn't talk much about his time in the Navy and I was curious to hear more.

He drummed his fingers on the steering wheel for a minute before answering. "Well, he's one of the best snipers I've ever met, pretty calm in tense situations, but he's got this sort of restlessness about him."

"What do you mean?"

He shrugged. "He just always seemed to be looking for the next bright, shiny thing. During our SEAL training, he would come up with these big elaborate pranks that pissed off our sergeant to no end. He never could figure out who was behind them." Cole smiled at the memory. "But, he took on every new specialty, went after every opportunity."

"Isn't that a good thing? Like, he's ambitious and wants to learn?"

Cole shrugged again. "You'd think so, but the way he went after everything, it was almost like he couldn't let anything pass him by. Like he was desperate to know it all. Drove the rest of us crazy. And he never slept. Even after BUDS he wouldn't need more than maybe four hours of sleep, and he'd still run circles around us."

Cole turned into the parking lot and backed into a spot before turning off the engine. "But hands down, he's the number one person I'd call for help if I needed it."

I nodded and started to get out but Cole growled, "Wait." He ran around and opened my door. I just shook my head at him, even though secretly it was kind of nice to be with such a gentleman.

He tugged me out and pressed his body into mine. "Just don't go falling in love with him, okay?"

Something about his tone caught my attention. Was he....*i nsecure?*

Before I could question him, a tall guy, even taller than Cole, whistled, and I watched as Cole's face broke into a grin. While they did that bro thing where they sideways hug with an arm folded in between them, I took the opportunity to check out his friend. Tall, slim but built. His chest filled out his aloha button-up and his tattoo-covered forearms showcased ropy muscles that made my heart pitter patter. I was a sucker for a good forearm.

"You gonna introduce me to your better half?" Glinting emerald-green eyes smiled at me in appreciation, and I reached up to fluff my hair. Cole frowned at me, and I dropped my hand.

Cole put his body in between us. "This is my girlfriend, Summer. Summer, this is Jeff. Behave yourself."

Giant hands encased mine, making me feel positively tiny and feminine. I'm pretty sure whatever aftershave he was wearing had pheromones in it because my skin broke out into goosebumps when I caught wind of it.

Jeff eyed me up and down and then tried to pull me in for a kiss before Cole intercepted him.

"Knock it off, Jeff." Cole sounded annoyed, his hands in fists at his side.

Jeff grinned unrepentantly at me, running a hand over his close-cropped brown hair, subtly flexing his biceps. "Just being friendly."

I smiled back at him. Cole cleared his throat and glared at us. If possible, Jeff's grin got even wider, his blindingly white teeth on display while a dimple on his right cheek popped out. He turned his gaze over to Cole and motioned toward the door. "C'mon. I got us a table already. It's in the back."

We followed Jeff to a table on the lanai, and I did my best not to notice how well his rear end filled out his shorts.

As soon as we sat down, a waiter came and handed us drink menus. The evening passed quickly, Jeff telling funny stories about he and Cole and their time in the Navy. Watching the two of them interact I sensed a deep bond, the type of brotherhood that I'd seen between my dad and his Ranger buddies when they got together.

"So, there we were, sitting on the tarmac, waiting for the next bird out of Somalia. At this point we'd been waiting close to twenty hours. Cole here decides it's not happening fast enough and comes up with a plan to masquerade as the U.S. diplomat's security detail. When his original detail starts questioning us, Cole flashes some bullshit badge at him that he bought off some kid at a market and tells him we're working with CIA and a high-level threat came in a few hours ago." Jeff shakes his head. "How he managed to get all eight of us on the plane still baffles me."

Cole snorted. "What baffles me is how you managed to sweet talk our CO out of throwing us in the brig."

Jeff sent him a shit-eating grin. I'm not going to lie; seeing Cole in this light made him even sexier to me.

"Do you want to check out the boat?"

Cole's question pulled me out of my head, where I had been wondering what a harem full of men would be like. I shook my head. No. Too much work.

"Huh?"

He repeated his question, Jeff watching me closely.

"Sure, why not?"

Jeff pulled out of the parking lot in a gray Ram 1500 pickup truck, the V-8 motor causing a shiver to run over me as he revved it. Cole noticed.

"Really?"

"I'm sorry. There's just something about that sound." I held my hands palms up as another delicate shiver danced down my spine.

He growled and ignored me for the short drive from Seafood Bar over to the harbor where Jeff's boat waited.

Jeff's boat was parked next to a large white sailboat owned by a mainlander who only came twice a year. One of my dive buddies once tried to buy it off the guy but no luck. On the other side sat a new boat, similar in size to Jeff's that I hadn't seen in the harbor before.

Cole whistled. "Nice set-up, man." He ran his hands over the fiberglass hull and teak accents. We hopped in, Cole helping me navigate the step down when my dress rode high up on my leg, Jeff watching with an appreciative glint. Cole caught him and narrowed his eyes.

Jeff held his hands up. "Dude, it's just that you have very good taste."

Slightly mollified, Cole motioned to me, and we followed Jeff as he gave us the tour. "It's a Regulator 41. She's got quad Yamaha 425 XTO's with 1700 ponies and all the power I need. She can go through some gnarly waters and skip right along."

I tried not to drool at the sleek deck with a center console and a tower with a hard top and bench seat. There was a nice little cabin with a small bedroom and galley combo and even a miniscule bathroom below. Above deck he had the boat outfitted with a Garmin GPS MAP 8617, a Fusion stereo unit, and an autopilot setting.

"Looks like you've got a great setup here, man. How long are you going to be on island?" Cole was practically drooling as he caressed the instrument panel.

"A couple weeks for sure but maybe up to a month."

"Your work let you take that much time off? I'm jealous," I blurted out.

Jeff turned to me. "I'm in between jobs at the moment, so it worked out." Something in his tone seemed off.

I cocked my head. "Oh, what kind of work do you do?"

"Just some odd jobs here and there right now," he replied before spinning around and leading us up to the stern of the boat and handing Cole something shiny. I leaned in and peered down at it. Cole held a knife; the silver blade etched with Cyrillic letters and an emblem of an eagle.

Quiet stretched out over us, and I watched Cole's face change from light-hearted, to serious, to sad. He sighed and looked up at Jeff, something indefinable in his eyes.

"Where'd you find it?"

Jeff fiddled with the fishing pole closest to him for a moment before answering without looking up. "Bulgaria. Just found it a couple weeks ago."

Chapter Four

SUMMER

NEITHER COLE NOR JEFF offered to enlighten me about the knife. Nothing more was said about it, and the silence stretched out uncomfortably. Before I could work up the nerve to ask what it all meant, a figure in the sleek boat next to Jeff's called over.

"Hey, Jeff. Did you see the forecast for tomorrow?" The figure moved into the light. A male, probably early 30's with short dark hair gelled to the side and shiny gold jewelry winking up at us stood there, a friendly smile on his face.

Jeff lifted his head and sent what looked like a forced smile in the guy's direction. "Hey, Kevin."

The man's eyes skipped over the three of us and immediately apologized. "Oh, sorry, I didn't see you had company."

Jeff waved off his apology. "No worries, man. This is my friend Cole and his girl, Summer."

Kevin nodded and said, "Hey," before turning back to Jeff. "It looks like the swell might be dying down. Diving should be good. Hopefully you'll get a good start in the morning with your charter."

My ears perked up at the word diving. "Are you a diver?"

Kevin nodded. "I've been diving since I was a little kid."

He gestured over his shoulder at the gleaming catamaran. I didn't know a lot about boats, but I'd drooled over this exact model when a friend of mine, Ty, was looking into starting his own diving and fishing charter business. The cost of a boat like that was eye watering. The $800,000 price tag wasn't exactly in Ty's budget, but it was fun to dream. Kevin and Jeff's boats bobbed up and down in the water next to each other, their nearly identical towers glistening in the waning sun.

"Came into some family money and decided to open my own dive operation. But unfortunately, I'll be driving the boat tomorrow, not diving."

My eyebrows rose. "Wow. It's pretty tough to not only get permits but also get a slot in the harbor for a boat of this size. Some friends of mine have been waiting two years to get one. Basically, someone has to die to nab a spot."

Jeff cleared his throat, and he looked distinctly uncomfortable while Kevin's face went from open to shuttered. "Uh, yeah. That's how I got my spot in the harbor. My uncle died."

Shit. "Oh, I'm so sorry." My words sounded lame even to me.

Kevin shrugged. "It's okay. We were really close when I was a kid, but once he moved to the islands our family couldn't afford the cost of airfare to visit him and we lost touch. I didn't even know he died until I got the notice that he left me his slip here in Kawaihae." He looked off into the distance and drew in a breath. "He never had a wife or kids, so I guess he decided to leave everything to me. The boat's been in drydock over in Maui for a few months now, and I'm looking forward to getting her out on the water."

Awkward silence filled the space. *Score one for me and my big mouth,* I thought.

Cole must've sensed my embarrassment. He put his arm around my shoulder and pulled me close. Either that or he was staking his claim; Kevin had thick brown hair ala Prince Charming, along with a physique carved from a lot of hours at the gym. He looked to be just over six foot tall with a bright white smile and little crinkles at the corners of his chocolate brown eyes. That reverse harem idea crossed my mind again, but I shook my head. Kevin was a little too polished for my liking.

Jeff broke the silence. "You got a charter lined up for tomorrow?"

Kevin nodded. "Yeah, a group of four. Sounds like they're pretty experienced which should help. My divemaster is new to the area and is still learning the sites."

"Oh, who's DM'ing for you?" I asked. The diving world was pretty small on the island.

He threw out a name, and I cocked my head. "Huh. They must be new; I don't recognize the name."

"Yeah, he just got to the island a month ago. He has really great credentials. He's dived all over the world and has close to four thousand dives logged, so I think his skills are solid." He looked at me closer. "I'm guessing you're a diver?"

"Yep. I sometimes work for Kohala Divers when they need someone to fill in."

"You looking to supplement your income at all? I could use an experienced DM from time to time."

Cole stiffened next to me, and I turned to look at him quizzically before answering. "Uh, my plate's a little full right now. I work for the county lifeguarding and my dad's business part-time."

"Well, if you change your mind, I could really use the help. Pay's really good compared to the other outfits in town."

I nodded noncommittally and took the card Kevin seemed to pull from out of nowhere. I'd seen a lot of small business owners come and go on the island. Once they experienced their first slow season and realized running a charter here required patience and perseverance, not to mention very deep pockets, they typically bailed.

"Why don't you hop on board and check out my set-up? Make sure I'm not missing anything."

My curious nature took over, and we all tromped off Jeff's boat and hopped onto Kevin's. Behind me I could hear Cole muttering, "Why don't you hop on board and check out my set-up?" in a high-pitched mocking tone.

I grinned. I probably shouldn't take as much joy in Cole's jealousy as I did, but it was more amusing than anything.

Kevin showed us the bench for divers to gear up on, along with the camera station, weights cubby, a spacious head, and hot showers. From what I could tell he'd spared no expense, down to the yellow rubberized weights that went all the way up to thirty pounds.

"Wow, you must have some big boys on boat for that much weight," I commented.

"Do you think I went overboard? I wanted to cover all my bases, just in case." He looked a little uncertain.

"I think you've got a really solid setup here. Maybe the only thing I might add is a dry area for bags and things."

Kevin seemed to take in my words before nodding. "Yeah, that's a good idea." He motioned to a space behind the captain's chair that could accommodate a big group of people. "Maybe I can put in a few benches and storage bins. Even a dry table."

My glance snagged on the clock shining at us from the captain's instruments panel. Knowing Cole had an early day tomorrow, I turned and tilted my head at the clock and raised an eyebrow in question.

Cole nodded and we said our goodbyes to Kevin and Jeff, with Cole promising to go fishing with Jeff soon. A boat was just coming in as we headed toward Cole's truck, and I recognized Mike, another dive operator out of Kawaihae.

He didn't have any clients on board which seemed odd. He noticed us and waved before tying up and jumping up onto the dock.

"Yo, yo-yo," he called out as he unloaded boxes from his boat.

"Hey, Mike. Howzit? I'm surprised to see you out here so late," I said. The sun had long ago sunk behind the horizon, and the stars were stark and bright in the moonless sky.

He shifted from foot to foot and avoided my gaze as he responded. "*Moonshine* needed some repairs, and I wanted to take her for a test run before my charter tomorrow."

My gaze caught on the small black boxes and flickered up to the darkened sky then back to Mike, who was studiously avoiding my gaze.

Headlights swept the parking lot just then and washed over us on the dock; a gray Toyota Tacoma with a rusted front fender drove past.

Mike tracked the truck with his eyes before lifting his chin and darting away. "Later."

Weird. While Mike wasn't talkative to begin with, this seemed abrupt, even for him. I watched him head to his truck. The Tacoma had parked right next to him.

"Ready?" Cole asked, and with another glance back I nodded and followed him over to where he'd parked.

As we drove out of the harbor, I couldn't help but stare as Mike stood talking to the driver of the Tacoma. Something about the truck seemed familiar, but I couldn't put my finger on what.

"So, what'd you think of Jeff?" Cole asked, interrupting my train of thought. *Why was Mike acting so shifty?* I pulled myself back to the present and looked at Cole.

I waggled my eyebrows at him and pretended to fan myself. "Hubba hubba."

Cole's face got red. I took mercy on him before his head completely exploded.

"He seems nice, friendly even. But also, kind of distant. Like, for instance, did you notice that any time the conversation flowed towards him or his personal life, he deflected the question?"

Cole hummed low in his throat. "Yeah, I did notice that."

"And, when I asked what he did for work, he never answered the question?"

"I noticed that too. I'll admit, I haven't stayed in contact with him as much as I should have. It came as a surprise when he reached out and told me he'd be in the area."

He was silent for a moment. "It was good to see him, though." His voice was low and filled with some kind of emotion I couldn't place.

"What was that knife? You both seemed intense about it."

Cole swallowed convulsively and seemed to be collecting himself before he answered. "It belonged to a friend of ours. The knife was stolen off his body in the middle of the desert after a mission went south. Jeff made it his mission to find it."

"Wow." I really didn't know what to say.

Cole made a noise of agreement. "Taco had a son. Jeff's mission was to find the knife and give it to him."

Chapter Five

SUMMER

My vibrating phone woke me from a restless sleep. After Cole brought me home last night, I attempted to talk him into having a grown-up sleepover, but he shook his head regretfully (or so I liked to think) and said he had to be in Kona early for new recruit PT. Poor guy. Eventually his chief would get his due, but unfortunately, until then Cole had to suffer his wrath.

Lying in bed, my brain whirled like a Ferris wheel, round and round and never stopping on any one thing. My first impression of Jeff was that of a person who covered up his secrets with blinding charm. But behind that smooth facade, something unsettling seemed to lurk. He'd been evasive about his employment, which in and of itself didn't necessarily mean anything. But for a guy who seemed to have the resources to travel and freedom to come and go as he pleased, there had to be money coming from somewhere. I knew it wasn't any of my business—I just didn't want to see Cole hurt if this guy turned out to be bad news.

And then there was Mike. Something about him last night struck me as off. Why had he been out on *Moonshine* at night if he was testing repairs? Wouldn't he want to do that in daylight? The way he abruptly took off also puzzled me. He wasn't a talker to begin with, but even for him, his sudden departure came across as strange.

My brain was still trying to puzzle out where I'd seen the Tacoma parked next to Mike when I finally fell asleep. It was the insistent buzzing of my phone that woke me up. The screen flashed with Lani's name, and I hit the red button to connect when I noticed the time. Even for Lani it was early.

"Hey. What's up?"

Lani's voice sounded strained as she answered. "Dad wants to hire us. Old Otis Peaks is missing."

My mind struggled to place the name. Then it clicked.

"Crazy Otis from the harbor? How does your dad know him?"

Crazy Otis was a local legend. He lived in his van down near Kawaihae harbor. He moved it every few days in order to stay out of trouble with the cops and had a pet goat he'd tamed from the time it was a kid after its mom ran off. Otis dressed her up in cute little outfits and took her surfing almost every morning when the surf was high enough. Beloved by locals and tourists alike, he kept to himself and lived humbly. People brought him food and water all the time, and the veterinarian up in Waimea gave her services pro bono to Paisley the goat whenever it was needed.

"Yeah. Dad said they served together in Iraq."

"Wow. Dang. I had no idea. I hope he's okay. Otis is such a sweet guy. I heard he helped Malii out when she lost her housing and had to live in her car for a while. He's like the unofficial guard down at the harbor." Since Lani's dad didn't talk much about the war, I hadn't even realized he had a connection to Otis. Lani's dad was an Army guy, honorably discharged shortly after he came back from the Gulf War in '91. As kids we weren't interested in wars that happened before we were even born, but now I felt a tinge of regret for not asking. Although, knowing Mack he probably wouldn't have told us much anyway—he wasn't exactly forthcoming with words. Getting him to talk about virtually anything was like trying to pull a stubborn donkey uphill.

Lani made a noise of agreement and told me he wanted to meet us at the office this morning to discuss the case.

"Sure. What time?"

"He said he'd meet us right at 9 o'clock when we open."

My eyes flicked over to the digital clock on the dresser. Red digits stared back. 6:12.

Tamping down my frustration, I replied, "That works. But why'd you call me so early?'

I heard her snort. "Because your weak, defenseless ass needs more training. Get up. I'm waiting for you in the parking lot."

Curse words colored the air around me as my irritation took over. She just laughed and said, "I have coffee!"

Damn it. My kryptonite. There was no way I was giving in that easy though and she knew it. I growled in response.

"Auntie Miriam stopped by last night and brought me some of her butter mochi." The smugness in her voice exasperated me, but, hell. Auntie Miriam's butter mochi.

"I'll be down in ten."

She laughed. "Not a second longer or I'm eating all of the mochi without you."

My arms were limp and nearly useless as I drove into the office. Lani was a tyrant when it came to teaching me self-defense. What was worse was when she'd flip me over on the floor and then lean over me grinning, not a bead of sweat marring her smug face.

Most people would look at Lani and think she'd be an easy target. She barely topped five feet, her stature owing to her mom's Filipino roots, but everything else was pure Hawaiian on her dad's side, from her long wavy black hair, sultry chocolate brown eyes, to the perfect posture and sassy sway of her hips. She was a pint-sized Hawaiian Aphrodite, and all the men currently watching her progress as she sauntered over to the water cooler across the gym were under her spell.

Unless you pissed her off. And then she became more like the goddess Pele—vengeful, full of wrath, and relentless. Her dad had trained her in primitive survival since she could walk. Lani could disappear into the jungle for months, and not just survive, but thrive.

He also taught her mixed-martial arts. But what she loved best was fighting dirty. He taught her how to use every advantage she had, as well as create her own advantages in order to vanquish her foes. His words, not mine—he went through a whole *Game of Thrones* phase when we were in middle school.

At any rate, I did my best not to groan too loudly as I exited my car, a Rav4 my dad bought for me last month as a dangling carrot to get me to come work for him at his thriving P.I. business. He'd moved to the Big Island only a few months ago, but owing to a reputation for getting the job done quickly and discreetly, his business took off more quickly than he'd anticipated and he needed help.

Enter Lani and me. Full-time lifeguarding not only wasn't paying the bills, but it had ceased to fulfill me. When my dad's offer came up, it seemed like the best of both worlds. I could still work part-time as a lifeguard but also train under him to get my P.I. license. After four years I'd qualify to become full partner in the state of Hawaii, along with Lani, who'd also joined my dad's practice part-time.

Our office stood in between Surf Camp Coffee and a chiropractor's office. *Of who's services I'd likely need if I kept training with Lani,* I thought to myself as I pushed through our office doors and was greeted by the sound of tinkling chimes and a gentle waterfall.

Lani stood next to the giant potted monstera, watering can in hand. She looked up and smirked at me as I flipped her the bird.

"I'm not sure if the coffee and mochi were worth it," I complained as I collapsed into the office chair next to my desk.

"Better not let Auntie Miriam hear that or you may never get her butter mochi again," she warned, her eyes alight with mischief.

"The only way she'd find out is if your big mouth told her," I replied crankily. Then thought better of it. "Please don't tell her." I begged.

Her only reply was a sniff and a fling of her head.

My attempt to grovel was interrupted when the door swung open, Lani's dad filling the doorway. Makoa 'Mack' Kawikani Davis's Hawaiian ancestry was unmistakable—he stood a solid 6'7" with broad, muscular shoulders and a thick barrel chest. His expressive honey brown eyes took in the office with a quick glance before landing on Lani, his eyes softening.

"Good morning, ladies." His booming voice reverberated off the walls.

I rushed to give him a hug, beating Lani by a step and throwing her a look of triumph.

He enveloped me in arms the size of tree trunks, swallowing me completely, which made me feel dainty, especially considering I was 5'7" and built like a farm girl from Iowa, blonde hair and all.

"Summer. How's my girl?" he asked, his words sounding like music as he spoke.

"Good. I'm glad to see you, even though the circumstances aren't the best."

He nodded and let me go to wrap Lani up in a bear hug. He murmured something too low for me to hear and then got down to business.

I think Otis is dead."

Chapter Six

SUMMER

"You're going to have to dive for the mooring, Summer," Ty called to me from behind the captain's chair.

Nodding, I motioned to him the approximate location of the mooring before donning my gear and jumping in, the mooring line clutched in my hand. Fifteen feet down I spotted the tag line and threaded it neatly into place.

"Nice work!" Elias called down to me when I surfaced and handed off the line so he could secure it.

The next fifteen minutes were spent getting clients kitted out in dive gear and orienting them to the dive site. After our briefing at the surface, I took my divers down below the warm, crystal-clear waters of the Pacific and into a wonderland not many people get to see. As I led clients around, showing them the underground playground of colorful reef fish, like the rainbow-hued parrotfish and the spunky Humuhumunukunukuapuaa, Hawaii's state fish, as well as hard and soft coral, and the occasional, white-tipped reef shark, my mind wandered.

Mack's absolute belief that Otis was dead caused chicken skin to rise on my arms, even underwater. He said he didn't have any proof, just a gut feeling. Lani and I spent the morning gleaning every detail we could about Otis's past and why Mack was so certain Otis was dead. Not to discount Mack's gut, but we were hoping for something, some kind of proof, or even a line of insight we could follow to get clues about Otis's disappearance other than the fact that he hadn't checked in with Mack in a couple of days, and no one had seen him down at the harbor recently. He showed us the last text Otis sent him:

> **The fish aren't the only thing that smells around here—I think they're on to me**

I understood Mack's concern, but the text without any sort of context didn't really help. Lani and I took down the sparse information Mack had about Otis and started doing some research, but there wasn't much about him online.

When the call came in from Kohala Divers that their afternoon charter needed a DM, Lani encouraged me to go, saying she'd continue to research more about Otis. Uncertain about bailing on her but desperate to get in the water, I fidgeted, clearing my throat and shuffling back and forth to the window several times until Lani snarled and told me to just go already.

Now, as I floated sixty feet below the surface, reflexively pointing out nudibranchs and moray eels hiding in little hidey holes, I couldn't help but wonder where Otis had gone. Was Mack right—was Otis dead? A massive shadow passed overhead of where I and my divers were stationed, the hum of a powerful motor rolling over our location and we all looked up. The shadow moved quickly past us, engine roaring, leaving a wake that reached us even at sixty feet down, causing a swell to push us up and down in the deep water. Anger and fear washed through me even as I threw a reassuring smile to my divers. Thankfully, none of them were new divers and weren't likely to ascend without checking the surface first, but still.

Checking my divers' air supply, I motioned it was time to begin our safety stop at twenty feet and then head to the boat. Everyone nodded, but their eyes were wide. After our three minutes were up, I wrote on my slate for everyone to stay put while I headed to the surface to make sure the coast was clear. I deployed my surface marker buoy just to be on the safe side and swam perpendicular towards the boat, only surfacing when I was practically underneath it.

"Dude, what the hell?" I screeched at Ty.

He shrugged, eyes tight in a red, angry face. "I'm not sure, Summer." He clutched at his hair in frustration, causing little strands to stick up oddly. "I tried to get a description of the boat, but it was going too fast. All I saw was a white vessel with a hard top tower." We both searched the area surrounding us to ensure no more boats were nearby before I dove back down and motioned my divers to surface.

Later, Ty, Elias, and I debriefed up at the captain's chair on our way back to the harbor.

"One of my divers was low on air. I'd just sent them to their safety stop when the boat went by." Elias shuddered. "I can't even imagine what would've happened if they'd surfaced just then."

"I'll call it in to the Coast Guard once we get back to harbor. All I got was a partial description, though. I was unplugging the toilet—someone threw toilet paper in it again—when I heard it coming close. By the time I got to the top, all I saw was a blur of white and blue and a whole bunch of wake behind it." He shook his head. "Any captain worth his salt knows when the flag is up to give a wide berth."

We all glanced up at the dive flag, its white slash through red unmistakable to any captain, experienced or novice.

As we pulled into the harbor, I chatted with clients and tried to downplay the seriousness of what happened. Once we reached the dock and unloaded our clients, Ty, Elias, and I made quick work of offloading the boat and rinsing gear.

"I'm going to head to the shop and let Tracey know what happened," I told them after we were finished. They nodded distractedly; I shrugged my shoulders and walked across the street to the shop, the cheerful frog statue at the front bringing a smile to my face briefly until I thought about what happened on our dive. I filled Tracey in; she said she'd pass the info on to Kohala Divers' other captains to keep a look out.

Heading out to the Rav, I saw Ty and Elias deep in conversation near Ty's truck.

"Hey guys, I'm headed home. I'll catch you later."

Ty and Elias both jerked back and hurriedly shuffled some papers out of sight. Weird.

"Cool. Thanks for filling in." Ty shifted and darted a glance at Elias before smiling tightly at me.

Sirens sounded in the distance, and we all looked in the direction of the noise and saw red and white flashing lights and an ambulance racing toward the south entrance. Squinting, I saw a crowd of people waving at the ambulance.

"Hmm. Wonder what's going on?" I murmured.

Ty and Elias both frowned.

"Not sure, but you should probably steer clear," Elias cautioned. "You seem to have a knack for finding trouble, and that situation over there doesn't look good." He gestured toward the distant lot just as two cop cars drove in, lights flashing.

Elias's warning only served to pique my curiosity more. Waving goodbye, I hopped in the Rav and drove down to the south harbor entrance, laser-focused on the crowd of people surrounding a stretcher near the rocky edge.

As I neared, I saw three uniformed officers helping two rescue divers wearing helmets and carrying camera equipment pull a body up the boat ramp. My hands were clammy on the steering wheel as I watched the medics transfer the bloated body onto the waiting stretcher.

Parking near the bathrooms immediately adjacent to the rocks, I jumped out of the Rav and surged toward the stretcher. Before I could get a good look at the victim, the medics covered the body with a white sheet.

Two fishermen I didn't recognize stood near me on the rocks, fishing poles hanging limply at their sides.

"What happened?" I asked.

The man closest to me, leathered skin the color of weak tea, eyed me up first and then answered. "They found a body."

"Uh huh." I tried to keep the sarcasm out of my tone in order to not offend him and maybe get more information. "Do you know who it is?"

He shook his head and then spat a huge loogie toward the rocks.

Recognizing he wasn't going to be much help I walked casually closer to a group of teenagers perched on the rocks. One kid noticed me and jerked his hand behind his back before nudging his buddy and nodding in my direction.

"Crazy, huh?" I jerked my head toward the stretcher being loaded into the ambulance.

The boys just nodded in unison, sharing a glance with each other before ambling off without saying a word.

Even more curious now, I strolled over to the officers clustered near their patrol unit in the hopes of overhearing some of their conversation.

"Damn, what a way to go," an older officer, graying at the temples with just a slight paunch hanging over his belt uttered.

"Yeah. Can't even imagine." Another officer, his hair gelled back and deep brown eyes somber, responded.

A skinny, dark-haired officer spun in my direction suddenly. "Hey, aren't you Peterson's girlfriend?"

I yelped and unconsciously took a step back. Busted.

"Uh, yeah, I'm Cole's girlfriend." Which still felt weird to say. We'd only recently made it official, although in my mind it had become official the second he walked through my front door and accused my best friend of murder. I mean, that's not why. If anything, that would've been a huge red flag, but even though our first meeting hadn't been smooth exactly, there was something about him that drew me in. And that ass. Ahem...Where was I again?

One officer, the older guy, grinned, the other one tilted his head at me curiously, and the officer who asked shifted from foot to foot, excitement dancing in his eyes.

"Oh boy. We've heard *all* about you at the station. Did you really take out Gonzalez all on your own?" The officer, T. Lopez was the name etched on the patch above his right chest pocket, asked me, moving in a little closer. "I heard Chief was *pissed* that you solved Wainright's murder and made him look like a fool to the FBI."

Officer Lopez was referring to a murder investigation that originally placed Lani as the main suspect. Cole, Elliot, and I teamed up to find the real murderer after we realized Takada was targeting Lani instead of searching for the real killer.

"I heard Gonzalez was getting sent to Oahu for sentencing. With our luck, he'll be back out on the streets in a few months." The older officer, Sergeant Jessup, pinched his eyebrows together and shook his head. "We finally catch them, and then they lawyer up and get off when a sympathetic judge falls for their sob story."

Cold chills swept through my body. Gonzalez was bad news. He and his accomplice held Lani and I at gunpoint in my own home last month. He had a criminal record full of violence—and I had hoped they'd locked him up and threw away the key for life. If what Sergeant Jessup said was true, I'd have a target on my back the second they let Gonzalez walk.

A whistle pierced the air, interrupting our conversation; we all looked in the direction of the ambulance, where one of the medics stood. "We good to take him?" the driver called over to where we stood.

Sergeant Jessup nodded and the medic swung up into the cab of the ambulance and drove off.

"Any idea who the victim was?"

The officer standing near Jessup, who'd been silent up until now, eyed me up and down. "What business is it of yours?" The name on his pocket was Tolten. I didn't recognize him and he seemed oddly hostile toward me.

Bewildered at his underlying tone, I tilted my head and frowned before responding. "Just curious. It's not every day a body gets pulled out of the harbor, and I know a lot of the people around here."

"Why don't you leave the police work to the professionals. You've heard what happens to the cat when they get too nosy, right?"

"Is that a threat?" I asked, folding my arms over my chest and meeting the challenge in his eyes with one of my own, but inside I couldn't figure out why he seemed not to like me from the get-go.

Sergeant Jessup and Officer Lopez jerked their heads back and forth between us like they were watching a ping pong ball.

"Of course not. Just don't want you getting confused about your role, that's all." With that parting statement, he strode back to a waiting patrol car without a look back.

I watched him go, my forehead furrowing in confusion as I flicked my gaze back toward the other officers.

"Eh—Don't worry about him. He's just a bit of a stickler for the rules. He doesn't always understand how things are done here on island." Officer Lopez patted me on the back then meandered toward the patrol car as well.

Sergeant Jessup hung back. "Word is, something's going down in the department, and you and Cole are at the center." He kept his voice low, his eyes concerned. Chicken skin broke out on my arms at his words.

"A little friendly advice—watch your backs. Takada doesn't seem like the type to let things go, and rumor is he's building a band of supporters to do his dirty work."

Little gasps of breath escaped me and my heart pummeled in my chest like a swarm of angry wasps were trying to escape as I watched him pause to send a look heavy with meaning in my direction before stepping into his waiting patrol truck.

Chapter Seven

COLE

"Peterson, I want the Chun report on my desk in fifteen minutes!" Chief Takada bellowed at me from his office.

My fists tightened and I felt the pull in my back as my shoulders tensed. *Just hold on a little longer,* I told myself.

My partner, Jonah, shot me a look of sympathy before burying his head in the file sitting in front of him.

Choking down on my temper, I managed a forced smile and replied, "Sure thing, boss."

The look he shot me through the window of his office was half suspicious and half smug. *Good, let him keep guessing.*

Checking my phone for the thousandth time, I tried not to let my impatience show. My buddy Jack, FBI agent and all-around good guy, texted earlier telling me he had new evidence in the case against Chief Takada. He'd promised to fill me in ASAP, but so far, I'd gotten nothing but crickets from him.

Noise from the bullpen drew my attention, and I saw Sergeant Jessup, Officer Lopez, as well as the new guy, Craig Tolten. Tolten was a recent hire, and one who hadn't done much to integrate into the department. I knew as much about him now as I did on the day he started. *Well, that's not exactly true,* I thought to myself. I knew Craig Tolten's hiring process and background checks were pushed through by Takada.

"Hey, Peterson. We ran into your girl up at the harbor." Lopez sat on the edge of my desk and grinned. "She sure isn't hard on the eyes, is she? That long blonde hair, those big blue babydoll eyes, and that mouth—" He squawked like a rooster at the chopping block as I held my open cup of coffee over his head, ready to pour.

Sergeant Jessup just grinned while Lopez stuttered, desperately attempting to backpedal. "Uh, what I meant was, your girl seems really nice."

"That'll teach you, buddy. You can think it, but you don't need to say it out loud, especially to this guy." Jessup jerked a thumb in my direction.

Lopez gave me an ingratiating smile, and I couldn't help but quirk my lips at him. He'd been one of the recruits I trained a few years ago, and other than not knowing when to keep his mouth shut was a pretty good kid.

"She sure is a looker, though." Jessup grinned at me, unrepentant. "Good thing you have a couple days off, you seem...tense."

"Grrrr...." I growled, only causing him to grin even wider, if that was possible.

Jessup leaned in close to me and murmured, "Tolten riled her up some. She was pretty upset. You may want to give her a call."

Throwing him a grateful look, I quickly texted to see if she had a minute to talk. Jessup and Lieutenant Kregness had been buddies on the force for longer that anyone could remember. Kregness had been pivotal in helping keep me out of HR's crosshairs last month after I assaulted another officer who'd targeted Summer and attempted to use his badge to intimidate and harass her. Kregness also had suspicions about Takada and spent a lot of time and effort helping Jack build a case against him. Jessup was acting as backup while Kregness was out of town and keeping an eye on Takada from a distance.

My phone buzzed.

> **I'm in the middle of something—wanna come over for dinner and talk then?**

Unbidden, thoughts of our date the other night came to mind, and I couldn't stop the grin that spread across my face. Or to be more precise, what happened before our date. The reason Lopez got under my skin so bad was the fact that Summer was way out of my league and I knew it. I didn't know what she saw in me, but I'd ride that train for as long as she let me, maybe even for the rest of our lives if she was interested in that. *Whoa.* I wasn't sure where that idea came from, but I found I didn't object to it in the slightest.

After typing out a quick response in the affirmative, I locked back into Lopez and Jessup as a thought occurred to me. "What was happening at the harbor?"

Lopez hung his head. "Pulled a dead guy out. A fisherman got his boat stuck in low tide and saw a body at the bottom, half buried in muck, and called us."

"Yeah, it looked like he'd been in the water for a while," Jessup remarked.

Pursing my lips, I looked at Jessup with raised eyebrows. "That doesn't make any sense." Gases build up in a body during decomposition and cause a body to float pretty soon after drowning. Weird it hadn't floated to the top.

Jessup shrugged. "The body was bloated, and it looked like some critters had been at it." He shook his head. "Definitely not the way I'd want to go."

"Peterson!" Takada roared from his office, and I felt my pulse race. Lips pulled back, I bared my teeth in his direction, but he'd already turned his attention back to the computer screen in front of him.

As I stalked over to his office, file in hand, I counted to ten. When that didn't work, I pictured what it would feel like when Takada was removed from his position.

"What's with the stupid look on your face, Peterson?"

Snapping back to the present moment, I dropped the file on Takada's desk and answered him. "Nothing, nothing at all."

I whistled on the way back to my desk, my mood shifting into something lighter as I anticipated seeing Summer.

Jonah stopped me before I left. "You know the evidence Kregness passed on before he left on vacation? The drug boat?"

Jonah was referring to a boat that was found partially sunk up near Puako a couple of weeks ago. The coast was tricky up there—it went from 300 feet to twelve pretty quickly. The captain must've misjudged the depth and slammed into some submerged lava beds. A local swimmer called it in. Normally the Coast Guard would handle the case but requested we partner with them after they found copious amounts of fentanyl-laced heroin and meth on board.

Both the Coast Guard and HPD created a task force almost a year ago after a steady supply of both drugs found their way onto the island. We'd had more deaths related to drugs in the past year than we'd had in the last five combined. The governor requested we work in connection with the Coast Guard and TSA to combat the problem.

Unfortunately, it seemed after cutting off one head of the snake, several more grew in its place. Last month, Summer helped uncover a drug trafficking operation and we'd put several scumbags behind bars as a result. However, the tide of drugs hadn't seemed to ebb.

Several officers sat nearby. Kregness had asked us to keep the details under wraps as much as possible until he got back. Considering Chief had a roster of toadies on the force, Kregness thought the fewer people involved the better. I motioned Jonah outside. We stood under the eaves as the late afternoon rainstorm typical of Kona swept through.

"What did you find out?"

"Another boat, a RIB again, was found earlier today down near Puna."

"How long do they think it'd been down?"

He shrugged. "Best guess? Three or four days."

Hmm. The working theory was that the drugs were coming from Oahu, but if that was the case, someone had made a critical error. Ocean conditions for the past week made it virtually impossible for passage in a rigid inflatable boat, aka a RIB.

"Either they're getting stupider, or more desperate."

Jonah murmured his agreement.

"Well, thanks for keeping me updated. What do you think about heading over to Pahala on Monday and shaking some Bois out of some coconut trees?"

Jonah smirked. "Only if we can stop at the bakery on the way."

A snort burst out of my chest, along with a broad smile. "Dude." My mouth watered as I thought about the doughy, sugary malasadas that were a particular weakness of mine.

We parted ways, and as I drove my truck up to Waikoloa Village, my thoughts turned back to the sunken boats. Chief Takada had seemed reticent on spending time or manpower investigating them, which threw up a lot of red flags.

Out of the corner of my eye, I saw Chief Takada in the passenger seat of an older gray Tacoma with rust on the rims two lanes over. For some reason, my spidey senses were tingling—he'd been up to enough shady shit lately that my instinct said to follow him and see what he was doing. I turned my blinker on to change lanes, but before I could make a move, the light turned green and the truck turned into Honokohau Harbor. At the next light I made a U-turn and doubled back, then searched up and down all three parking areas, but the truck had disappeared.

"Son of a ..." I slammed my hand on my steering wheel in frustration. Takada was doing his level best to make my work life a living hell, and I wanted to catch him in the act of whatever he was up to and get him kicked out sooner rather than later.

Heading back onto the highway, all thoughts of malasadas disappeared as I speculated what he could have been up to at the harbor. Nothing good, if his past associations with the Yakuza and several members of the Bois was any indication. I just needed to catch him in the act next time.

Chapter Eight

SUMMER

ON MY WAY OUT of the harbor, I stopped at the Pua Kailima o Kawaihae Cultural Surf Park to say a prayer for the drowning victim. Woowoo or not, I felt compelled to grab a handful of sand and wade out into the ocean, letting the sudden breeze that came through carry the sand off into the sea. My hair lifted off my neck in the stiff breeze and low chanting seemed to fill my ears.

Startled, I looked all around me but didn't see anyone else nearby. Just as quickly as the wind started it ceased, the chanting along with it. Chicken skin broke out all over my body and I felt a lump in my throat, mourning the loss of someone I might not even know.

On shore, I slipped my sandals on and picked my way over the lava rock back to where I'd parked my car. My eyes strayed back toward the harbor, and I thought of Otis. If something had happened to Otis, where was Paisley? With a sinking heart and another glance at the harbor I decided to start searching the shoreline for her.

My sandals made a thwapping sound as I walked along the edge of the shoreline in the direction of Spencer Park. The waves were starting to roll in, washing over the trail in spots. Every once in a while, I'd spy what looked like goat tracks, but around this part of the island there were so many wild goats that I had no way of telling if they were Paisley's or not. Once I reached the edge of the county park, sweating, cranky, and irritated with myself for not grabbing a water bottle, I decided to call it a day. Huffing back up the trail toward my car, I berated myself for being so impulsive. I knew better than this.

Mid-tirade, just as I started to catalogue all the stupid things I'd done since the seventh grade, I heard bleating. A piece of fabric colored bright neon pink was snagged in a Kiawe tree adjacent to the trail, catching my eye. Curiosity along with a sense of dread pulled me in to look closer. The bleating increased, almost panicked sounding, and I threaded my way through the thorny Kiawe branches.

There, trapped between a web of Kiawe branches, pear cactus, and agave stood Paisley the goat, her fuchsia sweater tangled in the bushes. She bleated at me, a mournful look on her face, almost like she was asking me for help.

I waded into the mess, thorns grabbing at my skin, and unwound her sweater from the tangled branch it was stuck on. As soon as she was free, she bounded out of the bushy mess like the goat she was, while I painstakingly picked my way back out, managing to incur even more scrapes and scratches than on the way in.

Paisley waited, munching on the scant amounts of grass on the edge of the trail until I'd freed myself before coming over and nudging me gently with her head.

"Paisley, what on earth are you doing here? Where's Otis?" Although, with a sinking heart, I looked back at the harbor and knew.

Upon hearing the word Otis, she perked up and started prancing around wildly, bleating and kicking. I made sure to stay out of her way until she settled down. Even after she stopped kicking, her head pivoted around, scouring the land around us, eyes wild and desperate.

My heart thumped painfully. "Come on sweet girl, let's find you a safe place to stay for a bit." She followed me sedately, her little hooves soundless as she tromped over the gravel and sand path.

On our way over to the Rav, I made two phone calls.

"Hey Richard! It's Summer. Is Evelyn around? I need to ask a favor."

"Sure, let me put you on speakerphone." I heard shuffling, then Evelyn's bright voice, touched with a soft German accent, came on.

"Summer! I haven't heard from you in a while—how are you doing, love?"

"Good. Hey, I know it's a bit of an ask, but can you do me a favor? I found a domesticated goat down by the harbor and I'm afraid it's going to get hurt on its own. She's imprinted on humans so..."

"Oh, we'd love to take her! Nanny passed away a couple of months ago, and we miss having a goat around," Evelyn answered. I could practically hear her clapping in excitement.

"I can bring her up to you right now if that works."

Richard's deep voice answered. "Absolutely, bring her on up!"

"Be there in fifteen minutes," I replied before disconnecting and making my next call. The one I didn't want to make.

"Hey, Mack."

He didn't bother greeting me back. "It's Otis. I already know. A fishing buddy of mine called me from the harbor."

The coconut telegraph seemed to work faster than anything else on the island.

"I'm heading to the morgue right now to identify the body," his voice held dual notes of resignation and sorrow.

"Oh, Mack. I'm so sorry. Lani told me you two were in the Gulf War together. I know this must be rough; let me know if there's anything I can do."

He thanked me, and we hung up. My head was getting steamy from standing in the sun, so I looked over at Paisley.

"Wanna go for a ride?"

She tilted her head and looked at me curiously, watching as I folded the back seat down to make room for her. I patted the trunk and motioned for her to get in, eyeing her as she stepped forward to inspect the space. She looped her two front legs into the back and then seemed to give up. Shoving her didn't really help—if anything, she seemed to resist even more, letting her back end go limp and causing me to tumble on the pavement.

Just then Cole texted, but I had bigger fish to fry. Or goats at any rate. I asked him to dinner and smiled at his quick reply before turning my gaze over to the edge of the gravel pullout, where Paisley stood, munching on the tall grass.

"Come here, sweetheart," I crooned.

She lifted her head to stare at me before dipping back down to the smorgasbord in front of her. A lightbulb went on and I grabbed a bottle of water from the floor of my backseat, pouring some into an old Tupperware dish buried underneath the seat.

This time she lifted her head, her nose twitching, and then took small, mincing steps in my direction. The second she was close enough I grabbed the white and pink collar studded with hibiscus flowers and wound a beach towel into a makeshift leash while she lapped at the water.

After she'd drank all the water in the dish, I lifted it into the back, pushing it all the way up against the back of the driver's seat and poured more water into it. Paisley hopped right in, turning to give me a smug look, if that was possible, before settling in, her head nestled against the wheel well, promptly closing her expressive black eyes.

I narrowed my own wary eyes at her and slammed the tailgate with more force than necessary before hopping in.

As soon as we hit the stop sign at the harbor exit, Paisley popped her head up between the seats and started foraging around in my console, looking for treats. I shoved her back. Pretty soon I felt tugging on my hair. My eyes shifted to the rearview mirror. My mouth dropped open in horror—Paisley had a hunk of my long blonde hair in her mouth, happily chomping away.

My car swerved as I swung the wheel off the highway and screeched. Paisley also screeched, dropping my hair out of her mouth and promptly pooping out little brown pellets all over the back.

"Paisley!" I scolded before tucking my now slimy hair up in a bun and out of Paisley's reach. Paisley's "deposit" would have to wait—I didn't want to take a chance of opening the back and having her jump out into the road.

Fifteen minutes had never seemed so long in my life. By the time I drove up to Richard and Evelyn's cattle gate my nerves were shot, and so were my olfactory senses.

Richard smiled at me as he leaned in when I rolled down my window and then wrinkled his nose, backing up quickly. He held his nose closed with one hand while waving me over to a goat pen.

As soon as I opened the tailgate, Paisley hopped out and ran right into the pen, eyeing the pile of fresh hay and goat chow that waited inside.

"Evelyn will be down in a minute. You want some help cleaning that out?" He motioned to the now very crusty brown back of the Rav. Nodding mutely, we set to work cleaning it out as best as possible.

Little barks and yips reached our ears, and pretty soon a tiny ball of white floof came barreling at me, prancing in circles around my feet.

"Buddy!" I cried, bending down to scoop him up and smother his soft fur with kisses while he wriggled happily in my arms.

I lifted my head and greeted Evelyn, whose face was split into a delighted smile.

"Oh, I'm so glad to see you," she said as she wrapped me in a warm hug.

Together, all four of us, if you counted Buddy, gazed at Paisley and watched while she munched on the hay, pure bliss shining from her coal black eyes.

Now that Paisley was settled, I took a moment to drink in the scenery in front of me. Fresh air filled my lungs, and tall grass shimmered like waves as the wind blew down from the mountain towards the sea. Richard and Evelyn lived in an old Coast Guard watchtower they painstakingly converted into a cozy cabin. The cabin stood high above the Pacific with an expansive view of the cobalt blue ocean. Boats bobbed far off in the distance, the white plume of fishing boats making foamy trails behind them.

"What a peaceful spot," I murmured, almost to myself.

"We like it." Richard wrapped an arm around Evelyn and spun her so we could look at the tranquil water together.

"It's not as peaceful as it used to be, but I wouldn't trade it for anything." Evelyn patted Richard's arm.

"What do you mean?" I asked.

"When we moved here thirty years ago, we hardly saw any boats. Now it's like the autobahn." She grimaced.

"Now, it's not that bad," Richard chided.

Evelyn's face went from grimace to reluctant smile, and she leaned her head on his shoulder. "Well, you're probably right. I'm just getting old, remembering the good old days, I suppose."

My phone buzzed, interrupting our sweet moment, and I saw I'd missed a text from Elliot.

> **Can you pick up some pasta on your way home? And a bottle of the Huihui flavor of Kuleana rum? I want to try a new recipe.**

My stomach rumbled and I realized I'd missed lunch. Making my goodbyes, I hugged first Richard, then Evelyn and hopped into the Rav, but not before agreeing to babysit Buddy next week when Richard and Evelyn had to fly to Oahu for the day for some medical tests.

With a last wave and a peek at Paisley, who had settled into a corner of the goat pen and looked to be fast asleep, I drove home, mulling over the body pulled from the harbor this morning. Logic told me it had to be Otis—he'd never leave Paisley unattended.

In fact, rumor had it that Otis turned down a solid housing option because they wouldn't allow him to keep Paisley.

The more I thought about it, the sadder I got. Poor Otis.

Just then a gray Toyota Tacoma with a dent and rust spots overtook me and swerved back into my lane so close I had to slam on my brakes, his front fender just missing the car coming in the opposite direction, the driver of the opposing car laying on the horn and throwing a one-finger salute out the window at the Tacoma's driver.

"What the hell?" I shook my hand at the truck in a useless attempt to berate them. They were out of sight in mere seconds.

My hands shook on the steering wheel on my drive back home. By the time I got to KTA to pick up pasta, my heart had stopped competing for the Triple Crown and the shaking was under control. Who on earth was driving like such a maniac? A thought niggled in the back of my mind, but I couldn't quite pull it forward into my consciousness. The nagging feeling continued though, and for the rest of the evening the back of my neck tingled.

Chapter Nine

COLE

SUMMER MET ME AT the door, a delighted smile on her face as she buried her nose into the bouquet of flowers I handed her, the scent of plumeria surrounding us.

"I heard you had a rough day." I buried my face into her hair and hugged her close.

"Yeah, the Rav doesn't smell nearly as good as these flowers do," she replied.

My brow wrinkled and I tilted my head. "Huh?"

"Even though Richard and I swept it out pretty good, it still smelled like goat poop on the way home."

I duckwalked her backwards into the kitchen, unwilling to let her go. "Hmm. We might be talking about two different things."

She angled her pretty face and looked at me with those crystal-blue eyes, one eyebrow lifted in question.

"I heard you had a run-in with Officer Tolten today."

Her mouth quirked and her eyes flicked up and to the right for a moment before her expression cleared and she laughed. "Oh, you mean Officer Meathead? Yeah, he's a treat."

Based on her reaction, she didn't seem too upset. Tension seeped out of my shoulders. Chief Takada targeting me at work had been a roller coaster that Summer got dragged into because of me. Instead of being upset, though, she seemed completely unbothered.

Elliot came into view as we rounded the corner. "Hey, man. How's it going?"

Steam from a pot on the stove surrounded him as he spun around at my greeting before spinning back and stirring something. "It would be going better if I could get this sauce to coat the pasta properly." He took a ladle of liquid from one pot and poured it into another one and stirred frantically.

"Smells incredible." I moved closer to take a peek, and he swatted at me with a wooden spoon.

"Back off!"

"Whoa, dude. What's got your coconuts in a nipper?"

Summer pulled me to the other side of the kitchen island. "Elliot's in a panic because TJ's coming over for dinner and he wants everything to be perfect. He won't even let *me* near the stove."

"That seems like the wisest course of action," I teased, then hopped out of the way before she could pinch me.

Summer's phone dinged just as the doorbell rang. Elliot let out a strangled screech and started stirring faster.

Biting my lip so I didn't laugh, I followed Summer to the door. TJ greeted us with a blindingly white smile and a chilled bottle of wine.

"Hey, TJ. I'm glad you're here—maybe you can tame the beast in the kitchen." Summer wrinkled her nose and jerked her head in Elliot's direction.

A frown furrowed his brow, but he followed Summer to the kitchen, me tagging behind. Elliot glanced up and then squawked when he spotted TJ.

Summer guffawed and Elliot glared at her. TJ just grinned and shimmied past Summer to give Elliot a kiss on the cheek before peeking into the pot on the stove.

"Amatriciana?" His face looked like Christmas came early.

Elliot nodded, as he looked down and shuffled his feet. "You mentioned you tried Amatriciana at that place near the Met in New York City and fell in love. I'm trying to re-create it for you." He glared down at the pot. "I just can't seem to get the sauce as silky as it's supposed to be according to the recipe."

TJ looked closer. "This looks divine. Honestly, I think you nailed it."

Elliot looked down at the pot and then up at TJ. "Are you sure?"

He nodded. "Yeah, this looks amazing. My mouth started watering as soon as I walked in."

Elliot's posture relaxed and his face softened. "Great. Why don't I plate it up and you pour the wine?"

"I can help," Summer volunteered.

"No!" Three voices melded together in a cacophony of fear.

"Har har," Summer responded, then dragged me on to the lanai, her pretty lips pursed into a pout.

We spent the rest of the evening savoring Elliot's pasta dish and sipping wine while we marveled at the wash of pink, orange, and red clouds spread out in front of us.

"So, my schedule is open tomorrow and I wondered if you might want to go for a ride on my boat." I leaned in close to Summer and snagged her hand.

"Eww, gross. Is that what you're calling it?" Elliot interjected, shooting me a cheeky grin.

Summer waved Elliot away, laughing. "I'd love to. My schedule is pretty loose for the next couple weeks."

Anticipation built up as I thought of the last time we went for a boat ride. Summer, reading my mind, grinned up at me wickedly, causing my shorts to tighten uncomfortably.

"Wanna stay over tonight?" She cozied up to my side, and I was sorely tempted.

I released a heavy sigh and shook my head. "I can't. I'd love to, but I need to hit the harbor early to get the boat ready."

Her lips poked out in another pout, and I kissed them thoroughly before grabbing my keys and heading toward the front door.

She followed and leaned against the door frame. "I'm glad we're going out on the boat tomorrow. I bought a new bikini and wanted to see if you like it. It's red and has a lot of straps."

With that she pushed me out of the doorway; the last thing I saw before she shut the door was a devilish grin.

⁓⁓⁓⧽ ⧼⁓⁓⁓

Dawn came early, and after a night of alternately picturing Summer in her bikini and wondering about my latest case, I needed a barrel of coffee to get out the door.

Stopping at Minnit Stop to grab a cup of coffee, I greeted the cashier, Maude, and pulled out my wallet to pay.

An iron grip on my hand halted my movement and I tensed, ready to fight.

"Give me all your money, punk." A low gravelly voice said in my ear as Old Spice wafted to my nose. Something tickled my memory, but by then I'd already leveraged my body weight into the perpetrator and trapped him against the wall, spinning around to face them.

Twinkling green eyes met mine. "Gotcha!" Jeff's lips twitched with suppressed laughter.

"Hey, man. Howzit?" We fist bumped and I threw a quick mahalo to the cashier as Jeff and I headed out to the parking lot.

"You got big plans for the day?"

"Summer and I are going out on the boat. Might throw in a rod and see what I can catch." I leaned against my truck and took a scalding hot swallow from my paper cup, which had the taste and consistency of black tar. "How about you? Any charters today?"

Jeff nodded. "Yeah, a couple my folks know from Oregon rented out the boat for the day. I'm just heading up to the harbor to open her up."

"Cool. Well, I'm sure I'll see you there. My boat's parked over at the boat yard by the Blue Dragon. I gotta run over and get her trailered up and check her out before Summer comes so it's ready to go."

"She seems like a keeper. I'm more of a catch and release guy myself, but it's nice seeing you with someone. You always were a one-woman kind of guy."

He twisted the paper cup in his hand, the cup making a crunching noise as he looked off into the distance, something almost envious in his tone.

"Aww, you just haven't found the right girl yet."

He shook his head, his eyes bleak. "No, I don't think there's a girl alive willing to put up with me. I'm never in one place for longer than a few weeks and if I get a call, I have to drop everything and be ready to go in an hour." He shook his head again, looking down. "I don't have much to give a woman right now but a few hours of my time."

"Maybe you need to find a different line of work." For some reason my heart sped up; something seemed off with Jeff, but I couldn't put my finger on it. Since arriving, he hadn't talked much about himself, and something about his evasiveness was setting off alarm bells.

"Hmm, yeah, I don't think they're going to let me go that easy. Too much invested in me at this point," he said bitterly.

The alarm bells had turned into a screeching bullhorn by now, but this was Jeff—indestructible, indefatigable Jeff. I couldn't imagine anything having that firm a grip on him. Before I could probe, he tossed the crumpled paper cup into the nearby trash and thinned his lips into a semblance of a smile.

"I better get going before the clients show up." He threw a wave and then hopped into his truck two spots over and left, leaving me with a feeling that Jeff had changed in ways I couldn't fathom.

Chapter Ten

COLE

Summer showed up at the harbor, picnic basket in hand just as I turned the motor over on my twenty-four-foot Radon that I didn't get to take out nearly as often as I'd like. Summer looked like a perfect dream in her frayed denim shorts that showed off legs a mile long and made for wrapping around a man. I shook my head. Nope, not the time, I told myself sternly as Summer smiled at me and handed down the picnic basket before hopping on board.

"Where to?" she asked brightly, as she unwrapped the bow line from the dock and coiled it neatly to the Samson post.

"I thought we'd head south for a bit and then maybe putter back up north."

"Hmm. Sounds like someone wants to do a little trolling." She unhooked the front fender and racked it on the captain's tower behind me, and I took a moment to admire her skill as a first mate.

"Busted. I figured I'd throw a line and see if we could catch some dinner while we cruise."

Summer watched as I got my trolling rig started and we stared at the line as it unspooled, forming a small "V" in the water behind the boat. I puttered south, inhaling the salty ocean air and letting some of the tension of the week fall away.

"I never get sick of it." Summer sidled up next to me, her arm automatically lifting to rub circles on my back. She motioned toward the Kohala coastline. "I swore when I was sitting in yet another criminal law class, listening to a professor who'd never even been in the field lecture us about proper procedure that I would live in Hawaii someday." She shook her head. "My dad was furious when I told him I was dropping out to move here." Her expression held something bittersweet.

"Sometimes, our gut knows more than our brains about what we need. Sounds like you needed to be here." I gestured around us at the stunning turquoise water. "And your dad ended up following you here after all."

Her head felt solid and warm as she leaned into my chest. "I think you are very good for me, sir."

"Sir, huh?" My lips quirked into a suggestive grin.

She twisted her neck to look up into my eyes, bringing her lips within reach. Shifting to face her more fully, I angled my head and brought my lips to hers, just a whisper of a kiss. A kiss Summer melted into, deepening the kiss and short-circuiting my brain.

The boat hit some chop and we bounced erratically. Kicking myself for losing focus, I shifted my eyes to the front and steered through a series of rough waves.

My body had other ideas, though, and that kiss kept replaying in my mind. Summer, who clearly must've been trying to kill me, stripped off her shirt and shorts, her honey-colored tan making a tantalizing backdrop to the barely-there red string bikini. She posted up just to the front of me as she surveyed the surface of the water in front of the boat.

White sails dotted the horizon, and I spotted several boats from the harbor bobbing around in the distance. Scouring the coastline wildly for a protected cove, I sussed out the perfect spot—a little inlet unreachable by land and C-shaped. I'd like to say I navigated the boat skillfully around the other side of the inlet, but truthfully, I couldn't even tell you what the depth was. We could've been sitting in four feet of water for all I knew.

Summer raised a perfectly arched eyebrow at me.

"I thought this looked like a good spot for a picnic." My little white lie clearly didn't fool Summer. She just grinned at me in that way women have when they know you're full of shit but are willing to indulge you anyway.

Before I cut the motor I dropped the anchor to the sandy bottom below. Summer lounged on the seat, her eyes following my movements. Anticipation rose up, along with other things, and I sat next to her, pulling her onto my lap. Her lips curved up at the corners, and she threaded her fingers through my hair, tugging me in close for a kiss.

My body heated and I wrapped my arms around her even tighter, delighting in every soft curve making contact with me when suddenly she shifted, her body tightening in surprise.

"What's that?"

It took a very long minute for me to realize she wasn't exclaiming in awe over certain parts of my body, parts that were currently saluting her. She was actually looking just past me at something in the distance.

Reluctant to let go of her, I shifted just enough to crane my neck and look behind me to see what she was pointing at.

There, partially submerged, was a gray, sixteen-foot rigid inflatable boat, the bow just barely breaking the surface.

Damnit.

Deep from within I sighed, knowing I'd have to check it out. If it was what I thought it was, I'd have to call it in. Summer listened intently as I told her about the recent rash of sunken boats, some filled with drugs and cash, all unregistered and their hull numbers sanded off.

She rummaged around in her bag while I maneuvered us in as close as I dared and dropped anchor again. When I looked up from my task I saw Summer standing on the bow, kitted up with a mask and snorkel, a dive knife strapped to her thigh. Before I could stop her, she dove in, the surface barely disturbed as she disappeared below.

My heart hammered in my chest; worry and anger fought for dominance. Yellow tangs and black trigger fish circled the boat, looking for a handout, and I strained to see beyond them into the murky water below.

Three heart-stopping minutes later, Summer's head popped up. She swam in jerky strokes over to the ladder. Racing to the back of the boat I watched as she came up the ladder, knife clenched between her teeth, clutching a black box the size of a small toolbox in her hands.

I took the knife and box from her and struggled to hold in the anger brimming below the surface.

She flipped her mask up and nodded to the box. "Found that in the bow hatch. Boat was pretty clean—I didn't see anything else on the boat other than some old mooring lines. Looks like the line got caught in the motor at some point—it's wrapped around it pretty tight. There's a hole the size of my fist on the port side where it hit some lava rock below the surface."

My brain understood she was saying words, but my ears were venting steam. I swallowed and tried counting to ten in my head.

A strangled laugh burst out of me as I stared at this woman I loved, equal parts exasperation, relief, and intense attraction warring with each other.

"Summer, don't ever do something like that again. When you disappeared before I even had the boat secured, I wasn't sure if I should follow you or wait. Not cool."

Her head lifted at my tone. She studied my face intently. Whatever she read caused her to drop the mulish expression trying to take root. She shifted her gaze down, her shoulders dropping.

"Sorry. I didn't think about it from your perspective." She licked her lips and lifted her eyes, anxiously studying me.

I nodded once, my teeth clenched hard in my jaw. After taking a few deep breaths, I turned my focus to the black box sitting on the seat, hoping for a distraction from my anger.

"Think we should open it?" Summer asked, her voice holding a note of curiosity.

I shrugged. "Might as well. You've already tampered with the evidence."

Her body jerked at the obvious reprimand. "I get it, Cole. I shouldn't have just jumped in. I acted before I thought and I messed up."

I closed my eyes and scrubbed my face, wishing I could take back my words. It was a low blow and a sore spot for Summer to call her out like that. Even though she hadn't said anything to me, I know it grated on her that Takada had taken credit for both of her investigations *and* insinuated she'd meddled where she didn't belong. She was working hard to learn the investigation ropes with her dad, but I know she was sensitive about her lack of experience.

"Summer."

She wouldn't look at me, busying herself stowing her gear.

"Summer."

"What?" she replied, her back to me and arrow straight.

"I'm sorry."

She spun around at this, turquoise eyes stormy and glistening. My gut hardened into a block of cement and my heart pounded a staccato rhythm in my ears. She was crying.

Shit. Summer's crying.

First rule in guy world is you never make your girl cry.

Gently, I pulled her toward me, ready to get slugged at any moment. I cradled her face in my hands and stared deeply into her eyes. "I'm so, so sorry. That was a low blow, and I shouldn't have said that. When you jumped in and I lost sight of you, I about had a heart attack. Forgive me for handling that so poorly. Please?"

For long moments she didn't say anything, and her eyes shifted away from mine. In microscopic increments I felt her body soften against me.

Eventually, she locked eyes with me and nodded. "You're right, though. I shouldn't have touched anything on the boat. That was dumb."

"I wouldn't say that," I replied.

She tilted her head at me. "What do you mean? I disturbed a possible crime scene."

"Yeah, but if you hadn't done that, we wouldn't be able to see what's inside."

Astonished, her mouth dropped open as she flicked her gaze down to the box then back up to me. "Really?"

She stopped short of clapping her hands in excitement and my breath resumed a normal pattern as I watched her.

"Let's do it," I said. "But afterwards, I need to get a photo of you with that knife strapped to your thigh. Nights can get cold around here," I joked.

Her smile was radiant as she looked at me, a devilish gleam in her eye. "We'll see."

I groaned. I knew it—she *was* trying to kill me, one feminine wile at a time. *What a way to go...*I grinned.

She knelt in front of the box and pulled me down next to her. We looked at each other and then down at the box.

"What do you think is in there?"

I shook my head. "I'm not sure. If this is one of the drug boats we've been chasing, it can't be anything good."

Summer reached behind her and grabbed a pair of gloves out of the hatch and handed them to me. She motioned mutely with her head. I drew in a deep breath; my eyes locked on the box.

"Here goes." I exhaled through pursed lips and unlatched the silver hatch on the box.

Water seeped out from around the rubber gasket designed to make the box watertight; someone hadn't latched it properly. Summer and I leaned forward to examine the contents. A two-inch-thick wad of soggy hundred-dollar bills lay rubber banded next to a Ziplock bag with four vials full of clear fluid. A fifth vial held about half the amount of the others.

"Summer, I'm going to make a call."

She nodded; her eyes focused on the contents of the box, her face white.

"Before I do, can I ask you a question?"

She nodded again, spinning her head to look in my eyes.

"Can you wear that bikini on our next date?"

Her eyes filled with laughter. "Sure, but you know the movie theater is air conditioned, right?'

"I'll bring a jacket for you."

I leered at her, waggling my eyebrows and laughing, ducking just in time to avoid the glove she threw at my head.

Chapter Eleven

SUMMER

WE SPENT THE NEXT hour after the Coast Guard arrived showing them the sunken boat and answering their questions. Cole told them we found the box floating on the surface. Afterwards, we drove back to the harbor, both lost in our own thoughts. As much as I was trying not to, Cole's criticism from earlier still clattered around in my thoughts. I kicked myself for touching the box, or anything on the boat, for that matter.

"Penny for your thoughts?"

"Just thinking."

"Uh oh."

"What do you mean 'uh oh'?" I raised an eyebrow at him.

"When a woman says she's 'just thinking,' it usually means a man is involved, *and* he's in trouble."

The hangdog expression on his face made me laugh. "No, not really. What you said on the boat about me tampering with evidence—"

"Summer, honey, I'm sorry. I let my emotions get the better of my mouth. When you disappeared under the boat before I even had it secured, I didn't know what to do, and, well, I was...scared. I could've handled that better."

"Maybe." She shrugged. "But you weren't wrong. If I want to make a go of becoming a full-fledged P.I. someday, these are things I need to consider before jumping headfirst into a situation."

"Literally, in this case." He gave me a lop-sided grin.

I waved my hand at him. "Yeah, yeah." My grin faded. "It's true, though."

Cole rubbed circles on my back with one hand while he steered us into harbor, lining us up within inches of the dock. I hopped out and caught the tag line, securing it neatly and throwing him a saucy look.

"It wouldn't hurt, though, if you're really sorry, that is, to buy me Pau Pizza to make up for it."

"Ah, a girl after my own heart," came a voice from behind us.

Jeff stood at the end of the dock, an army-green backpack slung over his shoulder.

"Oh, hey Jeff. Howzit?"

"Good. Great, actually. What's this I hear about pizza?" He sent a charming grin Cole's way.

Cole sent me a look, an eyebrow raised, and I shrugged slightly.

"Yeah, Pau Pizza up in Waimea. Some of the best pizza this side of the island."

"Sounds great. Mind if I join?"

With another searching look in my direction, Cole replied, "Sure, you're buying."

❧❧❧❧ ❧❧❧❧

After grabbing slices of ooey gooey cheesy wedges of heaven, we elected to sit out back at one of the covered picnic tables. A family of four sat two tables over; the keiki were feeding the hopeful chickens scraps of pizza crust.

"How'd the charter go today?" Cole asked Jeff.

"Great. Who knew cruising up and down the Pacific while charming unsuspecting tourists with made up lore could be so fun?"

I groaned. "Tell me you didn't."

He shot a sparkling smile at me. "Nah. Not really. I did a fair amount of research on the island and its history before I came. I might've embellished just a teeny bit on some of the history surrounding cannibalism." He held up his thumb and index finger an inch apart.

I narrowed my eyes at him, a groan rumbling through me. "You didn't."

His self-satisfied smile was answer enough. Seeing the thunderstorm on my face, Cole deftly changed subjects.

"We found a sunken boat today."

Jeff stiffened slightly, so slightly I almost missed it.

"Oh yeah?" His tone sounded almost bored, his face devoid of any expression.

"Yeah. I think it might be one of the drug boats we've been chasing along the coast."

He bent over to coax a rooster with a bright, velvety green plume closer with a piece of crust. "Interesting."

I could feel the deep 'M' form between my eyebrows as I watched him.

He stood so suddenly it startled the rooster, who ran behind the trashcan and squawked at him. "I didn't realize how late it was. I gotta go back to the harbor and get the boat ready for tomorrow's charter."

Cole tilted his head at Jeff, his forehead creased. "You sure, man? It's not even six o'clock."

"Don't want to be working in the dark." With that he sketched a wave and walked to his truck, roaring out of the parking lot.

"That was weird, right?"

I nodded mutely at Cole as we both stared in the direction Jeff had disappeared.

My phone buzzed on the table, bringing my attention away from the puzzling exit of Cole's friend.

"Hey, Lani. What's up?"

She didn't bother with a greeting. "My dad wants to meet with us tomorrow morning. He sounded really upset but when I pressed for more details, he just shut down and said he'd see us at the office tomorrow at nine o'clock sharp."

"Huh. Okay, not a problem. I'll meet you there. You okay? You sound funny."

"Actually, that's the other reason I'm calling. Time for some more self-defense training. I can't have you get taken out by some ninety pound chronic because you're a weak ass bitch."

I groaned, but her only response was an evil laugh and then the dial tone.

Cole, who'd gotten the gist of the conversation, smirked. "Sounds like you have your very own drill instructor."

"Yeah, one I didn't even sign up for," I replied ruefully.

"Oomph." The air escaped from my lungs as I landed hard on the mat. I glared up at Lani's leering face. "This is becoming a habit."

Instead of responding she extended a hand to help me up then grabbed a towel and handed it to me. She didn't have a drop of sweat on her, despite the fact that we'd been at it for over an hour and a half. Warm-ups, sprints, weights, then a mish-mash of fighting techniques. I shook my head and wrinkled my nose.

"Why are we friends again?"

"Lolo. Because without me, you'd be fish food by now the way you disregard personal safety in order to satisfy your curiosity."

I wrinkled my nose again, regretting telling her about my dive down to the sunken boat yesterday, but considering Cole's reaction, I had to concede her point.

"I'll grab coffee and meet you at the office," I told her after we'd both showered and were on our way out the door to the parking lot.

"And that's why you're *my* friend." She smirked.

"Should I grab something for your dad?"

"Naw. He thinks Surf Camp coffee is for tourists and millennials. Nothing but good old Red Lion medium roast for him." She rolled her eyes.

The drive went quick—nothing but a few Jeeps and a couple of wandering goats. When I got out of the Rav, I groaned as my muscles screamed at me for working them so hard.

Surf Camp was crowded when I walked in. The line snaked around to the tables by the back door. I wrinkled my nose and got in line. Ever since they'd opened, Surf Camp had a crowd.

Someone tapped my shoulder as I was checking my emails and waiting to order, causing me to jump, my muscles seizing up immediately. I groaned and rubbed my quads.

"Summer, right?"

I jerked my head up and saw Kevin standing in front of me.

"Oh, hey. Yeah. How's business? I'm surprised you don't have a charter today—conditions are fantastic."

Something ticked in his jaw and his face hardened. "My DM called off. Had to cancel the whole day."

"Yikes. I'm sorry about that. That really sucks."

He nodded and blew out a big breath. "Yeah. This guy came highly recommended, but he's a bit of a flake."

I was surprised—most DMs are pretty reliable. The pay wasn't always the greatest, but getting to spend your day underwater *and* get paid? Not a bad gig if you could get it. The problem was that scuba diving depended on good ocean conditions so DM'ing wasn't always a consistent source of income.

"Darn. I'm sorry to hear that." We moved forward in line.

"Actually," his eyes glinted, "I'm glad I ran into you. I know you said you had a full plate, but I'd be happy to pay you double the going rate to come work my boat."

My eyes widened. "Oh wow. As tempting as that is, believe me, I just can't commit. Can I give you my friend Kay's information? She might be looking to supplement her income."

Disappointment dimmed the light in his eyes, but he nodded. "Sure, that would be great."

I texted Kay first and got her okay before giving out her number, then typed mine into his phone as well. "I can't promise anything, but if I get a free day, I might be able to help out."

He let out a breath. "Phew—you're a lifesaver. I really appreciate this. I don't know what's up with the guy I signed on; some days he's great, other days he's like crazy manic, and today is the third day in the last week he no showed on me."

"Hang in there. There are some pretty great folks in the diving community. I'm sure you'll be able to find someone you can depend on soon."

He nodded, lips quirked with a ghost of a smile then ordered his coffee. After he paid, he lifted his cup in goodbye. "Thanks again, Summer—I really appreciate the lead." With that, he took a cup from the smiling barista and walked out the front door, shoulders drooping.

Checking my phone, I mentally pleaded with the coffee gods to hurry as I watched the barista steam the milk for my black sesame latte. Lani's dad was going to arrive any minute and I wanted to beat him there. Whatever he wanted to talk to us about had to be pretty serious if he was making another trek into Waimea—he wasn't a man for people and cities.

The barista handed over two paper cups, and I zoomed two doors down to our office, handing Lani her coffee and getting settled at my desk right before Mack walked in.

The grim look on his face caused my gut to clench. Whatever he came for, it wasn't good.

Chapter Twelve

SUMMER

LANI HOPPED UP, SLOSHING coffee and wincing when the scalding liquid hit her arm. "Dad, what's wrong?"

We ushered him into my dad's private office and flipped the sign on the door to closed.

Mack's whole body was tense, and the muscles in his jaw were tight as he made a brief effort to smile.

"Ladies, thank you for seeing me."

His tone was formal, which was strange coming from him. He leveled a gaze at me, his brown eyes full of sorrow and determination.

"The medical examiner in Kona's my cousin. He did me a favor and gave me a copy of Otis's report. HPD is calling his death an accidental drowning, despite the ME's report." He shook his head and rubbed a face over the stubble on his cheek. "After reviewing it myself, I'm convinced he was murdered."

Lani and I both stiffened in shock. "Whoa. Are you sure?"

He pulled out a sheaf of papers, but instead of handing them to me he placed them on his lap and looked down, his chest expanding as he drew in a deep breath. Somehow, he looked smaller to me, like he'd shrunk in the last 48 hours.

Lani and I both sat watching him; he looked lost in his own world, reliving memories we couldn't see.

"Can you tell us what makes you believe Otis was murdered?" I asked, my voice soft.

He lifted his head and searched Lani's then my face first before setting the papers on the desk. "Three things. One, there was very little water in his lungs. So little, in fact, that the ME found it suspicious but inconclusive. The ME made special note of it, but HPD is overlooking that fact. Secondly, there's the text I showed you two, alluding to someone being after him. Third, Otis wore his challenge coin around his neck on a chain. It's missing."

I raised my eyebrow at him.

He sighed. "The chain is a thing from when we were in the military. He never took it off."

My gaze shifted to Lani, and she shrugged her shoulders slightly.

"Dad, can you elaborate? Summer and I don't understand." Lani's voice conveyed patience, not something she was known for normally.

He shifted the papers around on the desk and cleared his throat. "Otis and I were involved in a top-secret operation in Desert Storm. We didn't know it, but it was a death sentence that higher ups planned in order to turn the tide of sympathy toward the Americans. Despite the odds, Otis and I survived." His laugh was full of irony. "They had a big ceremony for us, made a big deal even though Otis and I both knew the truth. Even had Dick Cheney, Secretary of Defense at the time, present us with challenge coins. The only two like it in the world." He snorted.

"After all we'd done, we decided to keep the challenge coins as a reminder. Otis never would've taken it off, but when they pulled him from the harbor it wasn't anywhere on his body."

My eyes widened as I listened. Neither Lani nor I knew much about his time in the military—he just didn't talk about it. The Plinko chips dropped into place though—no wonder Mack was so big on teaching Lani survival and fighting skills.

Quiet grief hung off Mack like a pair of gauze curtains. My heart squeezed—I'd never seen the mighty Mack like this before.

"Is it possible the chain fell off in the water?"

He shrugged. "Possibly. The chain was a solid Mariner rope chain, though. Nearly unbreakable. Neither the chain nor the coin were found on his body."

Lani raised an eyebrow at her dad. "How on Earth would you know anything about jewelry?"

He smiled wryly. "Otis said a girl bought it for him and showed it off to all of us at the barracks one night. We found out later that 'girl' was his mom." His smile dimmed. "She died shortly after we got back from Saudi."

Shit. "What can we do to help?"

Mack stared at me intently. "I need you to investigate and find out what happened to Otis. HPD is ruling this death accidental—Otis deserves the truth."

He reached into his back pocket and pulled out a wallet full of hundred-dollar bills. "I brought a retainer."

"Did you unbury one of the fifty-five gallon drums in the back?" Lani asked, amused.

He sniffed. "None of your business. Are you going to take my case or not?"

I reached across the table and squeezed his hand briefly. "Of course we are."

He stood up and both Lani and I scrambled to stand as well. He took turns looking between Lani and me, heartache awash in his expression. "Otis deserves justice."

With one last searching look at us, he turned and left the office, flipping the sign as he went.

"Shit."

Lani nodded in agreement. "Yep."

"Lani, this is big. How are we supposed to solve a murder that we don't even know for sure is a murder?"

She glanced down at the table then sighed. "I guess we can start with that."

The medical examiner's report lay on the table where Mack had left it. Medical jargon covered the front page, but down at the bottom I read "scant volume of water found in the lungs inconclusive with drowning as cause of death."

Lani and I poured over the rest of the report in detail. Bruises were found on head, face, and abdomen as well as red friction marks consistent with being restrained. The report mentioned microscopic fiber fragments found embedded in the lacerations on his wrists and ankles.

"How on Earth is HPD writing this off as an accidental drowning given this report?" I wondered aloud. "And who is making the call on that?"

Lani shook her head. "No idea. I can't imagine anyone dug too deeply into it though—in their eyes, he was probably just one of the many houseless people on the island. Those deaths never get much attention."

Heavy weight collected around my heart. "Well, this is one death that won't get overlooked."

Lani nodded and we both sat silently, sharing pages of the report and making notes. Mack put his faith in us—we needed to be as thorough as possible and find out what happened to Otis.

"Hmm. The toxicology report shows nothing in his system."

Lani nodded. "Otis didn't do drugs or even drink. Dad said when Otis first came to the island, he was a wreck, drunk all the time and acting a fool. Dad helped him get sober, and he's been sober ever since."

"Why do you think he lived in his van instead of finding a steady place to live?"

She shrugged. "Part of it was because of Paisley, I think. But also, Dad kind of alluded to the fact that Otis struggled to stay inside. Something to do with the war and one of their missions, but he didn't go into detail."

There was so much about Mack I didn't know. He was my bonus dad when I was a kid—a solid presence that was always there. I never really thought about him as a whole person outside the context of being a father figure.

"Do you think Cole would share any info with us?"

It was my turn to shrug. "I'm not sure. To be honest, I'd rather not ask. He's already in a precarious position at work, and I'd hate to cause more trouble for him."

She put her chin in her hand as she leaned her elbow on the desk, her eyes looking off into the distance. Suddenly she brightened. "Don't worry—I might have an in at HPD. I can ask him and keep Cole out of it."

We spent the rest of the afternoon compiling a list of questions and places we wanted to check out—places Otis liked to hang out according to Lani's dad when we texted him to ask.

After we came up with a good game plan for tomorrow, I gathered up my bag and shut my laptop. I lingered for a minute, fiddling with the pen cup sitting next to it.

"So, what do you think really happened to Otis?"

"Before I read the report I kinda thought maybe Dad was overreacting. After, though?" She lifted a shoulder, "A lot of things don't add up."

I sighed. "Yeah, I felt the same way. Besides which, other than a complete lack of trust in the government and clear prepper tendencies, your dad's not really known for pushing the panic button."

Lani smiled down at her Apple watch before noticing me watching her. She instantly pulled her face into one of complete disinterest.

"Who's texting you?"

She shook her head. "Nobody. It was just a funny spam text."

My eyes narrowed. "Uh huh. That sounds like you. The girl who has no patience for commercials or spam smiling at a spam text."

Suddenly, the paint on the wall seemed worthy of intense inspection. Lani kept her eyes focused on a spot just above her head as she replied. "People change. Maybe it just doesn't bother me anymore."

"That is the lamest thing I think I've heard all day." I kept my gaze steadily on her until she finally spun back.

She threw up her hands. "Okay, fine. It's Kalani."

Ha! I knew something was going on. "Oh yeah? How's that going?"

This time she couldn't hide the smile that broke out on her face. "Good. Really good. We've gone on two legit dates so far and they've been great."

"Lani that's awesome! I'm glad you guys took the plunge."

Her expressive brown eyes twinkled as she nodded. "Me too. We're still trying to keep it on the DL for now, but I can't remember ever having this much fun with someone of the opposite sex."

To prove her point, she did a little happy dance next to her desk. Mid-shimmy Dad walked in, broad shoulders filling the doorway, his athletic build still impressive at his age. Lani stopped, but not before he saw her and smirked. "If I'd known how happy you were to see me, I would've stopped by earlier."

Lani and I both rolled our eyes in tandem, which only made his grin wider.

"So, what are you girls up to today? Anything new come in?"

We shared a look before I answered. "Uh, yeah, actually. Mack hired us."

"Mack? As in 'the mighty Mack'? When Summer stayed with her mother during spring break on the island," he mock-grimaced. "She'd come home and talk about 'Mack said this, and Mack said that.' Have to admit, I was a little jealous."

He set his keys on the counter and checked the thermostat. "What's the case?"

This was the moment of truth. Last month we'd been thrown into a murder investigation unwittingly, but I wasn't sure how Dad would feel about us taking this one. We hadn't really talked about caseloads or what we were or weren't allowed to take on without his blessing.

I quirked my lips to the side. "Well, actually it's a murder investigation."

His eyebrows disappeared under his hairline and his posture stiffened. "Oh yeah? I'd like to hear more." He motioned for us to follow him back to his office where he pulled out an extra chair and closed the door.

We laid out everything we knew so far, as well as what our plan of attack was.

He leaned back in his chair, steepling his fingers in front of him. "Sounds like a solid plan so far. I think your instincts are spot on." He straightened an already straight pile of paper on his desk. "We should probably discuss taking cases ahead of time though."

I started to protest, and he held up a hand. "I know. Mack is family, and there's no doubt we'll help him. But the both of you are new to this. You showed good instincts on the Cameron case, but there's a lot involved in an investigation—especially one involving a possible murder."

My dad was referring to a reference check by a concerned father about his daughter's new boyfriend. The boyfriend turned out to be more than what anyone had realized at the time and Lani and I got caught up in the crossfire of his deception.

He continued. "Cases like Mack's require a seasoned investigator. You two are doing great, but there's still a lot to learn."

I bristled even though in the back of my head I knew he was right. Independence was my ride or die, and it was hard to admit at times that I might need help or guidance.

Lani, ever practical, responded. "Well, after hearing our game plan, what do you think?"

My dad threw her a grateful look. "Like I said, the plan is solid. I'd like to look at that report to see if there's anything you missed."

My nose wrinkled and I felt my forehead pucker. Lani poked me. "Your face gonna freeze like that, sis."

Dad's lips twitched. "I see the thunderclouds brewing on your face, but this is a part of investigative work you have to make peace with. In fact, I'd encourage you to try to make friends with the idea that if you want to get your P.I. license, for the next four years you're going to have to share your toys."

Grrr.... Just because he was right didn't mean I had to like it.

Chapter Thirteen

COLE

"PETERSON—DID YOU SEE THIS?"

Jonah shoved a flyer in front of my face. We'd agreed to meet for coffee before driving over to Pahala to rattle some gang members into giving up info on our sunken boats. Chief Takada's face took up most of the space on the flyer. Apparently, he was being honored at the HPD Officer's Ball.

"Jesus. You just can't make this stuff up."

Jonah snorted his agreement. "Right? How on Earth is he getting honored? He's hardly here, and when he is, all he does is have closed door meetings with his minions or harass you." He shook his head. "Remind me never to go into politics—I'd never be able to play that game."

"Same." Close up, the picture looked to be about ten years old; there was no gray in Chief's hair, and he didn't have a paunch hanging over his belt. With effort, I pulled my eyes away from the flyer and handed it back to Jonah. "What'd you find out about the boat Summer and I came across?"

"Unsurprisingly, the hull ID number was sandblasted off, and the coms were disabled. Just like the other three we found."

"If you had to guess, what do you think happened to this one? We hadn't seen any that far north yet."

He shrugged. "Couldn't say. It's too far north for any harbors, and coming around to the west instead of east is a death wish, especially given conditions lately."

"Hmm. Curiouser and curiouser."

Jonah bobbed his head just as the barista called my name. Grabbing our drinks we loaded up and started heading east toward Pahala and Punalu'u bakery. If the bakery was busy, it would be a lengthy detour, but worth it for the malasadas.

The winding road reminded me of Summer—I knew she was prone to carsickness. Now and then, ocean views peeked through the increasingly dense jungle forest. After a while the trees thinned, giving way to black volcanic rock and sweeping fields of golden grasses that could fool someone into thinking they were in Wyoming—if it weren't for the deep blue water in the distance as we neared South Point.

We drove through postage stamp-sized communities, green vegetation pushing through once again before we pulled into the bakery parking lot, the enticing aroma of malasadas wafting over to the truck, my mouth watering before we'd even gotten out.

Yeasty, sugary goodness in every flavor greeted us in the glass case at the service counter as we inched forward in the crowded line. An auntie with graying hair stuck under a hairnet took our order and then motioned us over to the register to pay.

As we stood waiting our turn, I caught a glimpse of a face. Dread filled me, my bones turning to brittle ice as I craned my neck to get a better look.

"Sir, your change."

Jonah nudged me and I turned back to the cashier, who was trying to hand me change.

"Oh, uh, sorry about that. Mahalo." I went through the motions and shoved the bills into my wallet and followed Jonah back to the truck on autopilot, still surveying the area around me.

"Dude, you okay? You went all Navy Seal on a mission on me in there."

With effort, I stretched my lips over my teeth in a poor attempt at a smile, but it must not have convinced him. He sat with keys in the ignition and stared at me.

"Yeah, I'm okay. Just thought I saw someone from my past in there."

"Wanna talk about it?"

I shook my head no, turned to face the front windshield, and took a gorilla-sized bite of the malasada in my hand, effectively ending Jonah's questioning. From the corner of my eye, I saw him study me for a minute before sighing and starting the truck.

Jonah turned on Detroit rock for the remainder of the drive, knowing how much I despise that genre. We shoveled malasadas into our mouths and washed them down with scalding hot coffee in the twenty minutes it took to reach Pahala, both of us silent.

Jonah sometimes complained that I kept my cards close to my chest; that it showed a lack of trust in our partnership. It wasn't that. Some things were horrors that no one else should have to experience. Jeff and I bonded so tightly in the Navy because we were a team and both got sent on some shitty missions, missions that ended with some of our team not coming home. I never thought about the successful missions, only the ones that ended badly. My closemouthed tendencies had more to do with wanting to spare anyone else from hearing about the shit going on in my head than trying to keep secrets.

We pulled into the auto parts store parking lot and Jonah found a spot to park.

"Okay, what's the plan?"

"Let's find Lennie and see if he's got anything he needs to get off his chest."

Jonah grinned at me. "I like it."

We ambled behind the Long's building and found Lennie in his usual spot, tucked up under an aging mac nut tree, peddling his wares. When he saw us, he shoved it all under the crate in front of him before standing up and shielding the crate with his body, a weaselly smile on his face as he repeatedly ran a hand through his greasy black shoulder-length hair.

"Gentleman, what brings you all the way out here on this fine island day?" He spread his tanned, skinny arms wide, the back-alley tattoos on them melding together, looking like a collection of slightly pudgy snakes, as he gestured to the cracked parking lot and rust-covered building next to him, surreptitiously kicking something under the crate with his foot.

"Lennie, my man. Howzit? Long time no see. Looks like you're staying on the straight and narrow. Haven't seen you in Kona in, what? Two months?"

Lennie's smile drooped for a second before snicking back in place. "Jonah, you wound me. I took your words to heart at our last meeting." He brought a fist to his heart, a look of complete innocence pasted on his face. "I am a family man now. My only goal is to be an example to the great keiki warrior my wahine carries in her royal womb."

"Boy, Lennie, you really missed your calling," I remarked. "You would've killed it on Broadway."

His posture stiffened ever so slightly, and he began jingling what sounded like change in his pocket. But props to the man, he kept trying to snow us.

"Detective Peterson, Cole. Can I call you Cole?" Before I could answer he continued. "I am merely a humble businessman doing my best to care for my local community." The shit was getting so deep I'd need a shovel soon.

Jonah and I shared a look. I snorted. "Great, Lennie. I'm so glad to hear that. I'm guessing then that you won't mind helping us gather information on some hoodlums running through the area." I showed him photos of two known Bois gang members operating in the area.

He shifted foot to foot, his eyes just as shifty, barely glancing at the photos before shaking his head emphatically. "Nope. Never seen 'em." He crossed his arms over his chest.

"Really? That's incredible. I guess the eyewitness we have that swears they saw you and these two gentlemen working behind 76 must be mistaken then?" Jonah scratched his head, quirking his lips.

Lennie licked his lips and rubbed the back of his neck, not meeting Jonah's eyes. "Well, uh, look, man. I can't say for sure I know those guys. A lot of people come around, asking for directions and things. I'm just doing my best to be a good citizen, you know?"

"Right. Of course. I can see that about you, Lennie. You really care about the people here." Jonah wandered next to the crate. Lennie shifted to keep his body between Jonah and the crate. Sweat broke out on his upper lip as he watched Jonah like a chicken watches a mongoose.

"You know, Lennie, Cole and I were talking earlier about what a good product you bring to market here in Pahala. Remind me again—incense and sage, right?"

Jonah feinted left and lifted the crate, Lennie one step behind him. Underneath the crate lay bongs of various sizes and colors, as well as a wide array of edibles. Displayed artfully next to the bongs lay dried marijuana leaves bundled in baggies with thin bamboo skewers of compacted leaves wrapped around what appeared to be hemp string in another pile on the table.

Next to the pile lay a neatly wrapped brick of weed. Depending on how the scales tipped we were either in misdemeanor territory or felony land. The bag of ice he kicked behind him tipped him firmly into one to two years mandatory at Kulani Correctional.

"Dude, it's not what it looks like. This is all CBD. I got a license and everything." Futilely, Lennie tried to cover up the table under the crate with a sarong.

Jonah lifted an eyebrow. "Really? Well, given what a fine, upstanding pillar of the community you are, you won't mind showing it to me then." I couldn't help but snort; Lenny had been picked up for selling weed to kids behind the high school as well as pimping out a few desperate wahine in the area. Not to mention the scam he devised to milk some elderly kupuna out of their SNAP benefits. Well-known to HPD, Lenny's reputation preceded him, but on occasion he was willing to give up information in order to lighten his sentence. This was one of those times; at least I hoped it was.

Lennie let out a squeak of manic laughter, his breath coming in quick gasps as he patted his shorts. He lifted his head and rubbed his hands together, his foot tapping out a chaotic rhythm.

"I don't seem to have it on me." His eyes shifted over Jonah's shoulder to a passing truck, then down to the highway, the speed of his tapping increasing and his weight shifting to his right foot.

"Oh, no. That's unfortunate. I'm afraid we're going to have to take you in until we can get this sorted out." Jonah made to reach for the cuffs in his back pocket.

The whites of Lennie's eyes showed as he watched Jonah reach back. I saw the minute he decided to run for it. His eyes shifted to the clump of trees behind him, and he raced toward the retaining wall, vaulting over it. One step behind him, I grabbed onto his T-shirt, but it was so slick with sweat, it slipped through my hands like a greased pig at a pig scramble.

I cleared the wall and raced after Lennie, Jonah close behind. Brush grew in heavier rows the farther back we pursued until it covered the trail almost completely. Glimpses of Lennie's white T-shirt and red basketball shorts drew us further in. Thorns from the Kiawe tore at my skin, leaving jagged scratches on my forearms.

A flash of red caught my eye and I nudged Jonah. Up in a tree, Lennie climbed higher, nimble as a spider monkey. Just like the hunting dogs on the island, we circled the tree, calling for him to come down. He shook his head resolutely.

"I ain't going back to Kulani. They'll kill me in there."

"Now, now, Lennie. It can't be that bad. It's minimum security, after all. If I were you, I'd be more worried about Halawa. Running from the cops—that can't be good. This is your, what, third time?" Jonah turned his back to the tree and pulled out his phone. "Three strikes you're out according to this."

Jonah's phone screen was blank, but the bluff seemed to be working. "You think they'll let me see my girl at Kulani?"

"Hmm. Maybe. I bet if we put in a good word for you they might."

I marveled at how good Jonah had gotten at the shakedown. When he first started, he'd been green as the Mauna Kea golf course. I whistled through my teeth, impressed. He learned quick.

He threw a grin in my direction as we watched Lennie climb down, and I winced as he got caught on multiple Kiawe thorns on the way.

My sympathy dried up the second I watched him vault over our heads like Julio Jones in the 2016 game against the Panthers.

Jonah and I looked at each other and shrugged, his wide grin matching mine.

❧ ❧

"I want a lawyer. I know my rights." Lennie sat on the ground next to Jonah's truck, his hands balled into fists at his sides.

"Absolutely. We'll get right on that." Jonah said, rolling his eyes and checking his phone. "The squad car should be here any minute, and once they've booked you through at the station you can use your phone call to find a lawyer."

I sat next to Lennie on the ground, wrinkling my nose at the smell of rotten fruit in the dumpster nearby. "Course, we might be able to make a deal with you, keep you out of jail. We just need some information. You'd like to see your girl tonight, wouldn't you?"

He sighed, dangling his head between his knees. He mumbled something.

"What's that?"

"Shit. That lolo wahine ain't going to let me in the house once she finds out about this." He slumped.

"Why don't you make this easier on everyone and give us some info. Listen, anyone in your position would do the same. You're just out here trying to make a living, take care of your girl. You just made a mistake. I'd hate to see this one mistake ruin your life." Myna birds chirped in the background as Jonah scrutinized Lennie.

"Tell you what. You tell us about the sunken boats and the guys in the picture, and we'll forget this whole thing ever happened."

Lennie's head snapped up, eyes shining like the Hope diamond. "Really?" he croaked.

Jonah nodded.

⁂

Lennie's singing rivaled the Myna birds nearby.

"Fruitful trip, eh?" Jonah grinned.

The corners of my mouth turned up as I looked over at him. "The student has surpassed the teacher."

He threw me a smug look before his face turned serious. "Now we just have to flush these guys out before more drugs end up on the island."

Chapter Fourteen

SUMMER

STARK YELLOW FIELDS OF grass and lava rock passed by on the highway as Lani and I drove up to Hawi. We'd decided to take a break from our investigation—after hitting a few brick walls we figured a break to regroup was in order, and I wanted to check on Paisley. Richard and Evelyn assured me she was thriving in her new environment, but I wanted to see her for myself.

We pulled up to the cattle gate, and I hopped out to unlatch it, lost in thought, stepping right into a massive cow pile, the squishy brown mess seeping over my sandal and releasing an earthy stench.

"Don't even think you're getting back in the car until you clean that off," Lani called over to me, grimacing as the smell wafted in her direction.

Mentally cursing myself, Lani, and the cow, I shut the gate after Lani drove through and walked up the long drive to Paisley's pen. Richard and Evelyn were waiting, filling feed buckets and water at the water trough.

"Aloha," Richard's booming voice hailed as I squish-squashed my way to where Lani, Richard, and Evelyn stood.

Evelyn looked down at my foot. "Oh dear. Let me help you with that," she said, her careworn face and German accent reminding me of a storybook fairy godmother. She held the hose and sprayed off first my shoe and then my foot, Lani chortling the whole time.

Paisley wandered over, a fuchsia pink scarf tied around her neck. She brought her head to touch my belly, just a whisper of a touch. My hand automatically rose up to pet her, her coarse, bristly hair tickling my hand.

"She's doing great. She made friends with all the other animals nearby. We caught the heifers crowded around her today. She stood up on her grain box braying down to them while they stared at her, transfixed. Personally, I think she's staging some sort of mutiny. Breeding time is starting and none of the heifers would follow me into the breeding pen after Paisley's little 'speech' this morning." Richard shook his head, looking mystified.

"Oh, now, Richard, that's silly talk. Our girl is doing no such thing. Are you, girl?" Evelyn gently scratched under Paisley's chin while Paisley looked at us with wide black eyes, the picture of innocence. I squinted at her, but she just looked back and nuzzled deeper into Evelyn's hand.

"Thank you so much for taking her. I'm sure Otis would be glad to know she was happy in her new digs."

"Poor guy. What a way to go." Richard shook his head, a slight shudder rolling through him. News of Otis's death had spread like wildfire in North Kohala.

Buddy came running down the drive, barking and snorting. As soon as he reached us, he started dancing around our legs, his white fluffy body looking like a tiny, out of control snowball. I leaned down to pick him up and snuggle him against my chest while he manically licked me.

Evelyn and Richard shared a look, and then she nudged him, pointing her chin in my direction.

"Umm, Evelyn and I have the dates for my visit to the doctor in Oahu next week. Are you still available to watch him for us? It would just be overnight."

"Absolutely! I'd love to have Buddy. Anytime. He's my little floofball, aren't you, Buddy?" I cuddled him closer and he snorted in delight.

While I snuggled Buddy, I noticed Lani feeding Paisley little handfuls of grain while she crooned to her. Paisley's eyes were rolling back in her head in ecstasy. Lani had always had a way with animals. It was spooky sometimes, the way they just followed her commands as if she was doing them a favor by noticing them.

After one last glance into Buddy's teddy bear eyes, I set him down reluctantly. "We'd better get going. We have some work to do."

Lani wiped her hands on her jean shorts and murmured something in Paisley's ear, Paisley listening intently before we said our goodbyes and headed down to the harbor.

"Let's stop in at Kohala Divers first and ask around. Maybe someone saw something or noticed something weird. Tracy and Meredith are around all the time; I bet if anyone saw anything it would've been them."

Lani nodded her agreement, and we took a right turn onto the dead-end street in front of the dive shop. The Kohala Divers truck was parked two spots away, loaded with gear. As we pulled up, I saw Elias grab a handful of wetsuits off the back, and I called over to him.

"Short trip, huh?" Normally the charter didn't come back until close to 2 p.m. It wasn't even noon according to my phone.

"Hey Summer, hey Lani. Howzit?" He adjusted the load in his arms. "Wind's picking up and it got too choppy. Charter was full of Discover Scuba students. We decided to call it for the day and try again tomorrow."

I hadn't noticed earlier, but as soon as Elias mentioned it, I saw the flag in the harbor parking lot flapping in the wind wildly as whitecaps danced on the surface of the water behind it.

"Rats. The report I saw a couple days ago looked more promising," I said as I gestured toward the frothy waves. "Hey, do you know who's working the shop today?" I asked.

Elias grunted as he threw a giant pile of heavy wetsuits in the dunk tank in the gear room where I'd followed him. "Meredith is around here somewhere."

Lani and I traipsed back through to the main shop where Meredith stood at the register, throngs of people surrounding it.

"Okay, if you were on the shortened charter today, I want you to line up over here so I can get you rebooked. If you have purchases, please line up over here and Kay will ring those up for you." Meredith pointed to Kay, a blonde pint-sized pixie with the enthusiasm of a Disney Princess. She smiled and held up a hand, and the line split nearly in half, with one half moving to Meredith and the other to Kay.

I turned my head to look at Lani and she looked back, shaking her head slightly. We backed out of the shop and regrouped.

"Should we go down to south harbor and see if anyone's around?"

Lani shrugged. "Probably not too many people around right now."

Good point—the fisherman had long since come in, and anyone else probably high-tailed it out as soon as the wind picked up. I tapped my chin, my thoughts interrupted by a thumping bass moving closer.

Lani and I watched as a cobalt blue late model Corvette pulled up, Kevin at the wheel. He spun a dial on his dash and smiled up at us.

"Hey, Summer. Fancy meeting you here. Change your mind about guiding for me?" His sparkling teeth were on full display.

"Hey, Kevin. My schedule just got busier, so I'm afraid not. Did you reach out to Kay?"

He nodded. "Yeah, what a sweetheart. Is she always so..." he threw out jazz hands, and Lani and I giggled.

"Yep. That's our Kay. She's going to cheerlead the whole world into happiness whether you like it or not."

"Nice ride," Lani said, running her hand down a fender.

Kevin's grin turned sheepish. "It's pretty flashy. And not very practical." He motioned to four Nitrox tanks in the back seat. "I kinda went crazy when I inherited all that money. Next week I'm going to head to Kona and see about trading it in for something a little sturdier."

"Just don't get a white Tacoma," I joked.

His expression turned quizzical.

"Everyone on island seems to drive a white Tacoma. I think it's a rite of passage or something." I said, smirking.

"Ah, gotcha. Well, thanks for the advice. I better go drop off these tanks."

We stepped back, but before he drove away, I asked if his divemaster was doing better. Something shifted in his face, and his eyes turned hard for a moment before his expression smoothed out. "Unfortunately, I think I'm going to have to hire someone else to replace him. I'm hemorrhaging money trying to cover his messes."

"Good luck," I told him, and he saluted before driving up to where Elias stood.

Lani and I hopped into her car. As we drove past, Elias swung his arm out toward the parking lot and shook his head. Kevin must've said something because Elias threw up his arms and shook his head again, this time even more adamantly before he slapped the side of Kevin's car and stalked off. My eyebrows flew up—what had Kevin said that got the normally chill Elias so upset?

⚶⚶⚶ ⚶⚶⚶

Lani drummed her fingers on the steering wheel as we gazed around the mostly empty harbor parking lot. A few trucks, empty trailers attached, sat parked, but no one was out and about.

Jeff's boat bobbed in the water in the fourth spot over from the loading dock. Huh. I noticed a thin layer of green scum circling the hull.

"Wanna walk around, do a loop?" Lani's voice broke into my thoughts.

With a last look at Jeff's boat, I nodded, and we hopped back out of the car. We started on the north end and walked along the rocks at the shore's edge, the ten foot drop to the water littered with cigarette butts and old fishing line.

What started as a reconnaissance mission quickly evolved into a clean-up as Lani and I snagged as much of the line as we could before it blew into the water and ensnared any sea life.

Something that looked like a cell phone caught my eye, and I clambered down the rocks, gripping tightly to the jagged lava rock. At the bottom in a small pool of water inches above the tide line was a collection of trash; the inside of a Cheetoh's bag, remnants of blue tarp, the edges feathery and worn, more fishing line, and a battered black phone case sans phone. Other than an Otterbox logo etched into the back, the case was empty of any kind of personalization.

I heaved myself back up the rocks carefully, the trash clutched in one hand while I scrambled over the lava rock with more care than on the way down.

When I reached the top, Lani stood glaring down at me, hands on hips. "Listen, lolo, if you're going to go on an expedition, it might be nice if you let your partner know."

I shrunk under her gaze and lowered my eyes, nodding. Without a word, she held the trash bag in her hand open, and I shoved all the junk I'd gathered into it. One glance over at the overflowing dumpster had her throwing the trash bag in the back of her car instead.

She put her hand up to shield her eyes and surveyed the coastline, turning slightly to take it all in. She let out a frustrated sigh. "I think this is a bust for today. No one else is going to be coming in for a while."

The breeze, which had been mild earlier, was picking up, and whitecaps were starting to froth more wildly on the surface of the water even on the inside of the protected cove.

"You're probably right." I blew out a breath. "This was a bust."

"Tomorrow, we need to get here before the sun rises and see if we can catch anyone who might know something."

As much as I hated to wait until tomorrow, I conceded Lani's point.

Lani smiled over at me, all of her teeth showing.

"Uh oh. Whatever it is, the answer is no."

Her smile widened.

Chapter Fifteen

SUMMER

"DAMN IT, LANI. I'M not going to be able to move tomorrow."

A white hand towel hit my face, and I looked over and watched as she daintily wiped her brow, the picture of innocence.

"You'll thank me when you and Cole get into some bedroom gymnastics."

A picture of Cole popped into my head, our interrupted moment on the boat causing me to smile.

Lani mimicked fanning herself, a self-satisfied smirk on her face.

"Hey, ladies, we're going to be setting up for the next class," the perky blonde yoga instructor informed us, and we rolled up our mats after quickly wiping them down.

"I like Bobby's classes better," I grumped to Lani as we walked out. Lani nudged me and jerked her head behind us. The bubbly instructor glared at me sourly, and I winced.

"Bobby's classes are for getting in touch with your body and your spirit. Willow's hot yoga class is designed to help you sweat out toxins and push yourself."

"Didn't we sweat out enough toxins this morning?" I griped.

Lani didn't answer. I looked up and saw her watching someone out front in the parking lot. Sidling up next to her, I watched as Kalani stood talking to a petite girl, long, shiny black hair rippling as she leaned forward to give him a kiss on the cheek and he beamed down at her.

Lani's face was a mask, but her stillness was a red flag.

"So, what's going on with that?" I pointed to the parking lot where Kalani stood. "I thought you two were dating."

"Apparently not." She grabbed my arm and pushed through the door, skirting where Kalani stood with the mystery woman.

We'd just reached her car when we heard her name shouted. She stiffened but refused to look up, hurriedly jumping into the car.

Not me, though. I stood right there and watched as Kalani dashed over to the car. I crossed my arms and narrowed my eyes at him as he approached, his bright smile dimming as he took in my expression.

"Uh, hey, Summer. Howzit?" Uncertainty colored his tone.

"You tell me," I said, as I jerked my chin in the direction of the girl he'd been talking to.

Confusion sprang up on his face as he glanced in that direction before his expression cleared and he smiled. "That's Sheila, she's helping—

Lani laid on the horn and yelled, "Summer, let's go."

Kalani put a hand on the car door, but I stopped him with a shake of my head. "Not now. If you value your life, you'll back off."

He looked crestfallen but didn't back down. He pounded on the window.

"Lani, you stubborn goat! Open the door. It's not what you think!"

The glare she threw him burned through the window. "Get away from my car. I'll run you over if you don't move!"

Rather than do the prudent thing, he went to stand in front of her car, leaning both hands on the hood, resolute.

"You are one wahine pilau! If you would just turn off the car and talk to me, you'd know that Sheila is my cousin's girlfriend and she offered to help me—"

Lani laid on the horn again and put the car in reverse. Kalani lost his balance and almost hit the ground, catching himself at the last minute.

"Lani, what the hell?!" he hollered.

Lani threw the passenger door open and I hopped in. She reversed further and then jammed it into drive, tires squealing as we exited the parking lot.

Silence reigned as Lani drove up towards the observatory. When I couldn't stand it any longer, I burst out, "Lani, for real. What is going on with you two?"

Instead of answering, she pulled over and jumped out of the car. She paced back and forth on the side of the road as the wind whipped from the big semi-trucks driving by and diesel fumes filled the air.

When enough time had passed and her steps slowed, I hopped out and leaned against her car, waiting for her to break the silence.

Before answering, she let out a string of cuss words and then kicked a tire. I did my best not to laugh—she looked like a Hawaiian fairy throwing a fit. But when she looked up, her face was full of misery.

"I caught feelings," she admitted, her body appearing to shrink in on itself.

If she wasn't so miserable I would've laughed out loud. "You say that as if it's the worst thing that could happen to you," I chided.

She swung her arms wide and then pointed in the general direction of where we'd just been. "Obviously it is. You saw him. He was with another girl." Her voice dropped at the last few words, and she hung her head.

Even though she hated to be hugged, I risked it anyway and wrapped her in my arms. "Yeah, but you didn't let him explain. It's possible she's just a friend." Even as I said it, I thought how badly I would feel if I saw some rando girl kissing Cole, and my stomach clenched.

She sniffled. "What's to explain? He found another girl."

My heart went out to her. Lani had grown up without a mother, and Mack, while a great dad, didn't do feelings well, either. He'd fix your car, build you a bookshelf, and go toe to toe with anyone who messed with you, but discussions on feelings were few and far between.

Lani ran from feelings faster than a mongoose running from a lawnmower. Last year she'd fallen in love with a nomad who did what nomads do best—leave. It kind of broke her for a while, and she'd only recently been able to admit to herself and Kalani in a drunken moment that she'd had feelings for him since she was seventeen. They seemed like a perfect match to me, and secretly I was pulling for them to work this out.

"Let me ask you a question." Sniffling was the only response I got, but I continued on. "Do you think Kalani is a good guy? Honest?"

She mumbled something.

"What?"

"I did." Her forlorn voice tugged at me, but the only way we were going to fix this was ripping off the Band-Aid.

"Putting what we saw aside, I also think Kalani is a good guy. So how about this—before you jump to any conclusions, wait to hear his side of the story." I quoted one of the textbooks from the online classes Lani and I were taking for our P.I. degree. "'The hallmark of good investigation work is gathering evidence but remaining neutral until you have a complete picture.' How about if we drive back and you call him?"

She shook her head, her face mutinous.

"Do you want to find love?" I asked, my voice low and serious.

Her body twitched and she wriggled out from underneath my arms, slipping into the driver's side without answering.

⁂

The next morning, I picked Lani up at her house. Mack stood on the front porch, his hair tangled and mussed, like he'd been running his hands through it. Lani burst through the front door and vaulted down towards my waiting car.

"Bye, Mack!" she sang and then jumped out of reach when he tried to swat at her. He hated when she called him that.

Before I could back out of the driveway Mack motioned for me to wait and shuffled down to the Rav. He leaned his head down. "How's the investigation going so far?"

Lani and I shared a look. More than anything I wanted to help Mack out and not disappoint him, so the thought of telling him about our lack of anything new curdled my stomach.

Lani jumped in before I could answer. "Right on track. We're following all of the leads we have currently."

Mack raised an eyebrow. "Girl, you know I know you, right? You honestly think I can't see right through you?"

My shoulders drooped and my eyes drifted over to several cars in various states of repair in the front yard. An idea occurred to me.

"Hey, do we know where Otis's van is? I think we should start there and see if we can find any clues to help us figure out what happened to him."

Lani hummed in agreement. "Great idea."

We both looked over at Mack. A glimmer of amusement shone in his expression before it died. He straightened. "HPD probably impounded it, but let me make some calls." He turned and headed into the small, green and cedar plantation-style home without another word.

Lani and I watched him go before turning to look at each other.

"How'd your night go?"

She toyed with the lid on her coffee cup, circling the rim over and over again.

"Fine."

"Did you talk to him?"

She shrugged. "Sort of. I texted him. He said he wants to talk in person."

Yikes. The way she stared pointedly over at the window told me she was done answering questions for now. I sighed and put the car into gear.

Sun rays were just starting to peek up over Mauna Kea as we drove down Highway 19 for the harbor. Even though it was early, a fair number of cars were also heading west, likely workers heading to the resorts that dotted the Kohala coastline. We turned into the harbor entrance and bumped along the rutted drive.

"Wonder when the county is going to fix the road and open the gate," I mused.

Lani snorted. "Shit, it's been closed since the big storm in August two years ago. I think they're just waiting until someone with big bucks donates enough to repair it without county money."

The Rav handled the potholes and ruts fine as long as I took it easy. It drove me nuts that there was a nice smooth road mere yards away that we couldn't access though. The storm had damaged a small portion of one of the speed bumps and was easy to avoid, yet the gate remained locked.

We drove through another gate and past the restrooms, parking down by the dock. In the distance I saw Mike flip the cover off *Moonshine*.

"Let's go talk to Mike. He might've seen something."

Lani grabbed her coffee cup and followed me down the walkway to *Moonshine*.

As we got closer, I could hear Mike muttering. He looked up as we approached, his expression going from annoyed to shifty.

"Summer. Lani. Howzit?" he asked, his hands staying busy setting up scuba gear.

"Hey, Mike. Everything okay?"

He whipped his eyes up to meet mine. "Yeah, of course. Why? What have you heard?"

My brow wrinkled and I tilted my head. "Um, nothing?" Lani and I exchanged a puzzled look.

Gear littered the deck of the boat and Mike increased his pace as he swung BCDs onto air tanks. "Cool. What's up?"

Other than this weird conversation?

"Uh, we were just wondering if you'd seen Otis talking to anyone in particular in the last few weeks? We have reason to believe his drowning wasn't accidental."

Mike's posture went rigid and his hands stilled. He rubbed his palms down the front of his shorts several times and then continued readying gear. "Nope. Never really noticed him, honestly. Most people down at the harbor kind of stick to their own business if you know what I mean."

Yikes. Message received. I thanked him and he nodded before turning back to the task at hand.

Lani and I walked back the way we came when I noticed two things simultaneously—Jeff emerged from the cabin of his boat, and a grey Tacoma drove into the parking lot, staying on the upper lot and moving slowly towards the locked gate.

Jeff noticed me at the same time I noticed him and he froze.

Geez, what is it with men today?

Narrowing my eyes, I marched straight over to his boat.

"Good morning, Jeff," I trilled in my most cheerful voice. Lani threw me an amused glance but kept quiet.

Before he could greet me back, a loud rumbling echoed through the parking lot, and the Tacoma I'd noticed roared away at a high rate of speed. Jeff's eyes followed it, his jaw tense and eyebrows furrowed.

Jeff returned my greeting, his attention still on the departing truck. I introduce Lani, but meanwhile in the back of my mind I wondered about the undercurrents I felt. His eyes tracked the direction the truck had taken before flicking back over to where we stood.

"What brings you lovely ladies out so early on this fine day?" His words were friendly, but there was something about his tone that didn't ring true.

"Investigating a death."

Lani looked at me like I'd lost my marbles. "Geez, you have such a way with words," she said.

I watched Jeff closely for a reaction. Other than a slight tic in his cheek, he remained still as granite. "Oh yeah? Sounds...interesting." Something about his tone made me bristle. "Well, good luck with that. I've got a fishing charter heading out soon, but if you all want to dive later, I could arrange it."

"Cool. We'll let you know." I had no intention of getting on a boat with him, but I pasted on what I hoped was an innocent smile.

Lani pinched me. "You look like a crazy babooze right now," she whispered.

I glared at her but attempted to smile more naturally. "Well, have fun on your charter," I waved at him before grabbing Lani's arm and pulling her up towards the bathrooms near where some shoreline fishermen were just getting set up for the day.

I could feel Jeff's eyes follow us as we made our way over to the brick building that housed the bathrooms and maintenance closet.

Chapter Sixteen

COLE

"Anything?" Jonah lifted a brow at me from across the desk, his laptop whirring softly, the glow of the screen reflecting off his face.

I pinched my lips together and gave a heavy sigh. "Not yet. All the records seem to stop about a year ago." I swung my gaze up in his direction. "I'm not saying that our perps," I looked down at the screen and read off their names, "Elijah Thompson and Eduardo Reeves, couldn't have somehow become model citizens, but given what we've seen so far, I doubt it."

Jonah's jaw clenched. "Yeah, not likely. The records I reviewed show a pattern. But the pattern seems to just...stop."

"Yeah, I don't get it. From what Lennie says, these guys are pretty much running every hard drug you can name all along the coast from Hilo to Kapa'au. There's no way they somehow got real smart in a year. Enough to avoid getting caught, that is." I gestured toward my screen. "These jokers seemed to get caught almost the second they got released each time. What changed?"

I scrubbed a hand over my face. I'd hoped to see Summer tonight, but it didn't look like that was going to happen. Jonah and I needed to figure out where these guys were living. Disappointment lived in my chest—work was consuming me lately.

Lennie had informed us the men we were tracking came around at random times of both day and night. "Listen, I don't want to get on their bad side. They don't mess with me and my operation, and I give them a wide berth. I'm just a little gnat compared to what they got going on." His tone held a note of envy.

I made a mental note to keep a closer eye on Lennie—while the amounts he was pushing weren't large, the willingness to target high school kids and the elderly revealed a deeper criminal bent than I'd suspected.

We'd left Lennie in Pahala but took his stash and entered it into the crime lab. I liked to think of it as insurance.

I thought about his words now. "Lennie seemed almost... scared when he told us about the spread of Bois members into the area."

Jonah nodded. "Yeah, I got the impression that if the guys knew about Lennie ratting, he might end up going for a swim."

Hmm. "Probably wouldn't hurt to have HPD keep a unit out there, just to keep an eye on things."

We ordered in pizza, and I sent Summer a text, letting her know I wouldn't be able to come over tonight. Regret beat at me. She'd quickly become the most important person in my life, and seeing her at the end of the day was the bright spot that kept me going. I held onto that bright spot through the roughest days. *Goddammit.* We needed to make some headway, and soon, so I could get back to spending time with my favorite person.

We combed through the records and even searched known associates, but nothing seemed to line up. Finally, after hitting nothing but dead-ends I threw my hands up in the air. "I'm calling it. I can't find anything."

Jonah ran his hands through his hair, grabbing a clump and staring at his computer. "Me either. It's like someone just wiped their records clean."

Something about his words caught my attention. "You don't think?" My eyes shifted in the direction of Takada's darkened office.

Jonah tracked my gaze and stared for a minute. "Shit," he swore under his breath.

Neither one of us said anything for a few minutes.

Jonah was the first to break the silence. "Timeline fits." He shrugged. "Didn't you say there were photos circulating of him fraternizing with some known Bois members after hours?"

My chair creaked as I sat up straight abruptly. Footage of Takada with known gang members had been sent to the DOJ anonymously, which is what started a deeper undercover look at his off-duty activities by the FBI. I stared blindly at my screen for a minute before looking at Jonah and nodding.

I lowered my voice, even though the only people left in the office were a few patrol guys in the break room. "Dear God, I hope we're wrong. He's done a lot of shitty things, but this? This is federal prison level stuff. And you know what happens to cops in federal prison."

"Dude, I'm not saying it's true, just that the timeline fits." Jonah threw his hands up as he leaned back in his chair.

Adrenaline coursed through my veins, my focus narrowing in on one thought: if we could finally get proof of Chief's misdeeds than this nightmare would be over. As I sat there deliberating, an idea occurred and I grabbed my phone, texting Jack, my FBI contact.

> Is it possible for T to scrub records? Just found two, Elijah Thompson and Eduardo Reeves, and I'm not seeing anything for the last year. Have you heard any rumors about him associating with the Bois on Oahu when he was with Honolulu PD?

His response was immediate.

> I'm firing up my computer now. You're going to allow access on your screen when I request it. Once I'm in, you're going to leave for the night.

Jonah didn't know I was working with the alphabet groups to bring Chief down, although I'm sure he suspected—he was a smart guy. Holding my cards close, I merely suggested to Jonah that we call it a night the minute I saw Jack had obtained access.

Jonah opened his mouth, and I stiffened at the thought of having to lie to him yet again, but after a moment he just nodded and grabbed his bag.

Our trucks were parked next to each other in the parking lot. I stood next to Jonah's door as he got in. "You know we can't tell anyone about this, right?"

A muscle in his jaw twitched and he nodded. When he looked at me, his eyes were furious.

"I know man, I know." The words seemed to get caught in my throat, sounding almost guttural.

Jonah nodded once, anger coming off of him in waves. He opened his mouth to say something, but then shut it, his jaw clenched. He jammed his key into the ignition before sketching a salute and driving off.

As I drove through the gates after him, I turned right instead of left. My thoughts were in turmoil and frustrated, angry energy burned through me; I didn't want to be still right now.

The bright lights of Forever Fitness came into view thirty minutes later, and I realized I didn't remember any of my drive. I grabbed my gym bag from my backseat and went in to sweat off the building fury inside me as best I could.

Was Chief really working with the Bois? Two months ago, he'd set off alarm bells when I saw him consorting with known Yakuza, and those alarms got even louder last month when he tried to pin a murder on Summer. So far, his behavior bordered on outright corrupt, but we had yet to gather anything undeniably damning.

But, if what Jonah and I discovered was true and he was wiping records, Pandora's Box had just cracked open, and an icy shiver ran through me as I thought about the chaos it might bring when the truth came to light.

Chapter Seventeen

SUMMER

OUR VISIT TO THE harbor had done nothing so far except raise concerns. Everyone seemed to be hiding something, and I was more confused than ever. While I was pondering the conversations I'd had with both Mike and Jeff, Lani nudged me and then whistled shrilly.

"Uncle Louie!" Lani called over to a barrel chested, middle-aged man with dark hair graying at the temples and twinkling black eyes.

"Eh, Lani girl. What you doing down here?" He set his rig down, dangling line and bait in the water as he stepped over to give her a hug. She managed to mostly contain a grimace, and I grinned at her. She shot me the bird behind Louie's back, and my face split into an even wider grin.

Louie asked how Mack was doing and they caught up on family news. Lani was related to approximately half the island's population, either by blood or marriage.

Doing my best to tamp down my impatience, I unconsciously started tapping my leg.

Lani flicked her eyes over at me. "Can I help you?" Her tone was dry and slightly irritated. Message received.

I shook my head, embarrassed. "My apologies. I'm not always the greatest at talk story, especially in this case."

Uncle Louie gave me a friendly smile. "Ah, no worries, sis. Don't let this one give you a hard time—there was a time I remember her buzzing all over the place like a mosquito on caffeine." He grinned and gestured toward Lani. "Never could get her to sit still."

Lani stuck her tongue out at me, and Louie guffawed loudly. "Ah, you young'uns are good for me."

My shoulders relaxed slightly. It was a daily struggle to fight my impatient nature on an island known for its chill vibes.

"It seems that you have something on your mind." Louie prompted.

"Uncle, did you know crazy Otis?"

His face drooped and his eyes lost their infectious twinkle. "Ahh, Otis. Good guy. Kept to himself. Shared fish whenever he could, even when he didn't have much himself." He shook his head. "He'll be missed around here."

Lani leaned closer into him. "Dad doesn't think his death was accidental. He asked us to investigate. Did you notice anything different going on before he died?"

Uncle Louie pursed his lips and cupped his chin, looking off in the distance. He seemed to be giving the matter some thought before he eventually replied, "You know, come to think of it, a few weeks ago Otis warned me to watch out for your cousin Joey. I asked him what he meant and he just said, 'they're after the lost.' When I asked him what he meant he just repeated his words, gave me a salute, and surfed off with that goat of his." He shook his head. "Craziest thing I ever seen—a goat surfing. In a dress, no less."

"Do you know why he would single Joey out in particular?" Curiosity wound through me.

Uncle Louie shrugged, his oversized arms covered in kakau tattoos spreading out. "No idea. I didn't even know he knew Joey."

"Anything else?" Lani asked.

He thought for a moment longer then shook his head. "Not that I can think of." He scratched his chin, his expression somber. "If what you're saying is true, I hope you gals catch whoever did that to Otis. He might've been crazy, but he was the good kind of crazy."

We nodded and thanked him. Lani suffered through another hug, and I heard her murmur, "Uncle, can you keep an eye on things around here? If there is a killer on the loose, they're going to slip up eventually."

His expression turned grave as he tipped his head and put his fist over my heart. "Don't worry, sweetheart. Me and your cousins will bird-dog down here until Otis's killer is caught."

In an uncharacteristic moment, I watched as Lani leaned into him, forehead to forehead. "Mahalo."

The rest of the morning we hung out around the harbor, watching the comings and goings. The wind had died down some, and the waves lapped lazily against the dock. Early whale watching boats were motoring in and out, taking tourists out for a day on the water in the hopes of seeing some of the ever-hopeful males of the whale variety looking to mate or pregnant cows trekking to the warm waters to give birth.

We talked to a few of the operators, but no one had anything new to add to what we already knew. I hated to burst Lani's bubble, but the Big Island was a small community, and news of our investigation would likely make it all the way to Hilo by lunch, despite wanting to keep it quiet. When I mentioned it to Lani, she frowned and rubbed the back of her neck.

She blew out a long breath. "Yeah, you're right. I don't know why I even thought for a second we could keep this a secret." She lifted her shoulders. "I guess I thought if we could fly under the radar, we could catch the killer off guard. But especially with this crowd," she gestured to the fishermen all clumped together on the shoreline and then over to the operators jabbering away at the wash station, clucking like chickens to each other, "there's no way to keep a secret. They're worse than *The Real Housewives* of wherever." She snorted.

Her phone vibrated and a disembodied voice said, "incoming text" from her back pocket. I raised an eyebrow at her, and she wrinkled her nose, refusing to meet my eyes. "Didn't want to miss any texts from Kal—, from my...dad."

"Mmhmm," was my only response.

Her face fell when she looked at the screen, but then her brow wrinkled before shifting her gaze back to me. "HPD never found Otis's van."

"Weird. He usually parked it just past the Kawaihae Shopping Center. Come to think of it though, I didn't notice it on our drive up to see Paisley."

My stomach growled just then, and Lani silently laughed at me. "Let's hit Surf Burger and then drive around and see if we find anything."

"Deal," I said as my stomach let out another gurgle. I pointed down at my stomach. "This is all your fault by the way. You've got me burning so many calories at the gym I can't seem to eat enough to feed the beast."

"You'll thank me later." She gave me a cheeky grin as we loaded into the Rav and headed north out of the harbor.

We stood in line at Surf Burger, tourists and locals alike waiting for their greasy, salty burgers. When it was our turn to order, the girl at the register, Hana, greeted us. "Hey ladies. Long time no see."

"It's her fault, she's trying to keep me on the straight and narrow." I poked Lani, grinning.

Hana grinned back and Lani fake frowned at both of us before ordering a burger bowl. I tilted my head to the side at her order before a lightbulb went on in my brain.

As we sat at the picnic table waiting for our food, I grilled Lani. "All this fitness stuff, it's because of Kalani, isn't it? Here I thought you were just trying to get me in shape, but it was really *you* who wants to stay in shape, isn't it?"

She sniffed but stared pointedly at the large screen TV on the wall. "I have no idea what you're talking about. I'm just trying to get your pansy ass in shape so you don't get rolled when some dude decides to have a go at you."

"Your nose seems to be getting longer by the second," I remarked blandly.

Hana brought over our food just then, putting a halt to our conversation as my eyes widened at the cheesy, greasy burger in front of me, surrounded by waffle fries. I pounced on my food like a cat pounces on a juicy mouse.

When I finally came up for air, I noticed Lani tapping away on her phone and grunted at her.

"You sound like a feral pig rooting through the dirt," she threw out at me irritably.

"Oink, oink." I watched her as she ignored me and focused on her phone screen. When I couldn't take it a minute longer, I burst out, "Okay, give. What are you doing over there on your phone?"

A knowing smirk covered her face. "I wondered how long it would take you to get nosy." She looked up at the clock on the wall. "About 4.8 seconds. Nice work."

"Yeah, yeah." I motioned at her phone. "What's going on?"

In answer to my question, she held her phone up. On it was a map of the island with little red pins at various spots along the Kohala Coast. I leaned closer to examine the points before raising my eyebrows at her. "Is this what I think it is?"

She nodded. "These are all the places either I or my dad could remember Otis having parked his van."

Excitement burst through me. I jumped up. "Sweet. Let's go."

Lani let out a long-suffering sigh but stood up and followed me out, waving goodbye to Hana as we passed by.

"You know, it really wouldn't hurt if we could just take a moment and methodically plot out our route versus just jumping in the car and driving around like all those chickens running around in Kauai."

My steps slowed as we got closer to the Rav. Shit. She had a point. I felt my face flush. "Right. Good point. Let's plot it in the Rav."

Once we loaded our route, starting with the closest and ending up near Pololu Valley, I turned to Lani. "I'm really glad you're my partner, if I haven't said that lately. I know I give you a lot of crap, but you help keep me on track."

She batted her eyes at me. "Of course I do. Someone's gotta keep your lolo ass from plunging headlong into danger."

"Phht. I am the picture of thoughtful action, you cow."

"Ha!" was her only response as we headed east to the first spot marked.

Chapter Eighteen

SUMMER

ELLIOT CALLED AFTER HE got off work to see what we were up to and asked if he could join. "I'm ten minutes away," he pleaded.

"You know we're going to be driving on dirt tracks and hiking in places, right? You might get your nice suit and tie a little dusty," Lani needled him.

"My workout clothes are in my car. Please? Pretty please and I'll make you carbonara for dinner?"

This last plea was directed at me—Elliot knew pasta was my kryptonite. "Fine. Ten minutes. Be at the Minnit Stop or we're leaving without you."

It was actually closer to fifteen minutes by the time he showed up, and I tapped impatiently on my steering wheel the last five of it. Did I mention patience wasn't a strength of mine?

Elliot's face popped up next to Lani's window. He knocked, causing her to squeak and fumble her phone, with which she'd been preoccupied for the last ten minutes, ignoring me and not answering any of my questions.

"Thank God you're here. Summer's driving me crazy," Lani announced to Elliot as she unlocked the door and he hopped in back.

"Yeah, I think that's one of her top five Clifton Strengths, 'ability to annoy everyone around her in less time than it takes for most people to brush their teeth.'" After the Fairmont paid Elliot to take the popular personality test, that's all he talked about for weeks.

"Har har," I said sourly. "Why do you want to go traipsing around with us anyway? Why aren't you hanging out with TJ and arguing about who's prettier?"

He sniffed. "We're both equally pretty. I have that whole hot, mysterious Asian look and TJ's a Ken doll come to life." He flipped his wrist at me. "It's that whole opposites attract thing."

Lani snorted. "Hot, mysterious Asian? Please. More like nerdy accountant."

He flicked her ear from the backseat. "Take it back."

She swung around and stuck her tongue out at him.

"Why is it when we get together, we revert to thirteen-year-olds?" I mused out loud.

"She started it," Elliot said sullenly.

I rolled my eyes and blew out a long-suffering breath. "Okay—here's the deal. Otis's van has been seen over the past six months parked at these locations. We need to check out each location. It's imperative we find his van. From what Lani's uncle told us, it sounded like Otis was concerned about something, and his van might give us clues about what that was."

Elliot shifted from casual to serious. "Alright, got it. I'm here to help. I didn't really know Otis that well, but I've heard a lot of stories about him and he sounds like a pretty good guy."

Luckily, Lani and Elliot seemed to come to some sort of a truce; they stopped arguing all the way to our first stop, a whole five minutes up the road from Minnit Stop.

Kiawe trees lined a narrow dirt path just off the highway. I parked parallel to the road and we got out, following the trail up a steep embankment of red volcanic dirt to a flat landing overlooking the ocean.

I made a slow circle, my hand shielding my eyes, and then looked at Lani. "Definitely not here."

She shook her head, "Nope." She let out a sigh, "at least it's a pretty view."

"Since we're here, we might as well take a look around and see if there's any trace of him."

Elliot, Lani, and I poked around in the dirt and bushes but didn't find anything but a few broken beer bottles and some cigarette butts. I blew out a breath. "Alright, on to the next spot."

We traipsed back to the Rav and headed off to the next several points on the map, but still nothing. We only had one more spot pinned. I drummed my fingers on the steering wheel. "Where on earth did Otis park his van? I found Paisley down by the harbor and Otis's body was pulled out at Kawaihae South. Much farther north and we'll be in Hawi. That's over fifteen miles away from the harbor."

Lani leaned over to look at the next spot. "Hmm. Good point. Something's off."

We decided to check the last point, but it was looking less and less likely we'd find Otis's van. Just past Richard and Evelyn's road we turned into the last pin on the map and drove down a graveled road toward the ocean. After about a mile, the bushes started to close in around the Rav, the high-pitched scraping noises of thorns running down the length of my car making me wince. We came to a downed tree that halted any forward progress.

"Well, no van here." I drummed my fingers on the steering wheel. I quirked an eyebrow at Lani. "Any ideas?"

She held up her cellphone, searching for a signal, then shook her head. "Nothing. Dad might have some ideas, but we're in a dead zone."

The Rav incurred more scratches on the way back out as I reversed to a clearing and turned it around. Each scratch felt like failure in more ways than one. I'd never had a new car before, and since Dad bought this one for me as a bribe/gift, it had been rear-ended, a tree branch fell on it, and now this. Insurance covered the repairs minus the deductible on the first two incidents, but per usual, my bank account was barely scraping three figures, and I mentally started adding up the cost of new paint.

On top of that, the mystery surrounding Otis's missing van was eating at me. My gut told me his van might hold some clues, but we'd never know until we actually found it. I leaned my head down on my steering wheel in defeat.

Elliot tapped me on the back, and I lifted a shoulder and looked underneath it at him. "Since we're already up this way, can we visit Paisley? I've never met her in person, and I want to get a selfie with her for my IG page."

I turned my head back to my steering wheel pillow and grumbled under my breath, before sighing. "Fine. I don't know if anyone's home, but once we're back in range, I'll call."

Richard and Evelyn answered on the first ring and told me they'd be delighted to have us stop by for another visit. As we drove through the gate, I lectured Elliot on goat etiquette.

"She's going to rush over and possibly nudge you a little with her horns—that's her way of saying hello. Hold your palm out flat and let her sniff you before you try to pet her."

Elliot dismissed me with a weave of his hand. "I'm sure I'll be fine. I have a natural affinity for animals."

Lani and I shared a look but said nothing.

Evelyn met us down at the goat pen with a big smile. She whistled and Paisley came trotting out of the pen and over to where we stood at the fence, her fuchsia scarf flowing in the wind.

"Oh my God!" Elliot squealed and clapped his hands together, a giant, slightly demented grin on his face.

Evelyn raised an eyebrow at him and started to say something, but just then her cell phone rang. She looked down and groaned before gesturing to her phone and stepping away to take the call.

When I turned back around, Elliot had climbed over the fence and into the pen. "Here, Paisley. Come to Uncle Elliot," he crooned in a high-pitched tone.

Paisley seemed to hesitate before taking mincing steps toward where he stood holding his hand out. She moved close and began to sniff his hand delicately then nudging it with a little more vigor.

Elliot, being Elliot, trilled out, "She likes me!" before pulling his phone out and leaning his head in next to Paisley's to get a selfie. He got off about two shots, crowing about how much she loved him when she suddenly stomped on his foot with her hoof, causing him to jump and hop around, screeching and grabbing his foot.

The screaming and hopping must've really freaked Paisley out because she reared up and started pawing at Elliot with her hooves. For once, he recognized the danger he was in and high-tailed it to the fence, vaulting over in a jump that would've made a kangaroo envious, landing directly into a large heap of fresh cow dung.

I'm pretty sure I peed my pants from laughing so hard. Lani was the same. Neither of us could even speak, and each time we tried, we convulsed into a fresh round of laughter. Poor Evelyn stood over Elliot and offered him a hand up, fussing and clucking like a little German mama bear.

When Elliot stood up, his glasses were crooked on his face, his hair standing up at all angles with brown dung smeared over the left side of his body. He attempted to pull together his dignity, but slipped in the pile, catching himself just in time and then followed Evelyn over to the side of the pen.

She pulled out the hose and handed it to him. "I'll be right back with some towels," she promised him before dashing up the drive towards the house.

Paisley stood in a corner of her pen and brayed at us, munching on hay, her eyes big and innocent. I patted the fence and she trotted over, nosing my hand. I gave her a good scratch and smiled down at the cute collar Otis had given her. Her name was surrounded by pink hibiscus flowers with a little leather Air tag holder. Seeing the Air tag holder punched through the amusement. Clearly, Otis had loved Paisley enough to make sure if she got lost, he'd be able to find her.

Hardcore squeals drew my attention away from Paisley and I turned to see Lani aiming the garden hose at Elliot. "You can't get into the car like that. Let me spray you down."

The whites of his eyes showed and he begged, "Just grab my clothes from the car. I'll change into those," he pleaded.

Lani angled her hand up as if to spray him, and he held his hands up in front of him, protesting. She threw a look in my direction and my lips curved up. She wiggled the hose, Elliot's cries hitting a crescendo before she set it back up on the pen door.

I went back to the Rav to retrieve his bag of clothes and set it on a shelf on the side of the pen that held brushes, collars, and extra grain buckets. "You're going to have to strip, spray yourself off, and then put your clean clothes on."

Evelyn came back down to the pen just then and set some towels next to his clothes on the shelf. While Elliot cleaned himself up, without Lani's 'help' which would've likely involved blasting him obnoxiously, Lani and I chatted with Evelyn.

"Have you girls had any luck today?" Her cerulean eyes pinched up at the corners, forehead furrowed in concern.

My shoulders slumped as I shook my head. "Not really. Lani's uncle told us Otis seemed a little worried about something, but it was pretty vague." I ran a hand threw my ponytail, tugging at the tangles. "We looked all over for his van but no luck there, either." I kicked a small piece of lava rock with my toe.

"Well, I'm sure you girls will find something soon," she encouraged as the wind lifted her hair, causing it to swirl around her face. The tall grasses in the field beyond the pen rippled wildly in the wind.

She cast a gaze around. "I sure hope Hurricane Luisa misses us. I don't think we can handle another storm so close to the last one."

Lani chimed in. "The forecast shows it going pretty far south of the islands." She peeled a piece of grass into pieces in her hand.

My neck tingled. "Let's hope so. We don't need yet another thing impeding our investigation."

Chapter Nineteen

SUMMER

AFTER ELLIOT WAS ADEQUATELY cleaned for the car ride home, we headed back towards Waikoloa Village. Evelyn had given us a trash bag to seal Elliot's soiled clothes in, but even so we kept the windows wide open which he complained about bitterly.

"You know I have a date with TJ tonight. My hair is already a mess," Lani had 'helpfully' sprayed out his hair for him, but it stood up in wild clumps now. "All this wind is going to tangle it so bad it's going to take *hours* to style it."

Lani mimed playing a tiny violin and Elliot glared at her. I smiled at their nonsense but then risked a look in the rearview mirror at Elliot. "Speaking of TJ, what did you decide about going on a trip with him?"

He sighed. "I don't know. The whole reason I wanted to win the cocktail contest was so I could use the prize money to take him on a trip, but now I'm not so sure. I don't want to rush things or make it weird with him, you know?" He quirked his mouth up in frustration. "The problem is that now TJ's so excited about the contest I feel honor bound to keep going."

Lani clicked her tongue. "Hmm. I'm with TJ—you can't quit now. You took on this challenge and now you have to see it through, champ." She reached back and patted him on the shoulder. "You got this buddy, I believe in you."

He scoffed. "You're only saying that because you want to keep drinking the cocktails I make."

"Can't I both be supportive of my friend's growth *and* enjoy the fruits of his labors?" she asked with a cheeky smile on her face.

He just folded his arms and stared out the window.

"If it's of any help to you, I agree with Lani about continuing on with the contest. Yes, there's a little bit of an agenda behind me saying that, but mostly if you quit now, I think it might cause TJ to worry that you don't finish what you start. Besides, you seem to really be enjoying it."

He leaned forward between the two front seats, chin in his hands. "I never thought about it that way. I don't want TJ to think I'm a quitter. And I *am* enjoying creating drinks." He pursed his lips.

"You know, you might want to consider gently introducing the topic with him and gauge his reaction. Even if you don't take him on the trip, maybe you could do something on island, like a cool tour or something."

Lani shifted in her seat and bounced a little. "You could take him ziplining at Oliver's." Oliver ran a ziplining business and was one of Lani's many cousins on the island. He'd been bugging us for months to come and take a tour. "Or, I heard about this UFO tour where they use night vision goggles and everything and they talk about the underwater UFO base offshore."

Elliot and I both snapped our heads in her direction. After a moment I said, "Umm, what now?"

Her head bobbed up and down in excitement. "Yeah, it's supposed to be really cool, and they tell stories of UFO encounters on the island and stuff."

A strangled noise came from Elliot. "She's finally flipped her lid. The chicken has lost her head." He turned to look at me and then Lani. "Have you been getting into the pakalolo again?"

She sniffed. "Just because you don't believe in it doesn't mean it's not real." She crossed her arms with a huff. "Besides, I don't touch that stuff. Gotta keep my senses sharp."

A gleeful laugh erupted from Elliot. "You've got to be kidding me. I can't believe you of all people believe in this."

'Wait. I can't believe you don't. Aren't you the same person that swore up and down the Menehune were stealing your socks?" My eyebrows rose in question at him.

He slumped back in the seat. "They were. And not all of my socks. Just one sock from each pair. I went a whole month without matching socks."

"Uh huh. But aliens are somehow unbelievable. Got it."

While we were talking, an idea took root in the back of my mind. Something about aliens brought it forward. I swung the Rav over to the shoulder, gravel flying, and took a hard U-turn a couple hundred feet north to a tiny little pullout. It hadn't been pinned on the map, but I remember hearing talk that Otis went through a period of talking about aliens.

"Damn it, Summer. At least warn us before you go all *Fast and Furious,*" Lani complained, rubbing her elbow.

"Shoot, sorry." I rubbed my hands together. "All your alien talk reminded me that Otis talked about aliens to us when I was down at Kohala Divers after pulling a shift. There's a cave not far from here that you can access from the higher road with a vehicle." I opened my car door and leaned in, "But there's also a foot path right off the road."

Lani slapped her head. "Oh my gosh, I can't believe I forgot about that."

We trekked uphill along the dirt and lava path, Elliot wincing as his shiny black Gucci loafers got instantly covered in red dust.

About a quarter of a mile in, the path jogged to the right and dropped down into a small gulch. Luckily for us it was dry. This time of year, it was hit or miss, but this summer had been abnormally dry.

We scrambled uphill again and came to a small, enclosed clearing. After shimmying through the Kiawe bushes carefully, the clearing opened up, and there, parked tight against the cave opening, was Otis's van.

"We found it!" Elliot crowed.

Lani and I spared him a glance and then turned to approach it, my pulse picking up.

Lani surveyed the area surrounding the van as we took careful steps toward it. Hoof prints surrounded it, along with large footprints. All three of us stood shoulder to shoulder staring at it. Elliot nudged my shoulder and motioned with his chin.

I wrinkled my nose at him but took the last few steps toward it, my hand hovering right above the door handle.

"Wait!" Lani said, and my hand stilled, millimeters from the handle.

I snatched my hand back as if I'd almost touched fire and looked at her, my body tilting away from the van.

"What if it's booby-trapped or something?"

"Shit. I don't know. What would your dad tell us to do?"

She reached into her back pocket and started tapping on her cellphone. I waited for what felt like hours but was probably only a minute or two. Lani shoved her cellphone back into her pocket and took a deep breath.

"Dad said we need to look for trip wires."

"What the...?" I scratched my chin. "Like in *Indiana Jones* or something?"

She nodded and we searched the outside of the van and all along the ground but didn't see anything out of the ordinary.

Once again, I found myself hovering above the door handle, girding my loins or something, I guess. With a deep breath I pulled the handle and jumped back, just in case. When nothing darted out at me, I leaned in to inspect the inside of the van, afraid to actually touch anything. Elliot and Lani crowded around me to peer in as well.

For someone who lived in his van, Otis was a neatnik. The van held homemade shelves with neatly organized Tupperware boxes, all labeled. Tentatively, I stepped into the van and shimmied between the driver and passenger seats to the back in order to slide open the side door for Elliot and Lani.

Elliot picked a box at random and opened it. Inside were goat supplements. Disappointment washed over his face, and he replaced it before grabbing another Tupperware box. This one had small, travel sized animal dishes.

"Dang it. I was hoping for something good, like gold doubloons or something," Elliot griped.

"It might help if you actually read the label before opening it," I suggested.

"Look at the labels—I can't read anything on them. It's worse than doctor handwriting."

I peered closer and saw what he meant. While the van and shelves were nicely ordered, Otis's handwriting looked like a two-year-old had gotten ahold of a sharpie. I sighed.

"Guess you're right. We'll have to look through each one," I said with a sigh.

"Maybe not." Lani's muffled voice came from up front by the driver's side seat. She pulled out a small, leather-bound book.

Elliot and I scrabbled forward as Lani flipped the book over in her hands, examining it from every angle. There was some sort of metal buckle on it. Lani tried to trigger the mechanism to unlock it, but nothing happened. She frowned down at it.

"Can I try?" Lani frowned at Elliot and then reluctantly handed it over.

He played with the latch as well, but it stayed firmly locked. Elliot handed it over to me to try. Silver knobs jutted out just above the buckle, which was about five inches long and two inches deep, running on the long end of the book. There were seven knobs in total, spaced out in a pattern on the buckle.

"It's almost like a bike lock or something, but I've never seen anything like it."

After studying it for a little while longer I set it aside. "We should check the rest of the van and make sure we didn't miss anything."

They nodded and we continued our search, but other than the strange book we didn't find anything else, not even a key to lock the van.

"I feel weird about just leaving Otis's van unlocked."

"Me too, but I didn't see a spare key anywhere and there's no way a tow truck could get down here." Lani swung her arms open to highlight the rugged terrain, the winding trail and rutted, rocky area too narrow for a tow truck to maneuver while pulling a car.

"Point well taken. What should we do?"

Lani shrugged. "I don't think there's much we *can* do for now. I'll let my dad know and maybe he and his buddies can figure out what to do with the van."

We shut the van and traversed back to the Rav, my feet dragging as I looked back several times to where the van was hidden.

Lani, sensing my reluctance to leave the van unprotected, clapped me on the shoulder. "Cheer up. Almost no one ever comes up here. I doubt we have to worry about anyone breaking in." She waited while I unlocked the Rav. "He sure did a good job picking a place to park his van, though."

I quirked my lips and raised an eyebrow.

She pointed across the highway to a barely visible trail leading down the ocean. "Otis could've easily hiked from the van and down to the harbor. That trail shortcuts right through and cuts off almost a mile. Probably only took him fifteen minutes or so to get down to the water."

Elliot hopped in the back, and we buckled up to head home. From the back, Elliot asked, "What do you guys think happened to Otis?"

Silence washed over us, neither Lani nor me sure how to answer Elliot's question.

"Honestly, I don't know." Lani finally answered.

My heart thudded painfully. Lani usually had a theory about everything. If she didn't have any guesses, then it was quite likely this case was well and truly screwed.

Chapter Twenty

COLE

AFTER SWEATING OUT MY fury and frustration at the gym I headed back to my apartment and crashed out in bed, exhausted. The following morning was spent impersonating someone who didn't know that the chief of police was possibly an even worse criminal than the guys we picked up off the streets every day.

When Takada called me into his office asking for an update on my latest cases it took everything inside of me to not reach across and choke him.

Jack hadn't reached out to me and wasn't answering my texts, so I was left in limbo on whether he found out who'd altered the records. By the time Jonah dragged me out of the office to get lunch, I felt like a cranky toddler who missed his nap.

Jonah had spent the morning reaching out to some of his other CI's, but so far no one knew anything about the boats or the guys we were after. Or if they did, they weren't saying.

"It's like they're ghosts or something. I keep hitting dead-end after dead-end. Even a few of the cousins I've talked to seem afraid of the Bois. The closest I got to a possible location of our guys was a sighting at South Point." Jonah ran a hand through his hair and let out a frustrated sigh.

"Do you think it's worth it to go poke around out there?"

He shook his head. "No. Elijah Thompson's cousin Ipo said he heard that Elijah moves around. The family tried to help, but Ipo told me Elijah's too far gone to listen to reason."

"What about the other guy? Eduardo Reves? Did the family have information about that guy?"

"Nothing much. They said Eduardo bounced around a lot as a teenager and pulled Elijah into the Bois right out of high school. There's no aloha in the family for Eduardo, that's for sure." He tapped his fingers on the console while we waited for the light to change. "Ipo promised to call me if Elijah shows up, but you know how that goes."

I did. Family connections on the island were strong, and sometimes it was hard to get family onboard to help. "Sounds like they're worried enough about him though that they might actually call."

Jonah shrugged. "Hope so."

My phone buzzed and I looked down to see a number I didn't recognize. "Hello?"

"Aloha, this is Nancy Fredricks with Waikoloa Realty One. Is this Cole Peterson?"

I pulled the phone in a little closer to my ear. "Yes."

"Mr. Peterson, I see that you filled out our online form expressing interest in several condos in Waikoloa Village. Is that correct?"

I nodded and then felt dumb. My voice came out hoarse. "Yes, I did."

"Well, I wonder if you have time to come in and discuss what you're looking for. We have some wonderful single-family homes that have just come on the market as well as several condo units, with golf privileges included."

My mouth went dry, and it took me a second to realize she was waiting for a response. "Uh, sure. When?"

The whole time I was on the phone, Jonah watched me, his eyebrows winging up at my increasingly muted responses.

She listed off several dates, and I picked the first one she mentioned, mostly because it was all I could remember.

After I disconnected the call, Jonah cleared his throat and gestured at me and then the phone. My first instinct was to deflect, but last month I'd dented our partnership a bit when I put in my resignation without telling him. Ultimately, I'd rescinded it, but the damage had been done, and Jonah and I were just starting to get back on track.

I took a deep breath. "I'm considering buying a house up in Waikoloa Village." Even saying the words caused my heart to beat at warp speed. My throat felt dry, my hands clammy. I hadn't felt like this since right before I asked a girl out for the first time in high school.

"Does it have anything to do with a certain hot blonde lifeguard?" A knowing smirk covered his face.

"Maybe. Sort of. But I also need to get out of my apartment and I'm tired of throwing money away every month."

Jonah let out a noise of agreement. 'Yeah, I hear that. It's stupid expensive to rent, but without a big downpayment, it's impossible to get financing for a house anywhere."

"Between savings and qualifying for a VA loan, I think I'll come out pretty square to where I'm at now."

Jonah clapped me on the shoulder. "That's awesome, dude! Congrats!"

I nodded slightly.

He tilted his head and narrowed his gaze. "You seem a little...nervous."

I shrugged, turning my head to look out the window.

"You do know you chase criminals down all day and, like, ran ops as a Navy Seal, right? I'm not understanding where this angst is coming from."

Jonah parked in the Kona Brewing parking lot and turned off the engine.

I rolled my shoulders, my gut churning. "This thing with Summer, it's serious. At least on my end. It's a big deal—if I'm lucky, maybe someday she'll live there with me. What if I buy something and she hates it?"

Jonah's eyes crinkled at the corners, as he quirked his mouth to the side. "Why don't you take her with you?" His tone implied I was missing the obvious—and maybe I was.

"What do you mean? To meet the realtor?"

He shrugged. "Sure, or if you want to spare her the boring parts, see if she wants to go look at some places with you once the realtor sets up showings?"

Hmm. "That's actually not a bad idea."

He punched me in the shoulder. "Yeah, I'm a real genius."

After lunch we headed back to the station. Jonah got a lead on another case on our way in, so I spent the afternoon studying case files and searching for any link that might connect to the drug boats.

By five my eyes were bleary, and I hadn't gotten any farther than where I started. I shut my laptop and called it a day, frustrated that I hadn't heard anything more from Jack yet.

My drive up to Waikoloa Village took forever. The closer we got to Thanksgiving and Christmas, the heavier the traffic got, and it was red taillights as far as the eye could see.

As the line of cars slowly snaked forward, a flashback to something Jeff said on the boat the other day crossed my mind. He'd said something along the lines of 'needing to fix the past.' At the time, I thought he was referring to getting Taco's knife back. But the face I thought I saw at Punalu'u Bakery made me think it might be something else. My hands tightened on the steering wheel, and I had the distinct feeling I probably didn't know Jeff nearly as well as I thought I did.

Scenarios flitted through my mind, scenarios that explained Jeff's comment. But I also thought back to right after we left the Navy. He'd struggled, probably more than the rest of us, once our active service contract had ended. Without the structure of the Navy, he'd been lost, ping-ponging through life somewhat. My mom met him once at one of the ceremonies she attended at Camp Pendleton when we finished our SEAL training. She'd remarked, "That one's never going to grow any moss, is he?" Something within Jeff craved adventure like a dying man craved more time.

When I received his call that he was coming to the island, I'd been genuinely excited. At heart he'd always been a good guy. I hoped that was still true.

My phone buzzed, interrupting my thoughts. "Jack, hey. What'd you find out?" Anticipation shot through me.

"Unfortunately, not a lot. Our team was able to backtrack and look at when the alterations to the records may have occurred. The IT signature we found belongs to an employee who died two years ago. The changes were made just under a year ago."

"What the...?" Frustration pulsed at me.

On the other end, I heard Jack blow out an exasperated breath. "My thoughts exactly. One thing I'll say about Takada, he sure is cagey."

"So, are we assuming he somehow found a way to access this dead guy's log-in to go in and change records? And if so—how many records has he changed?"

"That's the thing—we have mountains of data to comb through now. Any records with the IT guy's log-in have to be examined, but we've at least been able to narrow the timeline down to the past two years since he was, well, dead. I don't have any solid proof of Takada's interference, so we have to go through everything methodically. We're talking months, if not years, of sifting. I've got a team working on it, but we're short-staffed," he snorted, "and with the hiring freeze in place on all government agencies there's no light at the end of the tunnel."

I let out a strangled groan of annoyance. Takada was more slippery than an eel hunting at twilight.

Jack cleared his throat, and I was almost afraid to ask what other news he had. "We're getting a lot of pushback from the governor to wrap up this case before the next election campaign starts in January." A derisive snort echoed through the line. "He thinks putting a dirty cop behind bars might garner him a few more votes."

"You've got to be kidding me. Damnit!" I thumped my steering wheel in irritation.

"The policeman's ball is coming up next month." Jack's quick shift in topics threw me.

"Huh. Haven't given it any thought, but since Takada's the star of that show I figured I'd go do something more pleasant, maybe visit the dentist and get my teeth ripped out or jump in a nest of centipedes."

"Might want to reconsider. I'm getting reports of some very wealthy, and slightly shady backers attending. I could use a guy on the inside."

Chapter Twenty One

SUMMER

DINNER WAS A LIVELY affair. Cole showed up just as we were plating up Elliot's latest creation. He'd been experimenting with a guava chicken recipe and my mouth watered as we carried the plates out to the lanai, the intoxicating smell filling my nose.

I had my heart set on the promised carbonara, so when Elliot decided to switch up the menu and said to trust him, I tried not to pout. One whiff and I was glad I'd kept my mouth shut.

Cole smiled at the right moments and participated in the conversation, but something was off—there was a tightness around his eyes that worried me.

After dinner, I asked Cole if he wanted to go for a walk.

"Oooh," Lani sang. "Summer and Cole, sitting in a tree..."

I made a face at her and looked up at Cole. He nodded, his movements stilted.

He snagged my hand as we walked toward the golf course cart path, dodging a few overgrown bright pink bougainvillea on the way, their flowers brushing against my leg as we went.

"So, wanna talk about it?"

A muscle twitched in his jaw as I turned to look at him. He didn't say anything for what seemed like forever and then blew out a breath. "I can't." He shifted to look at me, pulling me in closer to his side, angling his head down to stare at the paved trail. "It's not that I don't want to."

I could tell by his tone he was fighting a war internally. I squeezed his hand and smiled at him. "Cole, you don't have to tell me everything. I know that I can be somewhat 'curious' sometimes." He snorted at this, but I continued after leveling a look at him. "But I know there are things that you aren't going to be able to talk about with me. It's okay, really."

The look on his face was equal parts hope and disbelief. I squeezed his hand again, then reached up and softly kissed his cheek. "Really. I promise."

His posture relaxed infinitesimally, and the smile he gave me was less strained than before which I took as a win.

With effort, Cole switched gears and asked me about my day. I wasn't ready yet to tell him much about the investigation. In the past, he'd walked the line of following police protocol, even going so far as to share facts about a case that were being withheld from the public. But with Lani's freedom on the line, Cole didn't hesitate to jump in and help us find the real murderer. As much I appreciated his help, my concern at present in accepting it was twofold. One, I didn't want Cole to put himself in even hotter water at work. And two, I needed to do this on my own, stand on my own two feet.

"Oh, you know, same old same old."

The look he shot me was one of pure disbelief. "Riiiggghtt." He drew out the word and narrowed his eyes.

"Hey, if you can have your secrets, so can I." I crossed my arms across my chest and looked up at him stubbornly.

"Summer, you know I'd tell you if I could." His chest deflated as his grip on my hand loosened. He held my gaze, silently pleading with me to understand.

Immediately I felt bad. "Cole, really, it's okay. The only reason I'm not giving you details about my case is because I'm trying to look after my client's interests and be discreet. Besides, I can't lean on you and wheedle help all the time. I'm a strong, independent woman," I declared and then immediately tripped on the uneven pavement.

Cole's strong arms encircled me so I didn't fall, and he looked down at me with the first genuine grin I'd seen from him all day.

"Yes, ma'am." He gave me a sizzling kiss, and I wrapped my arms around him, drawing him closer.

We broke apart after a delightful minute and smiled at each other before continuing our walk. The cart path took us past several different condo complexes, and I pointed out the crop of signs that had popped up recently. "Looks like there's a few new condos for sale."

He stumbled briefly, gripping my hand and then cleared his throat. "Uh, yeah, I noticed that. Actually—"

A giant black and tan Bernese Mountain Dog came out of nowhere and started barking and circling us, tail wagging as if he was playing the best game ever. A woman, dark brown hair in a haphazard bun and stained shirt, came around the corner pushing a stroller and yelling, "Bernie, you big doofus! Get back here!" All the while, a baby's high-pitched wail emanated from the stroller.

Bernie the dog grinned. That's really the only way to describe it. He grinned at us and then ran back and forth between where we stood and the woman with the stroller. As soon as he came within reach, she grabbed Bernie by the leash that was trailing behind him on the sidewalk, scolding him all the while.

"Sorry, guys. Bernie's still learning his manners. It's only taken him, what, eighteen months now, to get to the point that he doesn't run away when I call him." She grimaced. "Except for right now, obviously."

Her words were almost drowned out by the bawling coming from the stroller. Bernie ran over and started licking the plump little baby, eyes rimmed in red, tears falling in indignant outrage.

The woman looked down at the baby. "Henry, sweetheart, we're almost home. Everything's okay. Settle down." She picked the baby up and cooed at him, which only seemed to pacify him slightly.

Bernie was pulling on the leash, and I offered to hold him while she comforted the little guy.

"Mahalo," she said as she rocked the baby. "Henry's on a strict feeding schedule, but he must be hitting a growth spurt because he seems to want to nurse night and day. I thought I might be able to sneak in a quick walk for Bernie before the next feeding, but then Bernie decided to take off after a cat, and I've been chasing him all over the complex. And now, as you can tell," she gestured toward the baby, "we've missed Henry's next feeding."

My heart went out to the clearly frazzled mom. "Sounds like a rough day." I gave her a sympathetic smile. "If you ever need a dogwalker, I'm happy to help. I'm not home enough to have my own dog but I love dogs. And Bernese Mountain Dogs are one of my favorite breeds."

Her lips curled up at the edges slightly. "Me too. Probably not the best breed for the island though, with his thick fur. We got Bernie before my husband got transferred over here." The look she gave me was hope warring with embarrassment. "If you really mean it, I'd love to take you up on that sometime."

"Absolutely." I ran my hands through Bernie's soft fur and crooned sweet nothings at him while he looked up at me, togue lolling out the side of his mouth, happy as could be.

Cole stood a little apart, watching me with the strangest expression on his face. Before I could examine what that look meant, the woman reached into a diaper bag attached to the stroller and pulled out a pen and paper and asked if I could write my name and number down for her.

As I scribbled, she said, "My name's Sarah, by the way." The baby's cries had died down to the occasional whimper. I handed her back the paper, and we waved goodbye to each other before she tottered off, baby tucked into one of those front pack things that look like a human wedgie, pushing the stroller with one hand and holding on to Bernie's leash with the other.

I leaned my head against Cole's shoulder and watched them for a minute before turning to look up at Cole. Something hollow—and almost... hungry covered his face.

"Penny for your thoughts?"

His expression morphed into a mask and he deflected. "That was a nice thing to offer. That mom definitely could use the help."

I searched his face, but he just stared back at me blithely. "Uh, yeah. I guess." I shrugged. "I could tell she needed the help and besides that, you know how much I love animals, especially dogs."

"Yeah, she had her hands full. That's a lot to take on."

I peered up at him. "What? Motherhood?"

He nodded, reaching up to pluck a blossom off the ohia tree above his head.

I shrugged. "I guess it's par for the course. Sounds like she's kind of on her own; she mentioned her husband got transferred here so I'm guessing there's no family close by to help."

"Is that important, do you think? To have family close by?"

Something about his tone was off, but I couldn't put my finger on what it was that caught my attention. I tilted my head in his direction and studied him for a second, but he was fiddling with the flower in his hand.

"Umm, yeah, I guess. I think I'm lucky because I have Lani and Elliot." I smiled dreamily as I pictured it. "The baby would have its very own fairy godfather in Elliot."

As I thought about it, I realized we'd never talked about having kids before. Maybe that's why Cole seemed off. We'd only been dating for a little over four months.

He dipped his head in acknowledgement, and we continued our walk, both lost in our own thoughts. We came to a fork in the road, and Cole tugged me down the pathway that went left. I raised my eyebrow at him and he just shrugged.

The path led over to one of the newer condo complexes, complete with its own elevator and private pool, as well as pickleball courts and a community room filled with game tables.

"What do you think about this place?"

We stood in front of the building and gazed up at it. The outside was painted a cheerful yellow, and each unit had its own first and second floor lanai with beautiful pink bougainvillea bushes set in between for privacy.

"It's beautiful. I've heard it's pretty swanky inside, too. Elliot would kill for a kitchen this big."

"The units are almost 1400 square feet each and have Wolf ranges."

Surprise washed over me, and I turned to look at him more fully. "How do you know that?"

He cleared his throat several times and then scrubbed a hand over his hair before he mumbled something unintelligible.

"Huh?"

He cleared his throat again. "I said, I might be looking at buying a place sometime soon."

Delight and excitement ran through me. "Really?" I threw my hands around his neck and kissed him soundly. "That's awesome! You'd be so close!"

The clouds that Cole had carried over him since he got to my house brightened into the most brilliant sun. "Really? You don't think it'd be weird or anything?"

"Weird? No—not at all." I did a little happy dance, wiggling my butt, dancing just out of reach when he tried to smack it.

Our walk back was filled with talk about Cole moving closer and a few cool dance moves on my end, and some less cool, but very enthusiastic dance moves on Cole's.

Chapter Twenty Two

SUMMER

MY DAD TEXTED LANI and I first thing the next morning, requesting we swing by the office and fill him in on our progress so far. Lani got sick of my grumbling as we waited for him to show up, throwing me stink eye after the fifth time I whined.

"Girl, you were the first one to declare you wanted a complete separation of work and home with your dad. Right now, this is work dad, and work dad wants a progress report. That's what normal bosses require, you know." Her voice was huffy as she flounced off to fill the watering can and water the monstera plants spread throughout the office.

I wrinkled my nose. What she said was true; before I accepted the offer with my dad, I was very firm about keeping our work relationship separate from our personal relationship. Somehow that was coming back to bite me in the ass—and I wasn't happy about it.

I flung myself in my plush black office chair, a Costco special Lani had picked up when she helped Dad get the office outfitted for business. Thanks to her, we had actual real furniture and decor. If left to his own devices Dad would have a folding table, chair, and landline. Instead, homey touches lent a feeling of casual tranquility. Personally, I thought Dad was probably a little afraid of Lani and bowed to her wishes so as not to anger her. She had a way of sweettalking him into things and making him think it was his idea in the first place.

My leg swung wildly, and I lined up the pens in my pen cup in order of size. After what felt like an eternity, Dad breezed in, his hair a little wild and a wide smile plastered on his face. Immediately, I narrowed my eyes.

"Looks like someone had a good night," Lani said, sotto voice.

"Ugh, Gross. Can we not go there?" I grumbled. It was one thing to logically understand my dad was dating, but a different thing completely to see the proof of it in his self-satisfied smile first thing in the morning.

"Good morning, ladies. Keoki is going to be dropping coffee off in just a minute. He was backed up but promised he was just a minute or two behind me."

"How'd you talk Keoki into doing coffee delivery?" Lani asked.

"Since I opened a business account with Surf Camp. This way, I can use your caffeine addiction as a tax write off."

I rubbed my hands together in glee. All was forgiven. Clearly my dad was a saint, and I didn't give him enough credit. Yes, I'm that easy.

Lani, the girl voted most likely to die from being hugged, voluntarily hopped up and gave my dad a big Hawaiian-style hug. "Tom, you're the best boss ever!"

Dad blushed and got real busy checking out the thermostat. "Aww, it was nothing. Can't have you ladies missing out on your caffeine fix."

Keoki knocked on the glass door just then, and Lani ushered him in. "Tom, I can't thank you enough for opening up an account with us at Surf Camp. Between Lani and Summer, I'll probably be able to retire in a year or two," he grinned wickedly, his boyish face betraying him.

Once Keoki left, Dad gestured to his office and we trooped in.

"So, how's the investigation going so far?"

We filled him in on the good, the bad, and the ugly. When we got to the part about Elliot and Paisley, Dad's face turned red from laughter, tears running from the corners of his eyes. Once he caught his breath and swiped at the tears he remarked, "Things are never boring with you three, that's for sure."

"I talked to my cousin at HPD, but the report was super sloppy and lists cause of death as drowning. They're still waiting for the rescue diver photos, but he told me he doubted the photos would change the conclusion." Lani sighed and then pulled the black book from her hibiscus print backpack and handed it to Dad. Like us, he examined it from all angles, trying to figure out how to open it. After several minutes, he shook his head.

"It's some kind of legacy lock, but not like anything I've ever come across."

"Like in *Harry Potter*?" Lani leaned forward, her voice intense.

He frowned at the lock. "I'm not familiar with *Harry Potter*. This is a type of mechanical lock that requires a specific pattern or sequence to open it. Normally there are numbers printed or engraved on the buttons, but these don't have anything on them. In order to open it, we'd need to know the exact pattern." He shook his head. "There are probably 10,000 different possibilities."

I deflated in my chair. "Dang it. Do you know anyone who knows how to hack these?"

He sent me an amused grin before turning to stare down at the book in his hand, his expression sobering. "Not really. I knew a guy that liked puzzles like this, but I haven't heard from him in seven years or better." He spun to look at Lani. "Your dad was close with Otis—do you think he might want to give it a go?"

She nodded. "He's on his way here now. In fact, I'm surprised he's not here yet." Her mouth turned down at the corners, and she looked first at the clock on her phone and then at the door. She jumped out of her chair. "Let me just try and call him really quick."

Lani paced as she held the phone up to her ear. After several long moments, she pulled it away and tapped the red button and sighed, running a hand through her hair and peering out the window.

Even though Lani was related to half the island pretty much, she and her dad were an especially tight unit. After her mom died, Mack raised Lani on his own. Worry for him leaked out of her like oil from my old car.

Fifteen long and anxious minutes later Lani's phone buzzed and she let out a deep breath as she answered. "Dad?"

My dad and I shamelessly eavesdropped, but all we heard was Lani's one-word responses. She disconnected the call then wrung her hands nervously as she told us, "Dad's on his way. Had some car trouble."

Relief washed over me, but Lani paced like a caged tiger until her dad arrived, black oil streaks on his clothes and a small cut above his eyebrow.

"Dad!" Lani rushed up to him, and he enfolded her in his tree trunk arms, making her disappear almost completely in them.

"Shh. I'm okay, sweetheart."

"Mack, glad you made it. Everything alright?" Something about my dad's tone had me tilting my head like a dog does at a squeaky toy.

Nodding tersely, he responded, "All good. Just ran into a little trouble at the harbor."

My eyebrows winged up. "What were you doing down there?"

"Uncle Louie called and told me you girls had been down there to chat. He remembered a few things and asked me to come down there and talk." He snorted. "Old bastard didn't want to miss any fishing time, what with the hurricane coming and all."

My shoulders relaxed. "Oh, okay. Good. I'm sorry you had car trouble."

"Yeah, Louie asked if I'd help him grab gear from north harbor. Good thing I was with him. His brakes went out just as we went to park in front of the wash station."

"Damn. How'd you avoid going for a swim?" my dad asked. The parking spaces lined the edge of the dock, the parking barriers long since corroded and gone. Unwitting tourists were known to drive right off the edge, not realizing there wasn't a barrier.

Mack's face closed down, but a muscle in his cheek twitched. "Reached across and slammed it into park. Blew the teeth on the transmission, but at least we stayed dry," he reported grimly.

"I'm surprised that happened," Lani mused. "Uncle Louie's always been so good keeping up on maintenance."

Mack clenched his fists at his sides, his nostrils flaring. "Yeah, he is. He's really good about taking care of all of his vehicles. When I checked, it looked like the line had been cut."

Damn.

My dad asked, "Any idea who might've done that?"

Mack shook his head. "No names, but Louie told me after the girls visited, he and some of the other fishermen started talking. Turns out I'm not the only one who thought Otis's death was suspicious."

"Looks like you girls might've ruffled some feathers." My dad turned his gaze on me. "Better be extra careful next time you head down there."

Mack shook his head. "No. No more investigation. I'm not willing to put their lives at risk. Even if we find the murderer, it's not going to bring Otis back." He tilted his chin stubbornly.

Disappointment traveled down my spine. Not only was this our first big "legitimate" case, but I wanted answers about Otis's death, too. I pressed a hand to my temples and felt my chest tighten.

Before I could protest, Lani jumped in, her tone firm. "You hired us to find Otis's killer. That's what we're going to do. This is a professional commitment, and you signed a contract." The ice surrounding her precisely enunciated words caused me to shiver from across the room.

Mack's face got red and his chest puffed up. He and Lani stood toe to toe, which would've been hilarious if the situation weren't so serious; Lani stood just over five foot tall and looked like a dainty little pixie. Her dad was a mammoth of a man who, like my dad, played college football and could stop a man with just a raised eyebrow.

"Absolutely not. I'm not taking a chance that someone goes after you like they went after Louie. I'm tearing up my contract, and I'll consider the retainer forfeit at this point."

Lani put her hands on her hips, nostrils flaring, whites of her eyes evident around the circle of honey-colored brown. "You can't put me in bubble wrap and expect me to sit on the sidelines. You of all people should know better—you're the one who trained me to defend myself, to take care of myself. Are you saying that you don't trust me, even after all the time and training you've given me all my life, to handle this?" Lani's chest was heaving, and the volume of the exchange with her dad was rising.

Mack looked caught. "No. of course not. I know you're smart and can handle yourself. It's not that." He broke off and sent my dad a pleading look. "Help me out here, Tom."

Dad's face was a mask. "Girls, Mack has a point. We can't know for sure that Louie's brakes were cut by whomever murdered Otis, but neither one of us wants to take chances with your safety."

"So, what exactly are you saying?" Dread coursed through me.

Mack and Dad exchanged a look. "I think in order for this investigation to continue," Mack stiffened and opened his mouth to protest, but Dad held up a finger, "In order for it to continue, one of us needs to be with you anytime you're down by the harbor."

Pandemonium broke loose as Lani and I started arguing loudly against this. This went on for several minutes, back and forth, until Keoki pounded on our shared wall.

We all stood, red-faced, arms folded, Lani and I shoulder to shoulder, glaring across at Dad and Mack.

Dad held up both hands in truce. "Okay, okay. Listen, I get it. I'd like to offer a compromise."

Lani and I both stiffened in anticipation of a crummy deal.

"Can you both agree that: A.) you won't run into danger half-cocked; B.) every morning before you head out, we either meet in person or talk on the phone about your plan for the day; C.) if said plan changes, you update me; and D.) we have regular check in times several times a day just to allay our concerns."

"If we were men, there's no way you would have these stipulations. This is sexism," Lani said. Steam was almost visible coming from her ears. I was with her on this one. I bet if this were Cole investigating, Dad wouldn't require these conditions in order to continue investigating.

I said as much, and Dad's reply was, "Take it or leave it. This is non-negotiable. This has nothing to do with your gender, or the fact that you're my daughter. Once you have a little more experience under your belt, I might look at this differently, but for now this is the way it has to be."

Mack nodded his head in agreement with Dad. "And, as the paying client, I want to be included in each of these steps."

My mouth dropped open, and I looked at Lani. Her expression mirrored my outrage, but one look at Dad's face, and I knew that mountain wasn't moving. Lani must have come to the same conclusion. She shifted her eyes in my direction and gave me a subtle nod.

"Fine," we said in unison.

"But just for the record, I think this is unfair," I said.

"Unfair or not, this is how it has to be in order to move forward with the investigation," Dad replied.

Chapter Twenty Three

SUMMER

STILL SMARTING FROM OUR unfair treatment, Lani and I didn't say anything more than strictly necessary to Dad and Mack. After a while Dad got frustrated with us.

"Listen, ladies. This is real world stuff. You're going to have to deal with the fact that you can't always bulldoze your way through to get what you want."

My snort was long and sarcastic. "Says the original Caterpillar D11."

He continued on after throwing me a glare. "Sometimes you have to make compromises and work *with* the system instead of trying to fight it."

Lani and I kept quiet, both of us chafing at this obvious mansplaining event happening.

Dad, recognizing he wasn't getting anywhere, threw up his hands in the air in frustration and switched gears, asking us to show Mack the book we'd found in Otis's van.

Recognition lit on Mack's face when Dad handed him the book, and my spirits rose.

"Yeah, I've seen Otis write in this multiple times. When I asked him what he was writing, he told me he was 'keeping track.' Of what, he wouldn't say." He, too, tried pushing the buttons on the lock but had no luck.

"Do you guys mind if I hold on to this? I might know someone who can unlock it," Mack said.

Dad waved his hand in the direction of the book. "Feel free. If you don't have any luck, let me know." I could practically see the gears working in his brain. He continued, "I'll see if I can track down a buddy of mine from the old days," Mack and Dad exchanged a look, heavy with meaning, "see if he can decipher it."

Mack headed out, but not before stopping at the door to remind us to keep him in the loop.

After the door closed, Lani and I turned to look at Dad. He took one look at our faces and announced he had some work to do and ushered us out of his office, firmly shutting the door behind us.

"Well, this is straight bullshit if you ask me." Lani sighed.

"Agreed."

We sat down at Lani's desk and decided to go over the case and what we knew so far. "Maybe if we write it out, it will help us catch something we're missing."

Lani smirked. "You sound like a Gen-X'er right now. Okay, grandma, let me grab my scroll and quill."

I wrinkled my nose at her as she rummaged in her desk for a notebook and pen. As we discussed the case, no real pattern emerged, frustrating us more than helping us.

"Otis's body was found in the harbor four days ago. Official cause of death was listed as drowning, but we know based on the medical examiner's report there was very little water in his lungs. No alcohol or drugs found in his system. According to Louie, Otis seemed concerned about something happening in the harbor. Paisley was found wandering around the same day his body was found, but judging by her condition I'd say she'd probably been on the loose for a day or two."

I tapped the pen on my teeth and thought back over the last few days. "His van was pretty well hidden and looked untouched, so I don't think robbery was a motive."

Lani hummed in her throat as she stared at our list. "Honestly, I think he saw something he wasn't intended to see. Knowing Otis, if it was something that was illegal, at least by his definition of illegal, he probably said something or confronted someone and they offed him." Grief rested heavy on her face.

"It clearly had to be something going on at the harbor. That's where he and Paisley were most commonly seen at, and where Paisley and Otis's body were found. So what is it you think he might've seen?"

She lifted her shoulders. "Who knows? Maybe someone was messing with the boats, or dealing drugs, or pulling in illegal fish or something. Ever since the ban went into effect on taking reef fish for aquariums, the black market cost has increased exponentially. Maybe someone saw dollar signs and started taking them illegally, and Otis called them out on it." She sighed. "Who knows? I'm not sure how Joey fits in though."

I slumped in my chair. The only real lead we had other than the black book, which was a long shot anyway since we had no idea what was inside, was Louie's statement that Otis warned him to keep an eye on his son Joey.

"Why Joey?"

Lani swung her head in my direction. "Huh?"

"Why did Otis warn Louie about Joey in particular? What was it about Joey that made Otis worry for him?"

She screwed up her face in thought then shrugged. "I'm not really sure. From what I heard from my aunties, Joey was doing really good. He had a history with drugs, but the last I'd heard he seemed to be on the right track. He'd just got his commercial permit and was looking to buy a small boat to start running charters down south. He *finally* proposed to his baby mama," she said, rolling her eyes, "about time if you ask me."

"Now who sounds like a Boomer?"

"Hey, I didn't say Boomer, I said Gen-X'er." She swatted me on the arm.

"Hmm. I don't know then." I threw up my hands.

"You know what we need to do, right?"

My eyes shifted to where my dad had holed up in his office. "Yeah. But I'm not really interested in a shadow."

"I'm feeling pretty hungry right now. How about you?"

Her sudden shift of topic confused me. "What? It's not even eleven o'clock yet."

"Yeah, but we've been working hard. Don't you feel like it's time to take a break and grab some lunch?"

She was trying to convey some meaning, but the hamster was not running very fast on my little brain treadmill today.

"I heard that new coffee truck by Kohala Divers also serves breakfast sandwiches and burritos."

The light bulb finally went off. "Ooohhhh. Right. I have definitely worked up an appetite." I rubbed my hands together in anticipation. "Yeah, their haupia mochas are freaking elite, too."

I knocked on Dad's door, and he yelled for me to come in. I poked my head in and told him Lani and I were going to grab some lunch and then come back and hit it hard. He nodded but seemed distracted.

Curious, I stood on my tiptoes and tried to see what he was doing. His phone was on the desk in front of him and a pretty blonde woman's face lit up the corner of the screen. Dad was running his hand through his hair repeatedly and making a shooing gesture with his head at me.

Just then a woman's voice asked, "Thomas, did you hear me? Something's come up and I won't be able to make our date tonight."

Instead of leaving, I slid further into the office to openly listen to the conversation. Dad ran a hand across his throat at me, and I grinned back, leaning against the wall and pretending to examine my nails.

"Are you sure, Leslie? It sounded like you were really excited about checking out that new restaurant in Kona." Something about Dad's tone, disappointment and something I couldn't quite name, gave me pause.

"I know, Thomas. I'm so sorry. A friend came into town unexpectedly, and they're only here one night. Let's reschedule sometime next week or the following."

Dad's face fell, and what I heard in his tone, I saw in his face. Loneliness. Guilt engulfed me. I hadn't really thought about what it might be like for my dad to move away from the life he'd known for decades and start over here.

Dad ended the call and then looked up at me, a forced smile on his face. "You girls have fun," he said, and shuffled some papers on his desk, clearing his throat and making it obvious he wanted me to leave.

I shut the door softly behind me and motioned to Lani, remorse for lying to my dad weighing on my shoulders. We jumped in the car silently. After a while, Lani couldn't take it.

"Cheer up. You didn't lie to him, you just didn't tell him *where* we were going for lunch." Lani, reading my mind, tried to pull me out of my funk.

When I didn't say anything, she peered over at me. "What?"

Green shimmering fields interspersed with black lave rocks and the occasional beige cow passed by as we wound our way down the hill towards the harbor. I shrugged. "I overheard a conversation between my dad and the lady he's dating. Sounded like the old kiss off. I think Dad thought so too, but he was trying to play it cool in front of me."

She patted my shoulder. "I'm sure it will all work out. There's plenty of single ladies on the island. Your dad will find someone."

I wrinkled my nose at her words. While logically I under-stood my dad would like to have a partner to share his life with, somewhere deep inside I still felt a little weirded out by the idea. He'd been single throughout my childhood. Or, at least if he did date, he was discreet about it. I wanted him to be happy; I just needed to adjust to the idea of seeing him with someone other than my mom.

Before I went down that rabbit hole too far, we drove up to the Kawaihae Harbor gate. Matson shipping containers filled the side lot, and semis were driving back and forth, loading and unloading containers, beeping as they backed their loads into empty spaces along the fence. With the holidays coming up, commercial shipping had increased exponentially.

We drove all the way back to the dock at the very end, bumping along over the potholes as I scanned the parking lot for anything that seemed out of place. We drove slowly past the dock all the way to the locked gate at the end by the wash station. Everything looked...normal.

"What's our move?" Lani asked.

My forehead crinkled as I blinked at her. "This was your idea, Kemosabe. You tell me."

She telescoped her head like a groundhog looking for its shadow while she surveyed the scene in front of us. A handful of fishermen stood on the rocks, poles in their mounts while they chatted with each other, tour boats loading and unloading their passengers, although with the building wind chop, I was guessing their ride was going to be a rough one.

In the distance, the barge was being pulled by the tug, reminding me so much of a Chihuahua leading a Mastiff out to sea. The sky looked dark to the north, and I wondered if the clouds might reach down to the harbor and give the area a rare soaking.

"I don't see your Uncle Louie anywhere, do you?"

She squinted over at the fishermen, then searched beyond to the space over by the swim ladder then shook her head. "Weird. He's always down here."

A ribbon of worry passed over me. "You don't think anything happened to him, do you?"

Her phone buzzed and when she looked down, she stiffened and then did a near 360 with her head, spinning her neck around like an owl as she scoured the whole area, before focusing in on a clump of Kiawe trees nearly hidden by the berm of lava rock and dead coral.

"He's fine," she said through gritted teeth and showed me the text.

Sis, why you down here? I'm running surveillance!

The text came from Uncle Louie.

"Oh lord."

Lani nodded and frowned in the general direction of the trees.

"You don't think he'll tell your dad we were down here, do you? Cause if so, we're going to be in trouble."

"Well, we better make the most of it then." She hopped out of the car, and I scrambled out after her, easily catching up to her as she sashayed down to some local boat operators.

One man swung his head in our direction and went silent, the other three following suit, mouths hanging open as they admired the sight of Lani in her denim cut-offs that showed off her gently flared hips and perfectly tanned legs, along with a tank top that highlighted every curve on her top half enticingly as she made her way toward them, her hair loosened by the wind and cascading over her shoulders in soft waves.

"Hey, Lani." One of the men, a guy I'd met a handful of times around the harbor, called out, his voice cracking a little.

"Steve." she dipped her head at him like she was a queen acknowledging a peasant, and judging from the gob-smacked look on his face when she spoke to him, he was likely shocked and thrilled she even remembered his name.

The other men shifted, and she greeted them all by name. How she knew and remembered all these people, I'll never know. Faces I could remember, names I was a little spotty with.

Lani gestured with her head to me, shooting me a look.

"Hey, you guys notice anything weird going on at the harbor recently?"

Reluctantly, the men shifted their attention over to me.

"Weird like what?" One of the men, sporting blue striped shorts and a deep tan, asked.

I shrugged and quirked my lips. "Strangers coming around, more boat traffic than usual, any rumors. That sort of thing."

Something about my question caused the men to tense up and shut down. I caught two of them trade a look heavy with meaning. If they were wondering why I was asking, though, they didn't say—probably heard through the grapevine from Louie about our investigation.

Steve, the spokesman of the group apparently, shook his head. "Nah, nothing weird that I know of. Everything's fine." His words didn't match his expression, a wash of fear passing over it, his upper lip beaded with sweat.

Lani laid a hand on Steve's shoulder. "Is there anything at all that you noticed? Maybe someone acting out of character?" She practically purred at him, tracing light circles on his arm. I had to give it to her—she knew how to work her way around a man.

His face looked caught between delight that Lani touched him and alarm.

It was the alarm that gave me pause. Something was happening down here that had these men on edge.

Chapter Twenty Four

COLE

"IT'S TIME WE TALK about your performance here in the department."

Takada's beady eyes stared at me from across his desk. He'd called me in for my weekly review, something he'd put into place after I'd punched one of his lackeys last month. To be honest, I'd been lucky I hadn't gotten fired outright, but to be fair, there were extenuating circumstances. Such as the little twerp threating to lock Summer up based on nothing more than false rumors and a "tip" that was supposedly called in placing her at the crime scene.

I did my best to hold onto my temper, but after my conversation with Jack, it took everything in me to fight the urge to reach across the desk and slam my fist into his conniving face.

"Is there something you want to say?" He leaned forward in his seat, a challenging smirk on his face.

Guess I wasn't hiding my feelings as well as I thought. Damn, this was going to be harder than I thought.

With effort I pulled my face into what I hoped was a more sincere expression and shook my head ruefully. "Sorry, Chief. I've got the boat case on my mind, and I'm puzzling through a few things."

He made a noise in his throat. "Hmm. How's that going anyway? From what I could tell, it looked like some tourists went on a lark and crashed a few boats." He shrugged. "I'm sure it's nothing."

My eyebrows winged up. "Based on the amount of drugs we found on the latest boat, I'm fairly confident this is an organized ring bringing drugs into the island."

He waved his hand dismissively. "Ahh. I wouldn't waste too much time on it." He lowered his voice and leaned close, shooting a glance over my shoulder. "Actually, that's one of the reasons I wanted to talk to you. There are rumors about a local reporter, Kimo Hiroshi, who appears to be on a crusade to find corruption in the department. I'd like you to follow him, look into his past, dig up whatever dirt you can, and then report back to me. We can't have anyone undermining the department right now."

He watched me with measuring eyes to gauge my reaction. This was a test, and he wanted to see if I'd take the bait.

"If you think this is a better use of my time," I said blandly, shrugging my shoulder casually, all the while my heart pounded out a rapid rhythm.

"I need you to focus on more pressing things. No more patrolling with the newbies, and I'm going to have Jonah do the heavy lifting with the boat case. Between you and me, I think the Coast Guard is wasting their time on the drug boats anyway." He straightened up in his chair, the roll of his eyes telling me exactly what he thought on the matter.

"You're the boss. Wouldn't mind a little break from that case anyway. Nothing but lowlifes if you ask me." Stretching my arms over my head and yawning, the picture of bored contempt, I crossed my fingers and hoped he'd nibble.

He tilted his head, looking at me like a snake looks at a mouse. "Meet me after work down by the pier and we can go over it in more detail."

I couldn't help my eyebrows from winging up. Chief noticed. "I don't want anyone getting worked up around here if it's just a nasty rumor. Let's just keep it between us for now until we have anything definitive."

"Got it."

I felt the heat of his stare follow me out. As I shut his office door, I allowed myself a small smile of victory. If he was trying to recruit me for one of his pet projects, it could only mean one of two things: either I was being set up, or he needed more manpower for his corrupt agenda. I put it at 50/50 for either.

I whistled on the way back to my desk before stopping abruptly when I remembered how much Summer detested whistling. Said only serial killers whistled. Jonah looked up and did a double take.

"I thought for sure you'd come out here and punch something. At the very least kick a puppy or something."

"Har har."

"Well, I'm dying to know. How'd it go?"

The grin that popped out on my face couldn't be stopped. "Better than I dreamed."

The Kailua-Kona Pier surged with humanity. People from every country crowded the narrow sidewalk, the hum of a dozen different languages circling in the air as they stopped to window shop or gaze out at the azure blue of the ocean in front of them. Surfers paddled out, catching waves as the wind picked up. Seagulls stood like sentries watching for the chance to swoop in and swipe dropped crumbs off the concrete.

I'd gotten to the pier early. On my way I'd reached out to Jack and filled him in. "Go along with him for now, put on an act that you're open to something sketchy, but keep me up to date," Jack ordered. "Once we know for certain what he's asking you to do, we can go from there in determining how far your role will extend. As long as you're not breaking any laws but appear to be following his orders, we should be good."

Electric currents ran up and down my spine, and I nearly rubbed my hands together ala Mr. Burns from *The Simpsons*: soon Chief would be behind bars where he belonged.

Down an alleyway a street over from the ocean front, I thought I saw Takada talking to someone. Slipping in between the crush of people I crossed over and crept up behind the building for a better look.

Chief stood next to two men, one looked like he'd been ridden hard and put away wet. Teardrop tattoos traced down his cheek, in a pattern I recognized from some of the Bois who'd served time in prison, and his ropy arms were covered in loops and swirls of dark ink, the tattoos so old it was difficult to tell where one started and one ended.

The other man wore a crisp, navy blue polo shirt and tan slacks, his hair styled neatly, face clean shaven.

I closed the distance, slinking around the side, my steps slow and deliberate. Moving in as close as I dared, I leaned my head around the building. Chief's back was to me, and I took a mental snapshot of the two men in front of him. Their conversation was muffled, so I leaned further, turning my ear in their direction.

"Did you get the papers?" Chief murmured.

"Cost extra..."

"Make it look like an accident..."

"Perfect fall guy..."

Something tickled my leg, and I looked down at a tabby cat, currently rubbing against me and meowing loudly. I made shooing motions and pushed it away with my leg, but it only mewled louder and started kneading my leg with his claws.

"What's that?"

Shit.

My heart was running the Kentucky Derby in my chest and my mind raced. I reached in my pocket and pulled out my keys, shining a weak light on the ground from my keyring flashlight. The cat immediately pounced on it, and I carefully moved the light just to the corner of the building. The cat took a flying leap at it just as I took my finger off the light.

"It's a damn cat," Takada said, frustration lacing his tone. "I need you to focus. Can I count on you to get this done?"

I couldn't hear any replies, but they must've answered in the affirmative because Chief's voice carried over to my hiding place. "Great. I'll text you more details after I get things set up. Wait for my orders."

Footsteps echoed on the pavement, and I sprinted back the way I'd come, blending in with the sea of humanity out to catch the last rays of the red orange sun. I posted up next to a banyan tree and pulled out my phone, pretending to look at it while I waited for Takada. I didn't have to wait long. I had a moment of regret that Jack hadn't had time to set me up with a wire.

"Peterson. Glad you made it." Takada wore a smile full of teeth, reminding me of nothing so much as a shark.

Playing along I greeted him with a nod of my head. "Yeah, just got here." I shoved my phone in my pocket and straightened up, hands by my sides.

His politician smile remained in place. "Great. Why don't we head over to Quinn's and grab a drink. We're not on the clock," his glib words and hearty back slab put my radar system on high alert, the tiny hairs on my neck stood up as an early warning. He was being way too nice.

"Sure."

He gestured for me to lead the way and fell in step just behind me as we made our way to the popular oceanside bar and grill. One of the men from the alleyway, the rough-looking one, stood loitering just outside the bar, smoking a cigarette as he leaned up against a light pole.

Takada gestured toward an open table at the back of the restaurant near the bathrooms. We jostled for position, but I managed to snag the seat facing the door, my back against the wall near the kitchen. Judging by the way his lips curved down, Chief wasn't happy about it.

A young server dressed in a brown and orange T-shirt with the Quinn's Almost By the Sea logo on it and black pants smiled and asked for our order. "I'll take a Kona Big Wave."

She nodded and then turned to Chief. "Mai Tai, heavy on the rum, sweetheart."

Her face went still, and she took our menus without another word. Chief followed her with the eyes of a stray dog looking for a snack. When he caught me watching, he smirked. "Just cause I'm on a diet doesn't mean I can't look at the menu."

Some of the disgust I felt for him at that moment must've shown through my carefully controlled mask.

"What? You can't tell me you don't look at other women. That girlfriend of yours sure is a looker, though. I bet she's a tiger in bed," He leered at me and everything inside me went cold.

"I'd rather not discuss my girlfriend." I cracked my knuckles as I leaned forward, glaring.

He held up his hands in retreat. "Sorry, sorry." The self-satisfied glint in his eyes pissed me off. He'd taken a shot just to get me off balance.

A different server, a Hawaiian guy with kakau tattoos, dropped off our drinks, twisting the top off my beer and slamming a Mai Tai in front of Chief, sloshing liquid over the edges, which gave me a second to rein in my temper before I blew my cover.

"So," I said, my hand like a vise on the bottle in front of me. "What's going on with this case you talked about?" I leaned back in my chair and put on a bored face. "Some reporter's hassling the department? What's the big deal?"

He lips thinned, eyes hostile as he answered. "This damn reporter thinks he's Anderson Cooper cracking open the Epstein case or something. Waste of time if you ask me."

I refrained from rolling my eyes at the comparison. "The Epstein case or the reporter investigating the department?"

He snorted. "Both."

The ease at which he dismissed both one of the most egregious cases of child sex-trafficking in U.S. history, and our department being investigated caused disgust to surge through my body.

My phone buzzed and I pulled it out, my eyebrow furrowing at the unknown caller tag at the top. I shrugged and put it back on the table, but it started to buzz again. When I flipped it over, it was the same tag.

"You gonna answer that?" Chief asked, suspicion heavy in his tone.

"It's an unknown caller. If it's important, they'll leave a message." Just as I set my phone down, it started buzzing again. I sighed heavily and shrugged at Chief before stepping away from the table and answering the call.

"Hello?" I ground out.

"Don't say anything, just listen." Jack's voice was tinged with urgency. "We've got more intel on Chief's latest target."

I spun around and saw Chief watching me, eyes narrowed.

"I want you to play along—we've got an eye on things. The reporter in question knows he's being targeted and is taking precautions. Your job is to get Chief to think you're on his team."

"Got it."

"And Cole? Might want to work on your poker face." The line went dead, and I stared at the phone, not really seeing it as I wondered how deep this went.

Chapter Twenty Five

COLE

With Herculean effort, I pasted on a neutral face and returned to the table. While I'd been gone, Chief had another Mai Tai delivered. He tilted his head toward my beer. "Drink up, Peterson. You're already behind."

Chugging the bottle, I held it up to the server and she nodded. Seconds later another cold beer sat in front of me, and I did my best to appear relaxed and interested in Chief's exploits, of which he droned on and on without pause. My attention wandered; however, I pasted on an expression of interest.

By the time he'd downed the fourth Mai Tai, I couldn't take it any longer; at this point either he was going to get down to business or not. I decided to speed the process along. The table we sat at wasn't very sturdy; it only took a slight bump of my knee to pitch Chief's drink sideways, amber liquid flooding the table in front of us.

"Shit, sorry about that Chief. Here, let me help." I grabbed a napkin dispenser from the table next to us and made sure to smear the liquor off the table straight onto his lap.

"Stop it! You're making it worse." He grabbed the napkins from me and wiped off his hands. The server from earlier came over with a bar rag.

"I'm so sorry. Got a little excited and knocked over our drinks," I said sheepishly. The girl gave me a look that I interpreted to mean she would've done the same thing if she had to spend any time at all in Chief's presence.

"What are you smiling about?" Chief grumbled at the server.

She wiped the smile off her face and doubled down in cleaning up the mess. "Nothing, sir. Can I get you another Mai Tai?"

He waved her away. "No, forget it." He then turned his gaze over to me in slow motion. "Peterson, let's go for a walk." His words slurred slightly as he asked for the check. Signing his name with a flourish on the check, he stood up, swaying a bit.

The menacing look in his eye made me feel a bit like *Old Yeller,* but I followed anyway, surveying the area surrounding us, searching for the guy I saw him talking to earlier.

Just as we rounded the corner of a building, Chief surprised me and tried to shove something in my hand. It took two tries but I when I looked down, I saw it was a silver USB. "This has all the information you need about our target. Make sure you're not accessing any of this on your work computer though—if we ever get audited, I don't want any trace of it to show up. This needs to stay offline, hush hush. Got it?"

"You sure it's worth all this trouble? I don't understand how one measly reporter could be worth all of this effort." Inside, I celebrated, but I did my best to downplay the exchange.

The corner of his lip lifted in disdain. "You're not paid to think, you're paid to follow orders. I'm telling you, this guy needs to be eliminated."

I tilted my head. "Eliminated?"

He waved away my question. "Just dig up whatever dirt you can on him and report back to me. I want you to glue yourself to this guy like a damn tick. If he won't let up his campaign against us, then neither will we."

With that he stalked off, not even bothering to glance back. He hopped into his patrol car and drove away, almost clipping a light pole on the way out.

The USB in my palm glittered up at me, and I couldn't stop the little grin that crossed my face.

⚬⚬⚬⚬ ⚬⚬⚬⚬

I'd barely gotten into my truck when my phone rang. "Did he take the bait?"

"Yep."

"Terrific. I'll be in touch." Jack disconnected the call, and I shook my head at the absurd situation in which I now found myself. *It's like a damn James Bond movie or something.*

As I merged into heavy traffic, my eyes flicked up to the rearview mirror out of habit; I noticed a white Jeep Wrangler that had been behind me for two lights. I made a quick left as soon as the light turned and sure enough, the Jeep screeched through the intersection as well, tires screeching while drivers honked.

Chief pulling me into this scheme had my alert system screaming. A month ago, he'd tried to force my resignation, and now he was enlisting me to help him dig up dirt on a reporter? Something didn't add up.

Another point of concern was the FBI's handling of this investigation. I knew Jack was working night and day to handle this case, but the longer it went on and the more people that got dragged in, the harder it would be to maintain control. As a SEAL, our motto was to keep your team small and skilled. A bigger team meant more pinch points and more opportunities for error.

One thing I had to give Takada credit for—he knew how to manipulate people into doing what he wanted. If I hadn't already known what a piece of garbage he was, its possible I would've fallen for this "secret case, fate of the department rests on my shoulders" crap he tried to feed me.

Headlights followed close behind as I headed north on the highway. With a grim smile, I swung into the Honokohau Harbor and watched as the Jeep followed me in. I led him all the way to the dead end on the north side and turned off my lights. It parked right next to me, and the driver rolled down his window.

"First time?" I asked.

The agent, hair cut with military precision and an aloha shirt starched and ironed to the point it could probably take itself for a walk, bristled. "Jack wanted us to keep eyes on you."

"Ah. And you drew the short straw, I see."

He slumped as much as the shirt would allow. "He told me you'd notice right away."

"Better luck next time. Here's a hint, leave a car or two in between when you're following a subject." The corners of my mouth lifted in a smirk before I continued. "My next stop is my girlfriend's place, which I'm sure you have an address for. Let's see if you can do better on the way up there."

He gave me a self-deprecating smile and saluted.

To give credit where credit was due, he took my advice and stayed farther back, not crowding me but keeping close enough he was able to slide through a yellow light after me. On the way to Summer's, I called Jack.

"Pegged him right away, huh?" Jack answered his phone, his voice laced with humor.

"Sure did. Boy's pretty green."

"Trainable though," he replied.

I glanced up in my mirror and could just see the hint of his headlights behind me. "That he is. What's the tail for?"

"Well, you know how I told you staffing was garbage? I got creative. Doug's learning the fine art of tailing a suspect as well as acting as a witness to your whereabouts if Chief tries anything funny." He chortled. "I term this a 'twofer'".

"Gotcha. Thanks for the safeguards. Takada's definitely got something up his sleeve. He gave me a USB with all kinds of info on his target and warned me away from using department computers. Didn't want anything to get traced back to the department."

Jack snorted. "No, but it sure as hell would be traceable to you if it came down to it. Which I'm sure is exactly what he's thinking. When you get to Summer's, might want to hand that USB over to Doug. Just in case Takada embedded any viruses. I wouldn't put anything past him."

My headlights reflected off the condo's front window as I parked. "Sounds good. We just pulled up. Let me know what you find."

"Will do. For now, act like you're following his orders. Follow Kimo Hiroshi, around, make notes, all that garbage Takada's asking you to do. We'll be feeding you information along the way. Let's just hope Takada tips his hand and we can get it on record. I'd like to put this one to bed before I retire."

"Retire?" Jack had never mentioned retirement before.

"The wife wants to get out and travel more, go see the grandbabies. I'm getting a lot of pressure on the homefront to hang up my badge."

"You'll be bored inside of two weeks," I predicted.

"Yeah, yeah." Judging by his tone, I wasn't the first person to tell him this. He pitched his voice low, so I had to strain a bit to hear his next words. "Cole, keep your head on a swivel and do not relax your guard. Takada is in it up to his neck and we're still trying to identify all the players involved."

A rock settled in my gut as I listened to Jack's warning. Christ, the complicated web of deceit was getting real damn hard to follow.

Chapter Twenty Six

SUMMER

UNFORTUNATELY, WE DIDN'T GET very far in our line of questioning down at the harbor. The guys clammed up almost immediately and then both Lani's phone and mine started buzzing. After ignoring the first three calls, I finally answered the fourth.

"Summer Louise Jenkins. We had a deal. You get your behind back to the office now."

One glance at Lani told me she was getting a similar order from her dad.

On our drive out of the harbor, Lani slowed the car as we drove past the clump of Kiawe trees. "We know you told on us, Louie! I'm telling Auntie Miriam, and you'll never hear the end of it," she threatened through the open window.

Louie's head popped up, a World War Two era helmet perched precariously on top. His eyes were wide, face screwed up in horror, with a pair of binoculars clutched in his hand. "Aww, c'mon, Lani. I promised your dad I'd keep an eye on things." He held out a palm in front of him and begged, "Don't tell Miriam. I'm already on her shit list."

She waved at him dismissively. "Should've thought of that before you ratted on me. You know what the code is."

His only answer was to hang his head. I kinda felt sorry for the guy. He was smack dab in the middle of that rock and hard place—namely, Lani and Mack.

She drove off without saying another word.

"You're not really going to tell on him, are you?" Auntie Miriam was the island's unofficial Boss of Everything, and she ruled with an iron fist.

"I'll let him think about what he's done for a while, really let him get worked up, and then offer him a deal. Clear passage through the harbor without alerting Dad, and he has to answer all of my questions. I might even make him throw in an oil change and tire rotation to really teach him a lesson."

Secretly, I was kind of in awe of Lani. She really was a force of nature when she wanted to be. She played the chess game of life better than anyone I knew, except for maybe Miriam.

The drive back to Waimea was mostly silent, both of us lost in thought. I knew we were missing a piece of the puzzle; I just couldn't put my finger on what. Identifying a suspect came down to motive and opportunity. Who on earth would want to kill an easy-going guy like Otis? He kept to himself for the most part and was loved by most everyone in the Kohala area.

As we pulled into the office parking lot, I dragged my mind away from the rabbit hole of possible motives and braced myself for what was sure to be an invigorating discussion. I noticed Mack's truck in the parking lot. Even *more* invigorating, then.

"This is going to be fun."

Lani nodded and we parked, dragging our feet as we headed for the door.

After the blistering lecture we got from not one, but two angry dads, Lani and I decided a drink down at Seafood Bar was in order.

"I don't see what the big deal was. Because of what happened to Louie's truck, we knew to be on guard. Besides, Louie was there watching our backs the whole time." I pouted, holding my drink loosely in the air and gesturing with it for emphasis.

Lani clinked her glass against mine. "I'll take the heat on this one. It was my idea." She took a giant gulp of her drink, then set it down in the middle of the napkin and traced the rim of her glass with her finger. "I'm really sorry. I shouldn't have suggested we go down there and not tell them." She shook her head and blew out a breath. "I was just so *frustrated* at the way they were treating us! All because we were born girls instead of boys." She slammed the side of her fist on the bar counter and several other patrons looked over at her.

Nancy, one of the servers, stood behind the counter clearly eavesdropping on our conversation. "Far be it from me," she started, and Lani and I shot her a glare. She held her hands up in surrender. "I was just going to say at least it's nice you have someone watching out for you."

Nancy had a point, but my ears were still ringing after listening to my dad rant about our "careless disregard for his rules." Somewhere deep down inside I knew he had a point, too, but I wasn't ready to admit that just yet. Besides which, Lani *also* had a point. Our dads would never treat us like fine china dolls if we were men, and that really rankled.

Just as we were getting ready to head home, Cole texted that he was going to swing by for a bit. Lani dropped me off and I raced through the house up to the bathroom to swipe on a little mascara and lip gloss. Tearing off my Rip Curl T-shirt that may or may not have an avocado stain on it, I grabbed a casual black tank top with a silver buckle on one shoulder. Effortlessly relaxed, yet pretty.

Judging by the look on Cole's face when he came in, the shirt did its job. He drank me in with his dreamy sky-blue eyes, a sexy little smile on his face, and my heart danced a little jig at the sight of him.

Cole and I threw together a quick dinner of leftovers Elliot had stashed in the back of the refrigerator. We talked about our respective days, but it wasn't what he said as much as what he didn't say that caught my attention. Since the details I shared were just as guarded, I couldn't hold it against him.

At one point halfway through dinner, I let out a sigh on accident. Cole sat up straight and reached across the table for my hand, caressing it with his thumb and studying it intently.

"Everything okay?"

I shrugged and then nodded, my face twisting into a grimace.

"Wanna talk about?" he asked softly.

My shoulders deflated. I didn't *want* to lean on Cole for advice, but at the same time he had a lot of experience.

"We're running into some snags with Otis's investigation."

He didn't say a word, just watched me, waiting patiently. Sometimes it felt like he knew me better than I knew myself. As I wrestled with myself, I realized chances were slim I'd be able to keep my mouth shut much longer anyway.

I recited everything we'd found so far, including the journal in Otis's van and Louie's truck being tampered with. By the time I got to the epic lecture I'd gotten this afternoon, Cole was doing his best to control the grin threatening to erupt on his face.

He pulled me close. "Sounds to me like you're doing all the same things I would. Want some advice, even if you might not like it so much?"

I wrinkled my nose at him. "Well, when you put it that way....no."

He smirked and pulled me closer, snuggling me under his chin after kissing my forehead. "Your dad is your boss." I tried to squirm away, but he held fast. "Your dad is your boss, *and* he has a lot of experience to draw from. I know you hate being micromanaged, or hell, even managed, but in this case instead of fighting the power, you might want to work with it."

I slumped in his arms. "I know you're right. The second we started driving down to the harbor I didn't feel right about it." I turned and leaned away so that I could look in his eyes. "It's like I knew even before we went down it was the wrong move, but I couldn't help myself. I just *had* to go, you know?"

He studied my face for a minute then gave me a crooked smile. "You're like that lady on *Indiana Jones and the Kingdom of the Crystal Skull*—you just want to know everything."

"Exactly! Is that so wrong?" I asked.

He frowned. "You know how that ended for her, right?"

I waved my hand. "That wouldn't happen to me. The second that stuff started spinning I would've been out of there."

Before he could argue, my phone buzzed and I jumped up to grab it.

"Hi Evelyn. What's up? Is Paisley okay?"

Her voice sounded strained when she answered. "Hello Summer. Yes, Paisley is fine. It's Richard. He had some chest pain today and the doctor wants him to head to Oahu for a procedure tomorrow morning." Fear wended its way through her words. "Would you be able to come get Buddy tonight? I know it's last minute, but I don't have anyone else available."

"Absolutely." I looked over at Cole. "I can be up there in about thirty minutes."

"Oh Summer, thank you so much! Our neighbors are going to take care of the cows and Paisley, but Buddy needs to be with someone. He's never been left alone overnight."

"No problem—we'll be there soon."

"Oh? Are you bringing your friend Elliot?"

A smile flashed over my face as I thought of Elliot's last visit to the farm. "No, actually my boyfriend is coming with me."

"Oh!" She crowed in delight. "I look forward to meeting your young man."

We hung up just as I felt Cole pull me into his body. "I can't tell you how much I like hearing you claim me." His low, gravelly voice sent shivers up and down my spine.

"I have a pretty good idea," I teased, feeling his growing interest as our bodies pressed together.

"Summer," he growled, and I'm not going to lie, I completely forgot about Richard, Evelyn, Buddy, and Jesus himself for a few minutes as Cole ran his hands over my body and lined us up so I fit snugly between his well-muscled thighs.

"Wait," I said desperately when my rational mind touched earth for a minute.

Cole left the palm of his hand firmly planted on my breast and lifted his mouth from my neck, his eyelids hooded and heavy. Immediately I regretted saying anything.

Wait. Buddy. Richard. Oahu. Focus Summer, focus.

I put a hand on his chiseled chest and got lost for a minute as I explored the planes and valleys. Before they dipped too far south, Cole grabbed them and held them aloft. My lips curled in a pout, and he shook his head at me.

I licked my lips, and his eyes tracked the movement, pupils black and wanting. "Umm, Buddy. We need to go get Buddy," I blurted out.

"Who?" He cocked his head, brow furrowed into a 'M' shape.

"Grab your phone, I'll tell you on the way."

Chapter Twenty Seven

SUMMER

WE PULLED UP TO the gate and found Evelyn waiting for us. Her face was pinched, and her normally sunny smile was replaced by trembling lips and worried eyes.

"Oh, Summer. Thank you so much for taking Buddy."

I hopped out and gave her a hug. "Oh, you're actually doing *me* a favor. I love dogs, and Buddy in particular. Besides, with the way my case has been going I could use a little doggo therapy."

She thanked me profusely and ushered Cole and me up to the house. Richard was sitting on the couch petting Buddy. As soon as we walked in, the dog erupted into a cacophony of barks and yips, dancing around excitedly.

I bent down and he jumped into my arms. Cole stood awkwardly at the entrance, and I waved him in.

"I hear the old ticker's acting up," I said to Richard.

Richard's expression was sheepish. "I'm sure it's no big deal. Mostly I just hate for Evelyn to worry and fuss."

Evelyn bustled over and plumped a pillow behind him.

"Oh, there's no fuss. We'll just go on our adventure to Oahu a little earlier than planned." Her smile was bright, but her eyes carried the weight of worry.

He squeezed her hand where it rested on his shoulders, and I couldn't help the pang of wistfulness that ran through me. My eyes lifted to Cole who now stood just inside the threshold, quietly taking in the scene in front of him.

"Richard and Evelyn, I'd like for you to meet my boyfriend, Cole."

He stepped forward and shook hands with Richard before Evelyn reached up and hugged him, her arms barely able to reach around his neck. The gentleness in which he hugged her back cause my heart to swell and my stomach to clench. *Oh boy. Down ovaries, down.*

Buddy wriggled in my arms, and I set him on the floor. He rocketed straight over to Cole, sniffing him, his little tail wagging back and forth. Cole eased down to pet Buddy, but held his hand out first. Buddy sniffed his hand thoroughly and then circled him before coming to rest in front of him, body rigid and alert.

I cocked my head—I'd never seen Buddy greet anyone with anything other than frenzied enthusiasm. Evelyn and Richard exchanged a look of surprise.

Richard's face twisted in pain for a moment which he quickly tried to hide, but both Evelyn and I caught it. She said, "Oh, Papa let me get your pills."

He waved her away, but she dashed over to the prescription bottle on the counter and shook out a little white pill into her palm and held it out to Richard.

"Ahhh." He waved her away grumpily, but she just shoved the pill under his nose. He glared, but then winced and reluctantly took it.

Cole and I both watched, frozen and uncertain. After a few minutes Richard's pale, sweaty face pinked up some and he drew in a deep breath.

"Better?" Evelyn asked. Richard nodded and she sat next to him, her hands repeatedly smoothing the fabric of her linen pants.

"When's your flight?" I asked.

"First thing in the morning," Evelyn replied.

"Should you try to go sooner maybe? We're happy to take you up to Waimea just to get checked out." I didn't know much about heart issues, but Richard looked winded and tired.

Richard shook his head. "No, we've already spoken to the cardiologist and while he considers this an urgent procedure, it's not emergent. These little white pills will help until we get over to Oahu."

"If you're sure," I said, doubt evident in my tone.

He nodded. "I'm sure. I appreciate the offer, but this isn't the first time this has happened."

I caught Cole's gaze, and he also looked uncertain. "How about a ride to the airport in the morning, then?"

Evelyn shook her head. "Bobby's going to take us. He's flying out at the same time and is just going to swing by and pick us up on his way."

Richard and Evelyn, some of the most 'larger than life' people I'd met on the island, looked small and frail just then and my throat closed. I fought to keep myself from tearing up. Buddy barked for attention, diverting my spiral of thoughts.

"Yes, big man. You get to come home with Auntie Summer," I cooed as I bent down to pick him up again. He snuggled in my arms, his asthmatic snorts making me smile.

"You're helping us the most by keeping an eye on Buddy. We won't worry about him one bit with you taking care of him," Richard said, his words becoming clipped as he ran out of breath. He looked tired and he scrubbed a hand over his face.

"Well, we'll get out of your hair. Please be safe and let me know how everything's going, okay?"

Evelyn hopped up and grabbed a bag full of toys as well as Buddy's leash and dog food. "I wrote down the instructions for his food. Basically, he's going to give you sad puppy dog eyes and try to get a second breakfast. Don't fall for it." As she spoke, she gave Buddy a stern look. He just smiled back at her from the perch in my arms, his tongue hanging out.

Cole took the supplies, and we said our goodbyes, wishing them luck and reinforcing our offer to help if they needed anything else. On the way back to the Rav, I asked Cole to drive so I could hold Buddy.

Once we were settled in the car, Buddy stood on his hind legs, his front legs resting on the window frame as he watched Richard and Evelyn wave goodbye.

Shortly after we passed through the gate, Cole reached over to pet Buddy, but Buddy twitched at his touch and moved closer to the car door and out of reach, his face firmly in the other direction. Cole looked at me, mystified.

I reached over to take his hand. "Buddy's usually friendly with everyone." I shrugged. "Maybe he's just unsettled with everything going on."

Buddy swung around and used his nose to try and nudge our hands apart, his body vibrating as he stood on the console. My face broke into a grin.

"He's jealous!" I laughed. "I guess you're going to have to share me with another man after all."

Cole's lips quirked, half in amusement, half in exasperation, as he shook his head.

Once we got back to my place, we set Buddy's water dish up in the kitchen and watched as he explored, sniffing all the nooks and crannies downstairs. Cole and I took him for a walk to go potty just as Elliot pulled up in his Prius.

"You three look like a happy little family." Elliot bent down to pet Buddy, his face in shadow, but something about his tone sounded off.

"Hey, Elliot. How's TJ? I haven't seen him in a while."

In response to Cole's question, Elliot straightened and gave him a tight-lipped smile. "Fine."

Cole scratched his head and looked over at me, confused. Elliot normally ran in two gears—he was either a bubbly K-Pop star or a snarky, sarcastic thirteen-year-old. This Elliot was new to Cole.

"How did your talk go?"

Elliot's lips turned down at the edges and his eyes edged away to look over my shoulder. He shrugged, his shoulders drooping. "Fine."

After a quick look at Cole, we ushered Elliot into the house. I poured him a medicinal amount of whiskey before sitting him down on the couch, Cole and I bracketing him on either side. Buddy, sensing something was wrong, even curled up at Elliot's feet.

One he'd taken a few sips, I grabbed his hand. "Tell us what happened."

He swirled the liquid around his glass and sighed. "We had a nice dinner; I cooked for him and made some of his favorites. Everything was going really well—at least I thought so. We sat outside, snuggled together to watch the sunset on his couch. So romantic. Then I hinted about us going on a long trip somewhere together. He clammed up and said he couldn't take any time away from the store and volunteering at the theater, and basically a whole list of reasons why he couldn't go on a trip with me." He slumped down into the couch, his expression miserable.

"Huh. Do you remember what your exact words were?" TJ struck me as a pretty open guy, so that reaction seemed out of character.

Elliot rubbed his finger on the lip of his glass, staring glumly down at it. "Well, as we were watching the sun set, TJ made a comment about when he visited Italy six years ago, he tried to catch the sunset every evening. That seemed like the perfect segue into asking about going on a trip together, so I said we should run away to Tuscany right now. Grab our passports and go. The more I talked the more I got into the idea. I pulled out my phone and started looking at flights and car rentals and places to stay. That's when he told me he couldn't go because of the store."

Ah ha.

"Do you think it's possible that maybe TJ took you literally? He is a new business owner, so I imagine spur of the moment trips are probably not possible for him right now."

Cole asked, "What happened after that?"

If possible, Elliot slumped even farther into the couch, waves of misery projecting from him. "Well, I'll admit my feelings were a teensy bit hurt. I accused him of not loving me, and then we got into a huge fight and I left."

Elliot's phone had been buzzing intermittently while we talked, but only now did I connect the dots.

"That's him calling, isn't it?"

Elliot nodded, picking at a thread on his shirt and ignoring the phone completely.

"Elliot," I said gently. At first, he refused to look at me but eventually he gave in. "It sounds like maybe you overreacted just a teeny bit. I think maybe you and TJ need to have an honest conversation about where the idea for a trip is coming from, and go from there."

He let out a huge breath and straightened his shoulders. "I know. I knew the minute I left I blew it. He's going to be so mad at me."

Just then we heard pounding on the door and simultaneously my Ring app chimed on my phone and Buddy started barking. His yips sounded like a winded warthog, and I couldn't help but smile down at the ferocious beast living inside a fluffy, five-pound Pomeranian body.

TJ's voice carried through the door. "Elliot, I know you're in there. Let me in so we can talk and figure this out." His voice was half order, half plea.

Cole nudged Elliot toward the door and jerked his chin in that direction. "Sounds like TJ wants to work things out."

We both noticed the flicker of hope in Elliot's eyes as he looked at the door. He smoothed down his shirt and ran a hand through his hair and then walked over and opened it.

"Elliot, I can't believe you ran off like that! It's not that I don't want to go on a trip with you or spend time with you—I have a business that I can't just abandon in the spur of the moment. I made a commitment to running it." His argument was rational, but he looked miserable, like disappointing Elliot aged him ten years. In fact, it looked as if he'd raced down here after Elliot in a rush. He had two different sandals on, his shirt was untucked, and his eyes were suspiciously red.

When I glanced down at Buddy, he was dancing around TJ and sniffing excitedly. TJ spared him a smile, but he was so focused on Elliot he didn't give Buddy the attention Buddy felt he was due. I watched in horror as Buddy started to lift his back leg.

"Buddy, no!" I scolded. He slowly put his leg back down and threw me a look, wide-eyed and innocent.

I snapped a leash on Buddy and grabbed Cole's hand. "C'mon. Looks like Buddy needs to go outside again."

We left as discreetly as possible and took a long loop around the condos to give TJ and Elliot time to talk. I noticed Cole sneaking glances all around us when he thought I wasn't looking. When I finally called him out on it, he just shrugged.

"Cop habit, I guess." His smile looked forced, and I couldn't help but wonder what was really going on.

Chapter Twenty Eight

SUMMER

COLE LEFT SHORTLY AFTER we got back from our walk. TJ and Elliot disappeared into his room; I turned my fan on high and put in my noise-cancelling earbuds.

Buddy woke me up with little snorty kisses and dog breath and I jumped out of bed to take him outside. I passed Elliot and TJ in the kitchen, both of them working in tandem to whip up something that smelled mouthwateringly divine.

When Buddy and I walked back in, I could tell by the wattage of their smiles and the soft brushes against each other they'd cleared up any misunderstandings. *Phew*. I hated seeing Elliot miserable. He hadn't had many relationships, and learning how to navigate this one was important to him.

Buddy and I got ready for the day, which consisted of me finding something to wear that was reasonably clean and brushing my teeth and hair while Buddy snortled his way through his kibble, TJ and Elliot cooing at him the whole time. Elliot shoved a breakfast burrito topped with salsa, sour cream, and avocado in my hands as I gathered my backpack and keys.

"Here, you're going to need this today."

I raised an eyebrow at him. "Why's that?"

He tilted his head in the direction of my phone. Looks like your dad's been trying to call you."

Six missed calls from my dad. That couldn't be good. I snapped the leash on Buddy, and we did another potty run on the way to my car.

"Well, Buddy, looks like you get to be a private investigator today."

He beamed at me from the passenger seat, his little pink tongue hanging out of his mouth. It was kind of nice to have a dog with me.

My phone buzzed again, and I quickly texted my dad that I'd be to the office in twenty minutes. His reply was a thumbs up emoji. Then I knew he was mad—he almost never used emojis. I turned on the radio to Island Jams and swayed along to Bob Marley.

"You like reggae, don't you Buddy?"

He smiled back at me, and we rode like that, listening to music as I watched the rolling green fields of Waimea come into view. A commercial came on, followed by a news anchor forecasting Hurricane Luisa to make landfall near Mexico in the next few days.

"Phew, one less thing for us to worry about," I told Buddy. He sniffed and nodded at me.

When we arrived at the office, I held Buddy in front of me like a shield. "Buddy said we can only come in if you're not going to yell."

Luckily, my dad was a sucker for dogs. Buddy started to wriggle in my arms and I set him down. He made a beeline for my dad's legs and started jumping and snorting at him. Dad stooped low and let Buddy sniff him before scooping him up and cradling him against his chest.

"And who do we have here?" he asked Buddy.

"Buddy is a friend's dog. They had to go to Oahu for a medical thing, so I volunteered to dog sit for them."

His face broke into a grin, and he started murmuring baby talk to Buddy. It was kind of sweet to see this big lug of a guy turn into a marshmallow around dogs.

After a few minutes, he turned his attention to me. "I've been trying to reach you all morning."

It didn't sound like he was still mad at me from yesterday's shenanigans which made me wonder why the urgency to get ahold of me this morning. His next words cleared up the mystery.

"There's a rumor on the dark web that details about a black-ops mission from the Gulf War were hacked. Unfortunately, the identities of the team members that participated in that mission were compromised. Otis was one of the names on that list."

Dad kept his eyes pointed at a spot above my head and cleared his throat a few times, causing dread to snake down my spine.

"Mack was also on that list," he said, his voice soft. "The intelligence I've been able to gather so far reports that a terrorist group with ties to the Middle East is reportedly seeking revenge systematically. Three men on that list have died under suspicious circumstances already."

Icy cold fear swamped me as I thought about the implications. Was this group responsible for Otis's death? Even more concerning—were they going after Mack, too? With shaking hands, I pulled out my phone to call him, but my dad reached over and cradled my hands.

"Mack's safe. He was the first person I called."

Relief made my legs weak, and I stumbled over to sit down at my desk.

"Does Lani know?"

Dad nodded. "Yep. Here's the thing—we have no idea if there is a connection to Otis's death and this terrorist cell or not. I give it a 50/50 chance it's real. Regardless, Mack and I don't want you or Lani involved in this. It's too dangerous."

Buzzing filled my ears. I was nauseous from the roller coaster I'd been on in the last two minutes. This couldn't be happening.

"Dad," I protested, but even to my own ears my voice sounded weak.

He shook his head. "No, I'm sorry, Summer. Finding Otis's killer is not worth the risk to your or Lani's life." The quiet finality in his tone gutted me. It was probably useless to argue with him. Still, I tried.

"How about if we have you or Mack with us any time we're investigating?"

He gave a small shake of his head, his eyes resolute but sympathetic. "Listen, I know this comes as a blow to you." He placed a comforting hand on my shoulder. "Other cases will come along. You and Lani have great instincts and other than a bit of a struggle with impulse control, exhibit all the hallmarks of a good P.I.'s"

I rubbed a hand across my forehead, my eyes open but unseeing. After five minutes or so my dad cleared his throat.

"I'm going to run next door and grab us some coffee. Be right back."

Buddy pawed at my legs, and I picked him up, snuggling him against me as I attempted to make sense of everything. I was thankful Mack was okay, but heartbroken that our first real case got taken away so easily. When Dad came back, he deposited a paper cup on my desk.

"Dark mocha, extra whip."

Numbly, I took a sip then spread my lips into a wooden smile of thanks.

"While I was standing in line I had an idea," he said. "What if I flew you and Lani out to Arizona to train with some of my colleagues? They're the best in the business and they have a lot of cases there. You could really sink your teeth into the training."

With great care, I set my coffee cup back down on my desk and swiveled in my seat so I could look my dad in the eye. "This wouldn't be your attempt to get Lani and I out of the way, would it?" My tone was icy as I tilted my head at him.

A flicker of guilt crossed his face before he folded his hands across his chest and smiled brightly at me. "No, of course not. I just thought with your lifeguarding shifts few and far between right now, it might be a good time to get in some training. It would be paid, of course."

I mirrored his pose, folding my hands across my chest, narrowing my eyes at him. "I see. And what about Lani and her job at Napua?"

He dismissed my question with a wave. "I'm sure she can work something out."

"You just don't get it, do you? You can't treat us like vital members of your team on one hand, and then in the other like fine china the second danger is mentioned." I shook my head, anger and frustration causing tears to build up. "You either let us continue investigating, or I quit. This isn't right."

Even as I said the words, I knew I was letting emotion get the better of me, but now that I'd said it, I couldn't take it back.

Dad's face bloomed an angry red and he balled his hands into fists at his side. "That's not the way it works. As your boss, your *employer,* I make the decisions around here." His voice pitched low and resolute as he threw down the gauntlet.

I snapped Buddy's leash back on him and grabbed my bag. My dad watched, alarm growing on his face.

"Where are you going?"

The coffee cup on my desk was the last thing I grabbed before I turned and headed for the door. Over my shoulder I told him, "To look for a job."

❧☙

I drove around for hours, sad, worried, and pissed. If I was being honest and not petty, I knew my dad was just trying to keep me safe. My anger was intensified by the fact that there really wasn't anyone to be truly angry at, other than Otis's killer, of course. Dad made the call he did based on what he believed to be right. I didn't have to agree, but as my boss, he had a right to make the final decision. I knew that—but I didn't have to like it.

Buddy and I stopped down at Kawaihae Shopping Center so I could grab some sushi and let Buddy get out and stretch. My phone rang and I swiped to take the call.

"Hey."

"Hey. What are you doing right now?" Lani's voice wavered in and out.

"Licking my wounds."

Her snort came through loud and clear. "Same. Where you at right now?"

"Grabbing gas station sushi and taking Buddy for a walk."

"Stay put, I'll be right there." The phone beeped and disconnected. I stared at it for a minute, then shook my head and shoved it back in my pocket.

Lani pulled up into the parking lot a few minutes later and hopped out. Buddy strained at the leash to go to her, but there was too much traffic for me to risk letting him go.

She walked over to where I sat on the stairs, inhaling sushi, my chopsticks clacking together like a granny at a knitting bee. Standing over me, she gave me a look full of judgement.

"What?" I said around a mouthful of rice.

"I'm so glad you have Elliot in your life. Otherwise, you'd probably be dead by now."

She nudged me with her knee, and I scooted over so she could sit.

"How pissed are you right now?" she asked.

I set my chopsticks down and stared across the lot at a cement tower, sparkling whitecaps visible just beyond, before gusting out a long sigh. "Pissed. But also... I get it."

Lani nodded glumly as she picked at the hem on her shorts. "Yeah, I tried to talk Dad into going underground for a while and he blew up at me."

I rocked back and forth a little. "Dad tried to get me to agree to go to Arizona under the guise of 'training.'"

She gave a half-hearted grin. "Dad told me. It's funny how he thought it was completely acceptable to send me away but got pissed when I suggested the same thing for him."

We sat there in silence until Lani's phoned dinged with an incoming text.

She narrowed her eyes at the screen, her whole body going still and taut.

"What is it?" Anxiety, that old monster, started breathing the fire of fear at me.

She handed me her phone. Louie's text to Lani was basically a plea to spare him from Auntie Miriam's wrath in exchange for information.

I pursed my lips as I read and then handed it back.

"Uncle Louie trying to make amends?" I lifted an eyebrow at Lani.

She shrugged. "Might as well go meet him and see what he has to say."

We took my car the mile over to south harbor and hopped out just behind the rocks, where Louie could be seen pulling in line. Lani reached over and beeped and Louie jumped, bobbling the rod and just barely catching it before it hit the ground. He set it in its holder and picked his way over the rocks to the car.

Buddy was jumping and snorting, so I got out and let him sniff around before zeroing in on Louie. A giant grin broke out on his face as he leaned down and petted Buddy.

"Uncle, you said you had news—what is it?" I whipped my head around toward Lani. She wasn't normally this abrupt, especially with an elder. She caught my look and took a deep breath in and out before giving Louie a smile that didn't quite reach her eyes.

He scratched his head, shuffling his feet before looking her in the eye. "Them boys over there found Otis's phone the day he got dragged out of the water." Louie pointed to a cluster of teenagers I recognized from the day Otis's body was found. Louie whistled, and one of the boys, his shorts baggy and T-shirt loose, shuffled over and handed me the phone, keeping his eyes averted.

I turned it over in my hand, curious how they knew it was Otis's phone. Then I turned it over and saw the back had sticker on it of Paisley's face, fuchsia scarf included.

The boy ambled off, and Louie wrung his hands nervously. "Now we're even, right? No need to talk to Auntie Miriam about anything?"

I couldn't help but feel sorry for Louie. Getting stuck between family members was never easy, especially when it was Mack and Lani we were talking about. Lani flicked her gaze up to my face and I gave a small nod.

"Deal," she said, holding out her hand. Louie's trademark grin broke out, and he pumped Lani's hand up and down enthusiastically. He yelped suddenly, and I saw Lani had his hand pinched in a Vulcan death grip, which was a hilarious picture—a real David and Goliath moment. "That is, deal, as long as no one hears about us being down here."

Uncertainty colored his face, but confronted with Lani's narrowed gaze, he agreed.

A gust of wind blew a little dust tornado around the parking lot and I looked around, noticing for the first time a few tour boats coming in, jockeying into position on the downwind dock to unload their passengers. Jeff's boat was already docked and I spotted him breaking down gear for the day. Beyond him, several other captains were doing the same on their boats.

On a hunch, I wandered over to Jeff's boat and called over to him. "Aloha. How was the charter?"

The only indication he'd heard me was a slight twitch of his back muscles. He looked up, shading his eyes. "Oh, hey Summer." He used a cloth to wipe down the shiny aluminum frame as he replied. "Not too bad. Been harder to get charters than I thought but I've had a few good ones."

Buddy had gone still at the sound of Jeff's voice, and then he growled low and long. *Hmm.*

Jeff moved over to the stern of the boat and peered over at Buddy. "Cute dog. Cole didn't mention you had any pets."

Something about his words and tone of voice set off a warning in my head. Before I could process what it meant, Jeff asked where Cole was.

"Working," I said. "He's got his hands full with the chief and one of his cases."

Jeff threw a million watt smile my way. "Oh yeah? Which one?"

"You'll have to ask him for more specifics. I just know there's been an influx of drugs into the island and Cole's working to intercept them." I wasn't sure how much of what Cole had told me on the boat was public knowledge, so I tried to keep my words non-specific.

Jeff nodded, the corners of his eyes tightening and gave me a stilted smile. "Sounds tough." He'd stopped polishing the aluminum and now his hands gripped the cloth, wringing it out over the edge of the boat, the muscles of his forearms rigid.

Lani walked over and greeted Jeff before turning to me and leaning in close. "What do you think we should do with Otis's phone?"

Out of the corner of my eye, I saw Jeff's body go still. Lani had pitched her voice low—had Jeff heard somehow? Buddy's growling had increased, and Lani eyed first Buddy and then Jeff. Her scrutiny must've unnerved Jeff, he started polishing the area he'd already gone over with extra vigor.

Buddy was rigid in my arms. I'd never seen him like this before.

Chapter Twenty Nine

SUMMER

"Interesting," Lani remarked, eyes tracking from Buddy up to Jeff just as we felt the dock shift and Kevin sauntered over in our direction.

"Summer! I'm so glad to run into you. Is there any possible way you can pinch hit for me tomorrow? My guy disappeared on me, and I have some VIP clients coming to dive. I reached out to Kay, as well as several other dive masters she recommended, but no one is available. Five hundred bucks in cash plus tips." He held that carrot in front of me and my eyes widened at the amount.

"Wow, that's tempting. Can I get back to you? I'm dog sitting." I held Buddy up, who had settled into a vibrating mass of indignation and sharp teeth.

Kevin blinked down at Buddy and nodded. "Yeah, no problem. Just let me know as soon as possible." He grimaced. "I really don't want to have to cancel another charter."

"Another?"

He scowled. "Last week he bailed on me twice. Had to cancel two charters." He shook his head. "I had the guy scheduled pretty tight between the charters and running some errands for me." He shuffled his feet, his eyebrows squishing together, before shrugging. "Maybe I was working him too hard, I don't know. He said he wanted extra cash, though."

"What was his name again?"

"Jason Vargas." I looked over to Lani to see if she recognized the name, but she shrugged and shook her head.

"Hmm. Never heard of him. You know how it is on the island, though—people come and go as fast as trains in Japan. He probably said yes to the extra work to try to make ends meet."

Most dive masters on the island usually had a few different hustles going at once. Island life was expensive, and we all paid the price to live in paradise. I told Kevin as much and promised to get back to him as soon as I talked to Richard and Evelyn. I wasn't sure when they were getting back and I didn't want to commit to anything until I heard from them.

On our way back to the car I saw Mike coming into the harbor on *Moonshine*, but instead of Jess crewing, Tyler and Elias were at the helm readying lines. What the heck were they doing crewing Mike's boat?

"Earth to Summer." Lani knocked on my head, getting my attention.

"Sorry. What did you say?"

"I can watch Buddy if Richard and Evelyn aren't back yet. That's too much money to pass up. Especially now that we aren't working a case," she said glumly.

Buddy had calmed down, so I set him on the ground. He sniffed his way back to the Rav.

"Okay, cool. I'll let Kevin know." I swung around to call out to him, but I saw a trail of wake from the back of his boat as he sped out of the harbor, his back to us. I tilted my head as I watched him and then turned back to Lani with a shrug. "Guess I'll text him."

As we drove out of the parking lot, I noticed a gray Tacoma with some rust on the side and a memory niggled at me, but I couldn't quite grasp it. We waved to Louie who was still on the shoreline fishing; he waved back with a broad grin and held up a yellow-eyed surgeonfish attached to the line on his pole.

On impulse I asked Lani to stop in at Kohala Divers. She looked at me with a raised eyebrow but turned onto the dead-end street and parked in front of the shop.

Tracy was working the desk. "Hey, Summer. Howzit?"

"Good. How about you? How's business been?"

Her mouth turned down at the edges and her shoulders slumped. "It's fine. Could be better but the swell is making conditions rough enough we've had to cancel or cut short a few charters already this week."

Tourists started flocking to the island this time of year, but fall and winter conditions could be tricky for the charter business.

I looked around; there was a couple looking at masks in the corner but no one else. "Where's the crew? I figured they'd be back by now."

Tracy sighed. "We didn't go out today. Only one diver signed up. We had to call off crew last minute." She rubbed her neck. "I really hate making those calls."

The man who'd been looking at the masks came over to ask a question, and I waved at Tracy before heading back to Lani's car and poking my head in. She was trying to teach Buddy to shake, but he got so excited he just spun around every time she gave the command.

"Sorry about that, just had to check in with Tracy real quick."

Lani smiled at Buddy when he lifted a paw in her direction. "No worries. Buddy and I are refining our act for the circus."

I leaned farther in. "What do you want to do about the phone?" My gut told me Otis's phone might have something important on it.

Her shoulders rose and fell, and she let out a sigh. "We should probably hand it over to your dad."

A picture from this morning of my dad trying to package us off to Arizona rose up. "What if we took it back to my place? It might not even work anymore," I rationalized. "Besides, Dad will know we were down at the harbor if we take it to him right now. Let's at least see if it's worth the ass-chewing first."

Lani nodded and handed the phone to me through the window. Lani begged me to let Buddy ride with her back to my place and after staring at two sets of puppy dog eyes I gave in.

"Sure. You still have your key?"

She jingled a ring of keys at me with a sarcastic look on her face. "Of course. I can't believe you think I'd lose it."

I bit my tongue hard so I didn't reply. She'd lost her keys three times in the last year. Elliot and I made a half dozen copies just to have on hand in case she lost one again.

The sky had darkened considerably in the short time I'd been at the shop and talking to Lani. Fat raindrops hit the windshield of my car, the smell of ozone thick as I drove on autopilot towards home.

Foremost in my thoughts was getting kicked off the case. Regardless of the reason it still sucked. Dad had texted me several times, but I left the messages unread. I just wasn't in the frame of mind to respond rationally right now.

Cole also texted and said he wasn't sure if he'd be able to come over tonight, and my heart dropped a little. I'd gotten used to having him around and missed him on the nights he wasn't.

Bright yellow headlights appeared in my rearview mirror, and I noticed the truck behind me was close. Too close. I sped up a little, but it kept pace with me. I thought about pulling over and letting whoever was riding my ass go past me, but the shoulder on this stretch of the highway was almost non existent.

The sky opened up just then, and rain pelted my window so hard it sounded like hail. I leaned forward to see better and turned my windshield wipers on high.

The lights from the truck behind me glinted off my mirror, making it nearly impossible to see. Red taillights formed a line of color in front of me. I pressed my brake to slow down and *boom!*

My car lurched forward, and I swung the wheel to the right to avoid hitting the car in front of me. My heart pounded in my throat, and I broke out into a cold sweat. When I dared to look in my rearview mirror, I saw the truck fast approaching again, and I hit the gas, swinging my car even with the one in front of me, riding the shoulder and hoping I could squeeze past the mile marker pole.

I noticed a tiny face pressed against the window in the car I was now riding parallel to on the shoulder, the tires on the Rav thumping as I drove on the rumble strip.

I caught just a flash of dark silver or gray and some orange rust on the front fender before the truck that hit me swerved into the other lane. As I watched in my rearview mirror the truck made a U-turn, tires squealing.

The rain was coming down so hard I thought maybe I'd see Noah and his arc floating by. The truck had moved so fast in the low light I couldn't even be certain of the make or model, just that it reminded me of the truck I'd seen down at the harbor the night I'd met Jeff.

My hands shook so bad I could barely steer, but more than anything I wanted to get home and hide under the covers. I managed to steer back onto the highway, the whole time my heart racing painfully.

As I got in the turning lane to head up to Waikoloa Village, I didn't see yellow headlights in my rearview mirror and let myself breathe fully for the first time since I got rear-ended.

After making it home without incident, I pushed open my front door and let out a breath of relief, my hair dripping from the soaking I'd gotten walking from my car. Buddy and Lani rounded the corner and came running down the hallway to greet me.

"You guys are a sight for sore eyes." My voice came out weak and thready.

Lani ushered me into the kitchen and poured me a big glass of wine. "What happened?" Her concern was evident by the fact that she asked with zero snark in her tone as she handed me a dry towel.

I described my drive home and her face paled. "Maybe Dad's right. Maybe we need to drop the investigation altogether."

Her words hit me hard. I never considered that what we were doing was a game, but I hadn't imagined it would get this out of control. I shook my head, holding the bridge of my nose and wondering how to move forward. Every cell in my body told me we were getting close to finding something, but it didn't take a genius to figure out that the killer also recognized that.

Lani suggested I call HPD, but with so little information to give them, I figured it would be a waste of time. Besides, I wasn't exactly in their good graces.

"Damn it, Lani. This isn't how I wanted our first big case to go." Despite myself, an angry tear ran down my cheek, and I wiped it away impatiently.

"I know. Me neither." She grasped my hands. "The right case will come along." Not known for being the positive one, things must've gotten desperate if Lani was trying to cheer *me* up.

Nodding, I squeezed her hand and took a giant swig from my wine glass. I guess if we couldn't keep investigating the biggest case we'd had so far, I might as well drown my sorrows.

⚜ ⚜

Elliot came home soaking wet, raindrops making little rivers down the front of his shirt, to find Lani and I snuggled on the couch, a bottle of chocolate wine and a bowl of kettle chips in front of us as we watched *Karate Kid*. The original, not the new one with Jaden Smith.

"Oh shit. What happened?"

"Elliot!" I hopped up to give him a hug, only to tangle myself in the purple couch blanket I'd wrapped myself in.

"Hi, sweetie. What's going on with you two? You only break out *Karate Kid* when something really bad has happened."

I circled my hands around like I'd just watched *Daniel-san* do in the movie. "We're waxing on our good luck and waxing off our bad." I smiled winningly at him, the effect ruined by a loud hiccup I couldn't stop.

He glanced down at our snacks. "Looks like maybe you two could use some dinner, something to soak up all the booze."

Lani waved her hand at him in irritation. "We're fine. We are strong independent women who can handle ourselves without the help of a man," she declared, punctuating her words with a wide, wobbly karate chop in the air. She lost her balance and would've tipped over onto the floor if Elliot hadn't caught her.

"I can see that," he said drily. He ushered Lani and I over to the bar stools at the kitchen counter and ordered us to stay put while he started digging through the refrigerator and pulling out various meal-type ingredients, because according to Elliot there's a difference—food and ingredients are different. Food you can just eat as is, but ingredients have to be combined to make a meal. Who knew?

After plying us with sparkling water and pasta, Elliot finally pried the whole rotten story out of us. "So, what are you going to do?"

I slumped and threw my hands up in the air. "Give up? I mean, what other option is there?"

"Hmm." Elliot looked down and away.

"What?"

"That doesn't sound like the Summer I know."

"Well, what do you want us to do, Elliot?" Lani raised her voice, her tone livid. "The dads have kicked us off the case, besides which, they might have a point." She gestured toward me. "How many times can she get run off the road and survive?"

Elliot's head whipped over in my direction. "Run off the road? I think you left that part out."

His face got stormier and stormier as I filled him in about my drive home. "For once, I'm going to agree with Lani. Maybe it is better to retreat on this one. What did HPD say?"

Guiltily, I looked down at the floor. "Nothing. I never called them."

"What the hell? Why not?" he demanded.

His tone immediately set my back up. "Maybe because the Chief doesn't seem to like me very much? Maybe because he has lackeys on the force and who knows who would get sent out? Possibly because I have zero information to give them except it was a gray truck and had some rust on the front fender? And what do you think they'd be able to do with that information? You know as well as I do, there are probably 10,000 gray trucks on the island. Do you honestly think HPD has the manpower to sift through all of those owners and find one matching that description? Honestly, who even knows if it has anything to do with the case? It's just as possible some lolo was just in a hurry and took it too far."

"What about Cole? Did you let him know?"

After all my bluster, that question had me shrinking in my seat. I shook my head. "I didn't want to worry him," I whispered. "He already has so much on his plate and there's not much he could do anyway. Besides...I don't want him to know we got taken off the case. That Dad doesn't have faith in our ability."

The heat in my chest must've reflected on my face because Elliot handed me a cold paper towel. "I'm really sorry," his tone softened. "I know this case meant a lot to you."

I hung my head. This was it. No more case. I knew it, but for some reason it hadn't really sunk in until now. Suddenly everything felt too tight, too hot, too real. I jumped up and bid everyone goodnight.

"Got an early day tomorrow," I mumbled, leaving Lani to fill in the blanks about dive mastering for Kevin. On my way up to bed, I berated myself for ever getting excited about the case—who was I kidding anyway? Me, a P.I? I didn't even finish college. Might as well make peace with the idea that maybe I wasn't cut out for this line of work.

Chapter Thirty

COLE

"Good news or bad news?" Jack's voice sounded tinny as he asked.

"Huh?"

"You want the good news first or the bad?"

"Let's get the bad over with." I braced myself.

Jack's voice sounded like it was going in and out of a tunnel as he shared his latest news. "Despite our best efforts by multiple people working on the case, we are no closer to finding out how or who changed the records of the two guys from Pahala."

Before I could react, he continued. "There's more. The USB didn't have anything interesting on it that could incriminate Takada. What we found may be considered borderline stalking, but even that's a stretch."

"So, what do you want me to do?"

Jack blew out a big sigh, his voice tired as he replied. "Hold on. There's more. We're in a little bit of double jeopardy here. If you follow Kimo around and get caught or piss Takada off, he could flip the script and accuse *you* of stalking and harassment.

My guess is, he's thinking he'll get what he can on Kimo through you and then turn the tables the moment he starts to feel any heat."

Shit. What a weasel. I wasn't surprised, I'd had the same thought, but to hear it from Jack as well made all the muscles in my neck tense. "Any luck on any of the other leads?"

Jack cleared his throat and hesitated. "Well, that's where the good news comes in. We have pictures of Takada meeting with a known member of the Bois gang two nights ago down at Keahou Harbor. We dug around in his history and found an interesting fact—the man he met up with has a captain's license in the state of Hawaii."

Several missing pieces of the puzzle fell into place—Chief calling me off the case, the link from the gang members to the drug boats, and how we never could seem to catch them.

"You're pretty quiet on your end," Jack remarked. "All those Plinko chips lining up?"

"Let me get this straight—Takada is helping to somehow orchestrate the drug trafficking on island through the Bois?" Cold fury washed over me. We'd been fighting for years—*years* to stem the flow of drugs, and the chief of police on island was now helping to facilitate its presence?

"Tell me you have a plan," I ground out.

"Nothing yet."

The space around me exploded into a cacophony of swear words as I vented my frustration. Jack stayed silent until I quieted.

"Cole, we don't have enough evidence yet to make it stick. What we have are suspicious behaviors, but nothing downright damning. I need you to wait. He's going down, believe me," Jack promised grimly. "I'm not retiring until we get this piece of filth off the streets for good."

Long after we hung up, I sat on the edge of my bed, shocked at this turn of events. Every time I thought Takada couldn't get any dirtier, something new was discovered.

Unable to face going into the office and faking it, I headed to the gym to pound out my frustration on the punching bag instead of Takada's face. Thank God the gym was open twenty-four hours; not even the roosters were crowing this early in the morning, the sky inky black without a hint of sun yet.

On my way, I kept an eye out for Jack's tail, but either he was on a break or he'd actually taken my advice and gotten better.

While I pounded away on the heavy bag, I pictured various ways Takada would pay for his crimes. I landed on a cellmate named Bubba who really hated police officers.

So caught up in my revenge stories, I was taken off guard by a tap on my shoulder. Jeff stood behind me, grinning.

"I see you still got it," he jerked his head toward the bag.

I gave him a thin-lipped smile. "Hey, man. howzit? What are you doing here so early?" I took the towel he handed me and wiped the sweat off my face.

"Eh. Couldn't sleep." He scrubbed his face with a hand, weariness radiating off him. "The charters haven't been all that great, but I'm holding out hope it'll get better. I'm glad to run into you though—we haven't seen much of each other, and spending time with you was one of the reasons I agreed to take this gig in the first place."

I rubbed a spot on my chest that ached. I grimaced; the case against Chief took up most of my time, and everything left went to Summer. Jeff had been here for over a week, and the only time I saw him was when we ran into each other randomly or he reached out to arrange something.

"I ran into Summer yesterday." He coughed and wouldn't meet my eyes. "She said you've been pretty busy with one of your cases. If you ever want to bounce ideas off me, let me know. I've had a bit of experience in the last few years with drug runners."

The wording felt off somehow, and my face must've reflected my misgiving. "Or not. Just trying to help." He held his hands palms up, a thread of hurt in his tone.

"Actually, Jeff, I wanted to ask about your trip to Bulgaria. What were you doing in that neck of the woods?" I tried to keep my tone light, although inside I was burning with curiosity. "We haven't kept in contact much lately, and I'm curious what's going on with you. I didn't even know you had any experience with drug runners. It seems like you're living some sort of double life or something."

I was fishing, hoping to learn more about what was really going on with him. I hated to think he was up to something dishonest, but there were too many loose threads to his story. We were closer than brothers in the service, and I still considered him one of my best friends, but it occurred to me that our conversations had dwindled over the last year to just a few texts and some random memes.

Truth was, I didn't really know much about him nowadays.

A face flashed before my eyes, the man I thought I saw at Punaluu Bakery bringing a piercing pain to my heart—I really hoped I was wrong on this one.

I watched as his face closed down, going blank and flat. "Had a gig over there. Or nearby anyway, got some intel about the knife and took a chance." He shrugged.

"Oh yeah? What kind of gig? I'm curious." I wasn't buying it; he was up to something. Weights clanked on the bar as I shifted a few fifty pounders on each side of the bench. Without looking in his direction, I threw out a name. "You know, I could've sworn I saw Marquez, or his twin, down near Puna a few days ago."

Jeff gripped my arm so quick it reminded me of his nickname on the team—Viper. "Where?" Jaw locked, teeth clenched, this was not the easygoing Jeff the world normally saw.

"Why does it matter to you?" I asked, my tone mild as I took in his reaction.

With infinite care, he released my arm and turned away. "It doesn't. Not really, anyway. It's just not a name I was expecting to hear." The back of his neck was red, his back muscles rigid with strain.

Rage and frustration filled me, and I slammed him against the wall. "For fuck's sake, dude. Lie to yourself if you want, but have the common fucking courtesy to be straight with *me* at least."

We stood nose to nose, both of us breathing heavy. He was the first to drop his gaze. "I can't talk about it. Just...OODA at all times, okay? Some shit's going on behind the scenes, and until I've got a handle on it no one's safe." With that he pushed roughly past me and hightailed it out the front door, snagging his gym bag on the way out.

I stared at the exit, a myriad of thoughts cascading through my mind until someone tapped me on the shoulder. I spun around, hands up.

"You done with machine, mister?" A tiny Asian woman who barely reached my sternum stood, pointing at the bench.

I smiled through gritted teeth. "It's all yours."

I made a move to take the weight off the ends, but she waved me off and proceeded to lift easily twice her weight without breaking a sweat. My eyebrows rose and I stood close by in order to spot her.

She caught me staring and flexed a bicep. "Old age is a bitch but I kick its ass."

For the first time all day, I broke into a genuine smile.

Chapter Thirty One

SUMMER

MY ALARM RANG OUT with annoying regularity every nine minutes until Elliot pounded on my door and told me to "get my sweet ass out of bed already." It was still dark outside but during the Great Pity Party of the decade last night, I hadn't remembered to get my gear set out for leading dives on Kevin's boat today. He probably had everything I needed, but I preferred my own gear.

I rushed around, gathering everything up and waving to Elliot as I raced out the door and headed down to the harbor. At the very last minute before I stepped outside, I dashed back in and gave Elliot a hug.

"Thank you," I said. "Thank you for loving me and being my friend even when I'm being ridiculous."

He patted me, his face a combination of discomfort and delight at my words. "Of course. That's what I'm here for, babe." He spun around and handed me a Pop-Tart.

My eyes widened. "Where'd you get that?"

His grin was mocking. "I keep a stash for emergencies." He kissed my forehead and waved me off.

The clock in my car had me pushing my foot a little harder on the gas than normal, but I was able to pull in right at 6:30. The lights in the parking lot reflected off Kevin's boat, but I didn't see him anywhere.

I didn't feel right setting up without Kevin around, so before unloading my gear on the boat, I decided to poke around and see if I could find him.

Farther down the dock, I saw a few other captains readying their boats for the day, but it was dark and silent down on my end. As I passed by Jeff's boat, I saw no signs of life, but snatches of a heated conversation reached my ears. I couldn't tell exactly where the voices were coming from—*Moonshine*, Mike's boat, was parked in the day use slot on one side, and Kevin's boat on the other.

Not wanting to interrupt, I debated what to do—part of me, the nosy part, wanted to listen in. But the other part, the more prudent, rational part, warned me that whatever argument was happening was none of my business.

Before I could decide, I heard a male's voice. "Lost too many boats already. This is ridiculous. Should've been a simple operation."

An unseen man replied, "T promised us he'd make sure we had smooth passage. Not my fault he keeps switching the harbors. Ran out of gas three times now with all the changes."

The voices sounded as if they were coming closer, and I frantically looked around for somewhere to hide. My heart was beating double time so loud in my ears I worried everyone in a mile radius could hear it.

Out of the corner of my eye, I noticed a pile of ropes and tarp piled up near one of the fishing boats and raced over on my tip toes and dove underneath just as a light switched on.

The tarp smelled of old bait and fish guts, and I fought against instant waves of nausea. Two sets of footsteps walked perilously close, so close I probably could've touched them. I heard the rumble of their voices, but the tarp muted the sound enough I couldn't make out their words.

Once I was sure no one else was nearby, which felt like hours but was probably only ten minutes, I slithered out from underneath the tarp. I kept low at first and tried to brush off the remnants of whatever scaly fish species was now in my hair and clothes. Lights were starting to blink on here and there and the sun was beginning its slow rise in the sky over Mauna Kea, streaks of light visible in the distance.

"Whatcha doing?"

"Ahh!" I jumped and spun around to see Jeff standing over to the side of his boat, a smirk on his face. It took a minute for me to settle my racing nerves before I could answer. "Oh, Jeff, you startled me." I threw him what I hoped was a convincing smile. "I'm looking for Kevin. He asked me to DM for him today, but..." I pointed over at the still darkened boat. "No one's there."

With his eyes still focused steadily on me, he reached over with one hand and knocked on the side of Kevin's boat. "You got company."

Ten seconds passed before a tiny sliver of light shone from the berth of the boat and Kevin emerged. He was dressed in the uniform of captains everywhere—that is, he wore board shorts and a T-shirt with his company logo on it, a shark with a pirate patch grinning with all its teeth. He held a pair of sunglasses in his hand and wiped them repeatedly with his shirt, his face screwed up in irritation until he saw me. The smile he gave me didn't quite reach his eyes.

"Summer. Hey. Sorry—late night, and I guess I overslept. Hop on and we'll get you sorted."

Jeff's eyes followed me as I took Kevin's hand and stepped down into the boat. My neck tingled and my nerves felt raw as I thought about the conversation I'd overheard.

Just before I followed Kevin down below for a quick briefing, I risked a glance in Jeff's direction. He still watched me, something unfathomable in his expression. He held my eyes for a moment and then saluted me before turning back to his boat and setting up fishing poles.

Before the clients arrived, Kevin asked me what spots I'd like to moor up at for the dives. Judging by the light chop and swell, I chose two that were fairly sheltered but were known for critters that macro photographers loved to shoot. The area Kevin had set up for cameras included microfiber clothes and even extra sealant for any leaky housings and I surveyed it with approval before moving on to check out the gear set-up.

The spot set aside for weights was positioned at the front of the starboard side of the boat. Lani would've drooled at the organization. Yellow weights were stacked on a weight tree starting on the bottom with heavier weights progressing to lighter on top. The slots for some of the heavier weights were empty, and I searched to see if they'd gotten left under one of the benches. I finally gave up when Kevin told me they'd been missing for a while.

"Probably went home in someone's weight pocket on accident or something." He shrugged. "I have more on order, but it's Hawaii so who knows when they'll get here."

"Facts," I said with a mock grimace.

The morning passed in a blur. Kevin's dive set-up was top notch. It was probably the most boutique diving I'd ever seen. He'd put in place some of the changes I'd mentioned the first time we met, and it flowed nicely. The clients that morning had the latest and greatest camera and underwater housings, and we had fun looking at the photos in between dives.

As one of the clients, Bret, scrolled through his camera looking for a specific shot, one of his buddies made the comment, "Lot different than the usual photos, huh?"

He snorted. "You might say that."

Of course I had to ask, "What kind of photos are you normally taking?"

He looked up at Kevin, something unreadable in his expression, then pointed to himself and his buddies. "We're part of the Coast Guard's search and recover team. Those photos aren't nearly as fun."

After hearing that I resolved to make our second dive the most epic I could, and the ocean didn't disappoint. We found several rare species of nudibranchs, two frogfish cleverly camouflaged as coral heads, a giant moray eel cooperatively hunting with a silver and blue jack, and three octopuses. If that wasn't enough, a pod of dolphins came to entertain us with their antics on our safety stop.

Once we surfaced, the chop had doubled and the wind was blowing pretty hard. Kevin reached down to help the four divers into their spots on the boat and then took my fins as I climbed the ladder at the back of the boat.

"How was it?" he asked the group, a big smile on his face. I noticed that even as he made conversation, he secured the ladder and pulled the dive flag down. We were about five miles from the harbor—not a huge distance, but the wind waves and swell had built enough that the ride back was adventurous. Thankfully, the group was well used to adverse conditions and didn't bat an eye as we zigged and zagged our way into the harbor, trying to avoid the worst of the waves.

Bret shoved some cash into my hand as he and the other guys were disembarking from the boat. "Best dive any of us have had in a long time." He tipped his baseball cap at me and hopped into a red F-150 truck with shiny chrome accents.

"You're a lifesaver!" Kevin told me as we hosed down the deck. "Seriously, if you ever want a more permanent gig, just let me know."

"Thanks. I'll let you know." My mind drifted back to my argument with Dad yesterday.

We secured the cabin and stowed all the gear. "Want me to drop off tanks to get filled?" I asked Kevin. "I'm heading over there anyway, so it would save you a trip."

His gaze caught on the tanks, his brow wrinkled. "Hmm, thanks for the offer, but, uh, I think Meredith is working today." His face turned bright red.

"Ah, sure, no problem." I tried to hide my grin at his obvious crush on the long-legged blonde who worked at the shop. "Take care." I waved and slung my BCD over my shoulder, the metal from the tank straps clinking together as I made my way over to my car.

"Summer!"

My head popped up, and I saw Kevin standing on the dock, his hands cupped around his mouth. When he saw he'd gotten my attention, he held up something white and bounded over to me.

"Here. I almost forgot to pay you." He handed me a thick white envelope full of cash. I raised an eyebrow. "I didn't want to forget." He cleared his throat. "By the way, you and your friends are welcome to come out on the boat any time I'm not running a charter."

Something about his words tugged at my heartstrings. I knew what it was like to be new here. Thankfully I already had friends and family on island when I moved from Arizona, but I'd seen plenty of transplants come and go—this was a hard place to make friends when you didn't know anyone.

"Thanks." I held up the envelope. "Thanks—that's a really generous offer. I'll keep that in mind." I beamed up at him.

He nodded, his Adam's apple bobbing up and down like he was going to say something more, but in the end, he just smiled.

"Alright, see you around," I said, feeling ridiculously awkward and waving again before jumping into the Rav.

Once home, Buddy met me at the door, dancing around and snorting, his little doggy face split into a wide grin. Lani followed close behind.

"Wanna see what I taught him?" Her face was lit with excitement.

"Yes, please." I dropped my gear by the front door to take care of later.

Lani and Buddy scurried into the living room and I followed.

"Buddy, sit." He sat, his little butt plunking down on the tile. "Roll over." He dutifully rolled over and then sat up. Lani dropped a treat on the ground and Buddy eyed it closely but stayed in position.

"Housekeeping!" Lani trilled, and Buddy raced over and hoovered up the treat.

They wore identical expressions of pride. "Well done, Buddy!" I praised him. He spun in a joyful circle at my words.

Lani cleared her throat, loudly. "And well done, Lani," I said, tongue in cheek.

"How did it go today?" Lani wanted to know.

I spent the next fifteen minutes telling her about my day. I showed her the envelope loaded with five crisp hundred-dollar bills. Her eyes got big.

"Dang, I think I might need to get my dive master certs. Working at Napua pays the bills, for sure, but spending all day underwater sounds pretty good, especially if it pays that well."

Something occurred to me. "I noticed you haven't had as many shifts at Napua lately. It's not because of Kalani, is it?"

She shrugged but kept her eyes averted. "Plenty of people want shifts right now before the holidays."

My phone vibrated. I read the incoming message and looked over at Buddy, then Lani.

"Richard and Evelyn are back. They just got home and are anxious to see Buddy."

Lani's face fell.

"Let me grab a shower and we can run him up there. That is if you have time. Do you have to work the dinner shift tonight?"

She shook her head. "No, our numbers are down, so Brandon gave me the option to have a night off and I took it."

While I was in the shower I thought about my day. Diving was a passion of mine, but I'd never pursued full time employment as a dive master was because I liked keeping it as something to just enjoy. The only reason I'd agreed to work for Kohala Divers from time to time was the hefty discount on gear and tank rentals.

Today had been fun, though. Possibilities circled around in my brain. When I headed downstairs, I was just about to ask Lani's opinion, but the serious look on her face stopped me in my tracks. My throat closed up—what had happened?

"Dad texted."

A swarm of angry centipedes stampeded through my belly as I waited for her to fill me in, my mind going to the worst stories possible.

"He wants to meet us in the morning. He cracked the code on the journal."

Chapter Thirty Two

SUMMER

OF ALL THE THINGS that could've come out of her mouth, that was one of the last I would've expected.

"Did he say anything else?" I asked.

She shook her head.

"Why tell us? I thought we were kicked off the case." A trace of bitterness threaded through my tone.

She sat slumped, her chin cupped in her hand. "Who knows." She let out a gusty sigh. "But damn it, I'm curious."

The cushions on the couch shifted as I plopped down beside her and angled my head to read the text. Lani obligingly tilted it toward me, and I read it aloud.

"Cracked the code on the journal. Meet me in the morning at the office." I rolled my eyes and looked at Lani. "That dad of yours, such a chatty Cathy."

Lani and I debated on whether or not to meet with Mack on our drive up to Richard and Evelyn's to drop Buddy off, but ultimately neither one of us would be content without at least some measure of closure on this whole sad goat rope of a case.

Speaking of goats, Paisley came running up to the fence braying as soon as my car entered the drive. Evelyn's diminutive form could be seen towards the back of the barn, and we hailed her as Buddy burst out of the car and made a beeline straight for her.

Lani and I watched the reunion, and as happy as I was for Evelyn I knew I'd miss having Buddy around. From the look on Lani's face, she felt the same.

"Oh girls, I can't thank you enough for taking care of Buddy. It took a huge weight off my shoulders knowing he was safe with you." Evelyn's eyes glistened at the corners as she hugged us effusively. Paisley even got in on the action and stretched her head through the fence posts to lick my leg. I scratched her head and cooed at her. Her collar was looking worse for the wear.

"Do you want me to order a new collar for Paisley? There's enough fraying I'm worried if you need to move her on a lead, it'll break."

Evelyn leaned down to look while Paisley continued to lick my leg; she must like my coconut lotion. Evelyn inspected it and then unsnapped it from her neck.

"I have an old leather one that will work for now, but if you want to find her a fancy one, I'm sure she'd love that."

Evelyn disappeared into the barn for a moment and then returned with a serviceable black leather collar. From the look of disdain on Paisley's face, it was obvious she didn't like it very much. She immediately started to rub it against the fence post and bray in protest.

I laughed as I watched her antics—what a character.

Evelyn handed me the old collar. "You can use this to figure out the right size to get."

I tossed it into the backseat of the Rav and noticed something black on the floor. When I leaned in to get a closer look, my stomach dropped. Otis's phone.

I squeezed Lani's arm and said goodbye to Evelyn abruptly. Lani gave me a funny look, didn't say anything. As we got to the stop sign to turn onto the highway Lani turned in her seat and looked at me silently.

"Look in the backseat on the floor behind me."

She quirked her lips in annoyance but indulged me anyway. Her whole body contorted as she unbuckled and wiggled over the console to look back at where Otis's cell phone sat nestled just under the shadow of the drivers seat.

She jerked back up and sat in her seat. "Shit."

"Precisely."

"I forgot all about it."

"Me too. What should we do about it?" I rubbed my face with my hands as I waited to pull out onto the highway. We were going to be in deep shit with the dads.

"I suppose flinging it out the window and pretending we never saw it won't work considering Uncle is the one who gave it to us." She closed her eyes and took in a deep breath. I noticed her fingers form a yoga mudra.

"Umm, no offense, but this isn't exactly the time to meditate."

She cracked open an eye and smacked my arm. "It's the *perfect* time to meditate. Bobby always tells us that when we're at a crossroads and don't know the answer to look within. That's what I'm doing. Or would be doing if it weren't for my lolo noisy partner." She wrinkled her nose at me.

"Great. Whatever. Meditate away." I waved a hand at her as my thoughts raced, the most predominant one being my dad was going to freak out.

Which is why we were both up and at the gym at five a.m. the next morning, training our way through the anxiety. Lani dashed any hope that she'd take it easy on me, pounding me into the mat over and over again until I called a timeout.

I glared up at her; the light of victory shone in her eyes and smug smile.

"You're getting better," she remarked.

I turned a disbelieving gaze first at her and then at my current position, splayed on the mat like a one of Elliot's spatch-cocked chickens.

She offered a hand and I grabbed it, amazed at how strong she was for someone her size.

We showered quickly and decided to stop at Surf Camp first to fortify ourselves with caffeine for the upcoming thrashing we were likely to experience from the dads.

"Two twenty ounce full-fat mochas with whip," I told the girl at the register.

Lani raised an eyebrow at me.

"I have a feeling I'm going to need the extra caffeine."

She hummed low in her throat but didn't say anything. She angled in front of me and put in an order for a black sesame latte made with macnut milk.

"What size?" The girl taking her order asked.

"Twelve ounces," Lani said primly and threw a look at me over her shoulder. I stuck my tongue out at her.

Thus fortified, we walked over to the office. The lights were on inside, so we pushed the door open, both of us with our chests out, the picture of confidence.

Dad and Mack stood near my dad's office door huddled together, speaking in hushed tones. When they noticed us, they turned, both faces masked of any expression.

"Looks like you came loaded for bear," my dad commented with a nod at my double fisted caffeine trough.

Words got stuck in my throat now that I was standing face to face with him. We hadn't talked since he pulled me off the case two days ago, and I was equal parts upset at him and worried about his reaction. That's the trouble with working for family—even if you quit, you still had to see them occasionally.

Lani set her drink down on the nearby counter and took one out of my hands. She was the first to speak to the dads.

"Mack said he cracked the code on the journal but I'm curious why you called us in considering you took us off the case two days ago."

The two men shared a look, and then Dad suggested we settle in his office. He went to the front door and flipped the lock and turned the sign to Closed.

We sat at the conference table, Lani and I on one side and the dads on the other. I fiddled with my cup and did my best to appear uninterested. Judging by the glare Lani shot at me, I was failing miserably.

Dad cleared his throat. "It appears the intel I received several days ago was incorrect. We no longer believe Otis's death to be connected to the black ops mission I told you about earlier."

Mack took over. "With that, we both recognize we didn't handle things as well as we could've concerning your involvement with the case."

My eyebrows winged up as I looked at Lani, and she wore the same bewildered look.

My dad folded his hands on the table in front of him and leaned forward. "I've decided to reopen the investigation at Mack's request. My only requirement is that the two of you return to your previous positions as lead investigators."

Surprise swamped me. This wasn't what I'd been expecting.

Mack took over where my dad left off. "You girls have proven yourselves resourceful and capable, and I'd very much like for you to help find Otis's murderer." He pushed the journal we'd found in Otis's van across the table like the peace offering it was, with the lock opened, a yellow tab sticking out on one end.

"I marked the pertinent entries." He shifted in his seat, his expression one of discomfort. "Some of the entries are of a personal nature and I'm sure not something Otis would want anyone else to read. You can see there towards the end where I've marked it there are several entries that mention activity down at the harbor and Otis's concerns."

Lani picked up the journal and flipped to the entries, her lips moving as she read. My dad cleared his throat again, drawing Lani's attention away from the journal.

"We'd also like to apologize, Mack and me. We recognize we were heavy-handed in the way we handled things. Our only defense is that, well, we're dads, and sometimes our fear for your safety overrides anything else." My dad's finger tapped on the table, and he rocked back and forth in his chair. His expression looked pained.

Taking mercy on him, I reached across the table for his hand. "I understand, Dad. I really do. In the future if something like this comes up, maybe you can handle it differently, but I know you and Mack just wanted to keep us safe."

Dad's eyes took on a watery shine, as did Mack's. Our tender moment was interrupted when Lani exclaimed, "You've got to be kidding me!" All three of us turned to look at her but she was focused on the journal. Sensing our attention, she looked up.

"Otis wrote that he was tracking a smuggling ring down at the harbor. Our little harbor at Kawaihae." She shook her head. "I can't decide if I hope he's wrong or I hope he's right."

"He mentioned pictures in one of the later entries, but we never found his phone in the van. Which, by the way, we moved over to the family property in Hilo so we can clean it out and donate it." Mack drummed his fingers on the table. "If only we had his phone."

Lani and I shared a look which both dads noticed.

"Uh oh. That's Summer's 'I messed up bad' look," My dad commented.

I took a fortifying guzzle from my coffee cup before laying our cards on the table. "Well, a couple of days ago we might've accidentally found Otis's phone down at the harbor, but then we forgot about it."

"Forgot about it? Accidentally?" My dad's tone was icy as he glared at both Lani and me.

"A lot happened that day. It slipped our minds." I crossed my arms over my chest and narrowed my eyes.

"Let me get this straight. You forgot about a key piece of evidence in a murder investigation?" Dad's posture had gone rigid.

"Hang on, back off for a minute. You'd just kicked us off the case and threatened to send us to Arizona. We got a call and only responded as a favor to Un—" Lani kicked me under the table. "From one of our sources. When the phone came into our possession, it was dead. We'd planned on giving it to Mack the next day, but then I nearly got ra—" Shit. We'd just gotten back on the case. I didn't want Dad to know I'd gotten rear-ended on my way home. He'd be convinced it had something to do with the case and yank it away again. "That is, I ran into a friend at the dive shop who needed help the next day, and we both forgot. For what it's worth, it won't happen again." I finished, hoping to mollify my dad.

His face looked like a bright tomato and his hands were gripping the edges of the table. He nodded stiffly, but I could tell he was pissed. Hopefully his goodwill and guilt would carry over to this and just let it drop.

I fished the phone out of my bag and handed it to dad. "We tried charging it last night. It turned on this morning, but the lock screen was pretty glitchy."

Dad turned it over to look closely at it. "Hmm," is all he said.

Lani nudged me and I looked at the page she pointed to in the journal. "It looks like dates and boat registration numbers," she said.

"I came to the same conclusion," Mack said. "He also mentions two men specifically but uses nicknames for both. Big Gums and Sparky. When we were over in the Gulf, we had a team leader that couldn't stay still, always jumping from one thing to another.

We called him Sparky because he was like a live wire, sparking every time he landed on something."

Something niggled in the back of my mind but refused to surface at Mack's description. Before I could strain myself trying to connect any dots, Lani mused, "Big Gums makes me think of a shark, how when they open their mouths all you see is gums and teeth."

Dad's stomach growled and I smirked. He rocked back in the chair and shot an embarrassed grin at the table. "My stomach was upset, so I skipped breakfast," he said.

As soon as Dad mentioned breakfast my stomach growled in solidarity, and everyone laughed.

"How about I treat us all to breakfast at Hawaiian Style Cafe?"

Lani and I immediately jumped up before he could change his mind and headed for the door. I heard Dad laugh and comment to Mack, "Guess that's a yes."

Chapter Thirty Three

SUMMER

AFTER CONSUMING MY WEIGHT in coconut pancakes and thick, salty bacon, I traipsed back to the office with Lani, Dad, and Mack. We checked Otis's phone, and miracle of miracles, it turned on. The next order of business was figuring out a six-digit passcode.

"Any guesses?" I asked the group.

How about Paisley? Maybe he used her name," Lani suggested.

"That's seven digits, not six."

She shrugged. "Maybe he spelled it without and 'E'."

Anticipation grew as I typed it in, my heart pounding.

The buzz and jiggle of the wrong password crossed the screen. Dang it. Of course it wasn't going to be that easy.

Dad threw out a couple of guesses, and I wrote them down. When he asked why, I told him sometimes a phone will lock after too many unsuccessful attempts.

"Ahh, I see. That makes sense." He turned to Mack. "Out of everyone here you knew him best—wanna give it a shot?"

Mack pursed his lips as he thought, then threw out, "Zero, One, One, Seven, Nine, One."

I read it back and he nodded. Lani raised an eyebrow at her dad; he shrugged and responded to her unanswered question, "It's the date the first Gulf War ended."

After a few more minutes of throwing out ideas Dad suggested we take a look and start ordering them as most likely to least likely.

After finishing the list, we decided to just go for it, starting with Mack's first suggestion.

I passed the phone over to Mack. "Want to do the honors?"

He patted his pocket and pulled out a pair of reading glasses. My lips quirked when I looked at Lani and we smothered our grins before he noticed.

Using his index finger, he jabbed at each number, and from my vantage point I saw the screen light up with a picture of Paisley.

He slid the phone back in my direction. "We're in."

Otis had very few apps on his phone. The only texts he had were from Mack and someone named Sergeant. When I asked, Mack said Sergeant was one of their buddies from the service.

I tapped on the Picture icon and scrolled through. Most of the pictures were of Paisley and we all oohed and ahhed over her cuteness. As I swiped, I found a few blurry photos that were dimly lit and appeared to be of Kawaihae Harbor. I couldn't make out much and handed the phone off to Lani to see if she could spot anything. Mack offered, but we both just looked pointedly at the glasses perched on the end of his nose.

"Damn kids these days. No respect for their elders," he grumbled, causing Lani and I to openly smirk at him.

While Lani scrolled through the photos, I leaned in and pulled the phone closer as something occurred to me.

"Lani, those pictures are date and time stamped, yeah?"

She nodded and I snagged the journal and started reading off the dates while she matched up the photos. "Looks like they're split between what looks like smaller RIBS and then this boat." She spun the phone, and I leaned in close. The picture must've been taken from pretty far away—the footage was grainy. All I could make out was a tall sail and wide hull.

Dad was using two fingers to tap away on his keyboard, each jab punctuated by a loud clack which distracted me. "What are you doing?" My tone may have been a little pissy, but for real, you'd think at this critical juncture of the investigation he'd focus a little more.

"Checking the hull numbers in the DBOR data base to see if they match with the entries Otis made."

Oh. Oops.

A furrow marred his brow. "That's strange. None of the numbers are showing up with DBOR." He squinted at the screen and whipped out a pair of reading glasses from his desk drawer.

"Shut it," he warned Lani and me as we snickered.

"Huh. All the registration numbers in the DBOR database show they were either wrecked or sunk." I hopped up to look over his shoulder. The boats were all RIBs, just like the one Cole and I found last week.

"Shit. We need to tell Cole about this. These might be the boats they've been trying to catch." My call went straight to voicemail, and I left a terse message to call back ASAP.

"Lani, did you see anything else that caught your eye in those pictures?" I asked.

She shook her head. "No. The footage isn't great. About all I can say for sure is it's the south harbor."

"Speaking of pictures," Mack pulled a folder out from a shelf next to his head. "I got these yesterday."

When Lani asked what they were, he replied, "Photos my cousin, the medical examiner, passed on to me that the rescue divers took of the underwater crime scene. Not that they're calling it a crime scene." He blew out a frustrated breath. "Anyway, I thought you might like to take a look and see if you notice anything."

Lani's face blanched as she looked at the first picture and she squeezed her eyes shut before taking a deep, cleansing breath and opening them again to study the photos. She handed them to me wordlessly.

Bruises and a split lip covered Otis's face, making him barely recognizable. I'd seen dead bodies before, but it never got easier. Otis's body was just visible in the green muck, his eyes wide and staring. Bloat had started its progress through his body, his face swollen and white. I forced myself to study the photo even though my heart hammered in my chest. Small yellow tangs circled his body in the photo, and I noticed just the edge of something square and yellow poking out of the pocket of his shorts. Without meaning to, I shuddered.

"Poor Otis, " I whispered, my throat tight.

After staring at the photo until my eyes blurred, I handed it over to my dad. He took it from me and put it back in the folder. "I looked at it earlier, and about the only thing I can tell you for sure is that the cause of death wasn't drowning."

I raised an eyebrow, and he began pointing out the bruising and incongruencies with the medical examiner's report. "Also, there wasn't much water in his lungs—if it was an accidental drowning, they would be full. HPD's stance when the medical examiner asked was that there wasn't enough evidence to prove it *was* anything other than a drowning. Aside from that there's the giant lump on the back of his head. The ME detailed in his report the closed head injury and bleeding evident in the brain." He shook his head. "Whoever did this covered their tracks well."

Lani suggested we print out the photos and take them down to the harbor just to see if anything seemed to match.

"Great idea," Mack said. "We can take my truck."

"We?" Lani and I both spluttered.

Dad jumped in. "Yeah, we figured we could come down with you, do some poking around on our own, see what we can shake loose."

Steam was surely coming from my ears as I protested. "I thought you trusted us, that you weren't going to be so heavy-handed? What happened to all of that?"

He laid a hand on my arm and said quietly, "I do trust you."

"Sure doesn't feel like it."

Mack and he shared a look. "Summer, any employee I have is subject to random ride alongs. Not because I don't have faith in them, but because it gives me an idea of their investigative style and how their minds work, which helps me learn how best to support them on cases." He straightened. "Mack had a good point earlier. We've been treating you like our daughters, but when you walk through that door that needs to shift to employee and employer."

Grrr... I didn't like it but at the same time it was exactly what I'd been asking for. Cole basically said the same thing to me a few days ago. My shoulders slumped a little, but I gave Dad a tight nod.

"Fair. It's your business to run how you see fit."

Dad's posture relaxed, and he smiled before clapping me on the shoulder. "Cheer up, you'll get to see your old man in action, maybe learn a few things."

I'm pretty sure my eyes rolled right out of my head at his bragging, but I felt a little sliver of a smile erupt.

"Lead the way, oh wise one," I said, grabbing my bag and praying this wasn't going to be an absolutely embarrassing shit show.

⚜

"You kill anyone lately?" I asked Mack, holding a rusty machete up in the air. I'd had to move various things out of the way in order to sit down in the backseat of his truck. So far, I counted two rolls of duct tape, a fifty-foot-long rope, the machete, three pickaxes, two shovels, and a blue tarp with a suspicious odor.

"I'm so embarrassed you saw that." I thought Mack was talking to me, but I realized he'd directed that statement at my dad. "I normally take much better care of my tools. Can't believe I let that one get rusty."

"Well, it was shoved halfway under the driver's seat in the back." I volunteered. "You probably didn't see it. Especially if you weren't wearing your bitchin' spectacles."

Both Mack and my dad turned around and shot me a whole lot of stink eye, but Lani and I were rolling around, laughing so hard I barely noticed.

After we'd settled down, which took longer than expected because damn, I could be real funny sometimes, Lani looked at her dad.

"I get why Tom came, but why are you venturing forth on this little field trip? You're not an employee or employer."

"Technically, I am your employer in that I'm paying you to investigate. That being said, Mostly I just want to go and give Louie a whole barrel of shit for not telling me you showed up down there."

"Aww, take it easy on him. I threatened him with Auntie Miriam."

Both men gasped and grabbed their balls, looking at each other in horror. Miriam was not a woman to be trifled with, and they both knew it. As the favorite niece, Lani had her ear more so than almost anyone save Mr. Sam, her retired Yamaguchi mob boss boyfriend.

"Poor Louie, you really had him by the short hairs there, huh?" Mack hummed low in his throat then announced, "Alright, I'm still going to give him shit, but I'll go easy on him."

We pulled up to the harbor just as Louie was packing up his fishing pole. The wind whipped his hair into a salt and pepper bird's nest. When he saw Mack pull into the parking lot, he hot-footed it towards his truck, but not before Mack's truck caught up. Mack parked in front of Louie's truck and hopped out.

"Cuz, howzit?" Mack lifted his chin at Louie. "See you packing up to go. Why you leaving so soon? Seems you had a lot to say earlier to Lani. Why not spend some time talking to me?"

Louie held his hands up in front of him. "Eh, now Mack. I just trying to help your girl. You know she one lolo Wahine if she don't get her way."

I shifted my eyes in her direction, and she lifted her shoulders and smiled that shit-eating grin—the same one she gave me when she flipped me onto the mat at the gym.

"What can I say? It's a gift."

Mack cuffed the back of her head lightly, but the corners of his mouth tipped slightly up. He turned his attention back to Louie.

"You hear anything new?" This time his voice was pitched low and serious.

Louie answered back in kind. "No. Been quiet. Less charters through here since the weather picked up. My boys been running patrols through here at night but nothing so far."

Mack clapped him on the shoulder. "Great job. Thanks, man." He leaned farther in and murmured. "I heard she threatened you with Auntie Miriam." A shudder ran through him. "I woulda talked, too."

Louie's face broke out into a relieved smile. "She one scary lady." He pointed at Lani. "That one gonna be just like her."

The look of horror on Lani's face was almost worth all those mornings of getting thrown to the mat by her.

Chapter Thirty Four

COLE

"NICE OF YOU TO join us, Peterson," Jonah cracked as I slung my bag on my desk.

His pretty boy hair looked like a winged bird had taken up residence in it this morning and his shirt was untucked and more wrinkled than a Shar-Pei's fur.

"Did you sleep here last night?"

"Nah, I went home for a few hours but got called back in for another sunken boat down by South Point." He sighed and rubbed his face, exhaustion coming off him in waves.

Guilt made my stomach churn. In my pursuit of nailing Chief, I'd ignored my duty to the department, and even more importantly, my partner.

Jonah interrupted my mental whipping. "I'm heading out there now." He stood up and shouldered his bag.

My gaze slid over to Chief's office which was dark and I made a split decision. "Want some company?"

He caught my glance at Chief's office. "He's out until this afternoon for some 'official business.'" Jonah snorted. "His words, not mine."

I grabbed my laptop and shoved it in my bag.

Jonah leaned forward. "You sure, man? I know you're working on something big."

I smiled at him, tight-lipped and nodded. "Let's do this."

The ride to South Point took us just under two hours. We stopped to fill up on coffee and donuts; I was grateful we weren't in uniform because the cliche was too much to handle today.

Jonah, recognizing there was a lot I couldn't talk about, kept the conversation light on our drive. Mostly we talked about hockey and his Gran, who was recovering from a broken hip.

"She's walking circles around everyone." His voice held a note of pride. "Mom says she can hardly keep up."

The compulsion to unburden myself to Jonah about the investigation into Takada was overwhelming, but I kept my mouth shut. No point in burdening him with it. Besides, the less people who knew what was going on the better.

We drove slowly past the top of the South Point complex next to the cliffs overlooking the deep blue water below and bumped along over the rutted, and in places, washed out dirt road to the end of the path. Breathing in the deep salt air, I felt a whisp of tightness unwind in my gut.

"So, where's the boat supposed to be?"

Jonah pointed down the steep trail to Papakolea Beach below. Most people were familiar with its other name, the Green Sand Beach. The hike down could easily take a couple of hours.

"You sure?"

He nodded. "The report that came in said a sunken RIB similar to all of the others was noticed at dawn by witnesses out for a beach walk. My theory is they were attempting to make it to the Kaulana boat ramp. It's only a quarter mile away from the beach by boat."

"Damn, I didn't prepare well for this." I grimaced, pointing to my long pants and button up shirt.

Jonah reached into the back of his truck and pulled out a backpack and shoved some water bottles in it without another word, and we hiked down, the sun blazing hot on our backs.

We spent the next three hours sweating our balls off between the hike and searching the waters from the shoreline.

"Could've used a boat for this," I commented.

Jonah frowned. "The report said the witnesses saw the boat just offshore where it drops off to ten feet." He shook his head, irritation plain on his face. "If it was here, we'd be able to see it." He swung around and gestured toward the calm blue ocean in front of us. "Nothing, not even a trace of a boat."

"It's shallow enough that if it was here, we'd see it. Guess it could've floated away." The look Jonah shot me said it all. Sunken boats don't usually float away in ten feet of water.

The hike back up was mostly silent as we navigated the rough, rocky terrain and guzzled our remaining water. Back at the truck, Jonah slammed his pack into the backseat, frustration swirling around him like a tornado.

I clapped him on the back. "No worries, bro. It was worth checking out at least."

His lips thinned as he narrowed his eyes and responded, "Another freaking dead end."

I tilted my head. "Another?"

He nodded grimly. "Second one this week." He punched his seat. "I should've dug deeper before dragging us out here."

By now my stomach was loudly protesting our missed lunch, and we decided to stop off for a quick dinner on the way back. When we finally got back to the office around 7:30 p.m. only a few souls were left, typing away and talking in muted voices. Shit.

"Peterson!" I heard my name being roared from the vicinity of Takada's office and instantly my back tightened. I looked up in the hopes of divine intervention. Nope. No luck there.

"Good luck, man," Jonah murmured, patting me on the back.

"Where've you been all day?" he asked, his tone accusatory.

My fists tightened of their own accord as I thought of how dirty he was. Gritting me teeth so hard I was sure I'd need to visit the dentist, I responded, "running down a lead with Jonah."

His eyes were cold as he leaned forward on the desk. "I thought I was clear on what was expected of you." A vein pulsed at his temple.

"Oh, you were clear, alright. But here's the thing." I sat and crossed my arms over my chest. "What's in it for me?"

He cocked his head, face red and angry. "Excuse me?"

I settled into the chair more comfortably, the picture of nonchalance. "That's right. Seems to me like what you're asking me to do really toes the line of appropriate use of department resources. I'm game to follow this guy, but what do I get out of it?"

He stared at me for a moment, his look probing before answering. "I would think knowing you're serving your community by getting this scumbag off the department's back would be compensation enough."

"You'd think so." I said no more, letting him fill in the blanks.

He sat, leaning back in his chair and steepled his fingers, his gaze never wavering from me. "What is it you want exactly?"

"We can negotiate terms tomorrow. I'll be down at the pier at 8:00 a.m. Let's go over specifics then."

My heart pounded loudly as I stood and sketched a salute at Takada before heading out of his office and grabbing the bag on my desk.

"How bad was it?" Jonah pitched his voice low.

With a subtle shake of my head, I said nothing, and wisely, Jonah took the hint. Just before I exited the department, Takada called out, "Tomorrow at 8, Peterson."

I threw a curt nod over my shoulder and hightailed it for my truck, anxious to fill Jack in. Getting Chief on tape would fast track the case against him and hopefully have him out of the department that much sooner.

My phone showed a missed call from Summer four hours ago. She must've called when I was going through a dead zone. Damn it. My call back went straight to voicemail, so I left her a message.

"Hey beautiful, I got your message. Sorry I missed your call. It's been a long day, but I'm hoping we can get dinner together tomorrow and you can fill me in on what you found. Take care, and, uh, I love you. Bye!"

The next call I made was to Jack. After I filled him in on my conversation with the Chief, he was silent so long I thought the connection had dropped.

"You there, Jack?"

He cleared his throat. "I'm here. Just taking it all in." I heard what sounded like cheering in the background and then footsteps and a door slamming.

"Did I catch you at a bad time?"

He laughed. "Leave it to you to not realize today's UH's biggest game of the year against UNLV."

"Dude, I can call back. I didn't realize you had company."

"Ha. Company? I wish. That's my wife and daughters in the background. They're bigger fans than I am." He chortled then cleared his throat and got down to business. "I'm surprised you went a little rogue on this one, but it may actually work in our favor. I'll get a few guys on the ground. Meet me at 7 at my place, and I'll get you wired up."

"Sounds good. Anything else you need?"

"Yeah, I need you not to pull anymore crazy stunts like this between tonight and tomorrow morning."

The line went dead, and I grinned down at the phone in my hand. Jack wasn't pissed—not really. My guess is he was just as anxious to nail Chief as I was. I whistled on my drive home until Summer's words flashed through my head about whistling and serial killers. The whistling stopped abruptly as her pretty face swam in front of my face.

We'd had more than our fair share of drama since she and I met. Once Chief was out of the picture, I hoped to have more free time to spend with her. The realtor had emailed me some listings up near Summer and Elliot's condo, but I'd had to put it on the backburner for a few days. Summer's reaction to my buying something near her warmed up an empty spot in my heart. We fit together really well. She may exasperate the hell out of me when she pulls crazy stunts like diving off my boat and disappearing into a sunken ship, but there was something wild and spontaneous about her that called to my own renegade spirit.

As I pulled up to my apartment building, I was greeted by peeling paint and a dim lamp post casting a somewhat depressing shadow on the potholed parking lot. I realized how much the warmth of Summer and Elliot's home filled me. The apartment was just a landing place to sleep and shower, but Summer...she was home.

⚜

"Once you make contact with Takada, I want you to twist this little nob." Jack showed me a dial on a tiny device that looked just like my truck's key fob. "That will activate the Bluetooth device on your shirt button." He pointed to the collar button on my aloha shirt.

"This is sick, dude," I said. "Can I keep it when we're done?"

Jack frowned at me and I smirked back. I'd definitely be combing the internet to find one of my very own as soon as we were done with this—this was a first-rate gadget.

"Focus. Now, what I need from you is to lead the conversation towards the USB and then have Takada explain in detail what he wants you to do. Bonus points if he mentions anything about killing Kimo."

"Got it."

"Meet me back here when you're done. Agents are posted near the meeting point and will only assist if you say the words, 'the moon sure was bright last night.'"

After I climbed in my truck, I took a moment to consider what I was about to do. Would this lead to Chief being charged? Anticipation coursed through me at the thought that the nightmare might soon be over. I could have more free time, spend time with Summer,—hell, maybe even go fishing once in a while. The weight I'd been carrying for so long suddenly felt lighter.

Of course, the biggest challenge would be getting him to admit to all of it, not just the vendetta against the reporter, but also colluding with known criminals, aiding and abetting, and accessory after the fact. This guy needed to go away for a very long time.

I parked just down the boardwalk from the pier and meandered over to it. It was still early, and the normal bustle of people wouldn't start for another hour or two. A few surfers were catching waves in the bay, the wind pushing them along. The normally blue sky was concrete gray and the air felt still and electric, adding to the foreboding feeling of what I was about to do.

The closer I got to the pier the more my heart rate kicked up. As I crossed the street, I saw Takada was already there, leaning against the wooden railing.

As I approached, he swung his head in my direction and said, "You've got some explaining to do."

Chapter Thirty Five

COLE

Ice ran through my veins at his words. For a split second I wondered if he knew about Jack, but I discarded that idea. I'd been careful—*really* careful—to make sure I covered my tracks.

I gave Takada a tight-lipped smile and angled my head at him. "How's that?"

He motioned with his hand to encompass the pier and the two of us. "This meeting. I thought I was very clear on what I expect from you." He held his body stiff.

Jingling the key fob in my hand, I used the side of my thumb to flick the dial to 'on.' Instead of answering his question, I asked one of my own. "How'd you find out about Kimo Hiroshi's investigation of the department? I don't know the guy personally, but I've seen his stuff—he's a pitbull when he's on a story from what I hear."

The smile he sent my way was chilling. "You'd be surprised at how much information I can gather." He leaned in close. "You might want to remember that the next time you try to bargain with me."

His tone was low and threatening, his meaning clear. My heart sped up.

Instead of responding right away I leaned against the railing and studied him. Going with my gut, and knowing Jack was going to freak out, I disclosed, "I know about the Bois and your, ahem, affiliation with them. The boats too. Is that what Kimo dug up?"

He stilled. "You don't know shit," he ground out, a vein bulging in his neck.

"I know several suspects in the drug boat case have had their records wiped. I know you're living in a more expensive zip code than a Hawaii police chief's salary can handle. I know you have a penchant for buying baubles for pretty young girls. Girls your wife doesn't know anything about. Money's coming from somewhere and it sure as hell ain't coming from the state of Hawaii."

His hands were white where he gripped the railing; his face mottled with so much rage I wouldn't have been surprised if he stroked out right in front of me.

He shook his head. "That's quite an accusation." His words were tightly controlled through his clenched jaw. "You have no idea what you're talking about."

"Oh, I think I do." I leaned in. "And I also know how to gather information." My implication was clear.

"What is it you want exactly?"

I relaxed my posture at the railing, even though my heart was beating so loud my ears vibrated. "It must've been pretty easy to recruit those guys in Pahala. After all, you're a police chief. You can make their lives easier or harder, depending on their answer. Not much of a choice, if you ask me."

Not ready to show me all his cards yet, he side-stepped. "You surprise me. I've never seen you take this kind of initiative before. I could use a man like you to help in some of my, let's call them, side pursuits."

"Hmm. You want another little chess piece?" I shook my head. " I don't think so." I straightened. "But if you're looking for a partner, I'm all ears."

"Where is all of this coming from? I thought you were as straitlaced as they came, with your big 'I'm a Navy Seal' white knight complex I never figured you for someone who'd be willing to look at alternative means of money-making."

The question seemed genuine, and I knew I had to get the tone just right or he'd sniff out my deception immediately.

I shrugged casually, even though my mouth felt like the inside of Mercury. "I'm shopping for a home. I got the girl and now I want the white picket fence, 2.5 kids, the works. Hard to do on a policeman's salary alone."

He shifted slightly and when I dared to look at him, I caught the briefest glimmer in his eye. He bought it. Not only did he buy it, but I suspected he was trying to figure out how to leverage it.

He turned and stared out at the surfers, the waves rolling and growing. "What makes you think I need a partner?"

I snorted. "Here's the thing, Chief. If I could figure out your little side gig, I'm betting other people can too. People who can make your life very difficult. Having someone on my end of things might help smooth the way." A final piece of the puzzle fell into place as another realization washed over me. "Just like when you made sure Jonah chased his tail for the last week by sending in false reports of sunken boats. Pretty clever, by the way."

As much as Takada was trying to play it cool, I could tell he wanted to brag. "I had to keep him busy somehow. You and your little girlfriend caused a lot of problems when you intercepted Cameron last month. Only way to make money on a product is to get that product in the hands of paying customers."

Disgust locked my throat. Cameron and his flunky Gonzalez had kidnapped and attempted to kill Summer and Lani. It took all the strength in my body not to choke Takada where he stood.

He clocked my reaction and waved a hand. "They went a little off script, I'll admit. Turns out Cameron was trying to run his own hustle." He grunted. "The guys I got now know what's expected of them. And what will happen if they screw up."

The bared-teeth grin he gave me brought to mind a hungry shark.

I matched him grin for grin. "I want in."

⚹⚹⚹⚹ ⚹⚹⚹⚹

"Of all the lame-brained, *stupid,* reckless things to do, this takes the cake." Jack paced in his living room, berating me. He stopped and looked at me, his face screwed up. "You could've jeopardized the whole damn case!" His eyes tightened. "I told you to *listen.* Not jump with both feet into the corruption stew he's cooking and offer to partner with him. This was a recon mission only, for Christ's sake!" By now he was gripping handfuls of hair on his head in frustration.

When he finally ran out of steam he asked, "Well? What do you have to say for yourself?"

"All's well that ends well?" My charming smile seemed to have no effect on him, but I noticed the junior agent smirking in the background.

He pinched the bridge of his nose and let out a deep sigh before plopping down on the couch across from where I sat.

I'll turn in what we have to the Attorney General and go from there." His face was haggard.

"Jack, you okay man?" I'd thought this would help the case, but judging by Jack's reaction, I was missing something.

He waved a hand and raised tired eyes to look at me. "The Attorney General and I don't always see eye to eye. She may decide we don't have enough to proceed with a case. If so, Takada skates."

"Wait—what? I basically got him to admit he was involved with known felons and was running a drug operation."

Jack's look made me feel like a dimwit as he spoke slowly, enunciating every word precisely. "Cole, Takada alluded to corroboration but there's nothing a good lawyer couldn't poke a seine net's amount of holes in. He kept his words couched in innuendo and allusion, never any sort of full confession."

His expression changed from perturbed to deadly serious as he took me by the shoulders. "He could turn this around and say *he* was the one trying to catch a dirty cop. *You.* Don't you see? The game you're playing is dangerous. Takada has a lot of aces up his sleeve, and we don't know who else he's working with. If we can't get him to admit to what he's doing explicitly, he could blow our whole case out of water. Easily."

Aghast, I just looked at him for a full minute with my mouth open, every fiber of my body in denial.

When I could finally speak, I ground out, "What do we need to do to make the charges indisputable?" There's no way I was willing to take the chance on Chief walking.

Jack sighed, his shoulders slumping. "Get someone on the inside, get him to confess to everything." His laugh wasn't really a laugh. "Know anyone willing to put up with him long enough to get that? To get that close?"

I closed my eyes and scrubbed my face with my hands. I knew what I had to do to end this, but *goddamnit* I really didn't want to.

For the first time I understood the phrase 'no good deed goes unpunished'—and I didn't like it one bit.

Chapter Thirty Six

SUMMER

Dad, Mack, Lani and I spent a fruitless hour checking registration numbers on boats down at the harbor to see if they matched the ones in Otis's journal, but with boat traffic picking up along with the wind we had a hard time staying out of the way and looking harmless.

I noticed *Moonshine* bobbing in the water on the day use mooring again and I wondered if Mike had an afternoon charter. With the way the whitecaps were building I would've been surprised, but who knew? He was one crazy Russian, and I'd seen him do some crazy things—like wrestling a hook out of a baby whitetip reef shark's mouth in a cave at night. Mike was probably one of the most blunt, gruff people I'd ever met, but when it came to animals, especially the ocean variety, he turned into a puddle of mush.

Sand and grit were pelting my arms and legs when I finally called it for the day. No one in the group looked especially upset as they were just as frustrated as me that we'd come up empty handed.

I missed a call from Cole while I was in the shower before bed. The house was quiet, and I couldn't decide if I liked it or not. Now that Elliot was spending more time with TJ, he wasn't around as much. He still left little notes for me and made sure I had food. We had a good gig going—I would rather clean than cook, and he was the opposite.

As happy as I was for him, I felt the shift in our 'normal' and it was taking me a minute to get used to. I'd tried to talk Lani into staying, but she had laundry to do and a certain hot bartender to meet up with.

Cole had left a voicemail for me- we seemed to have a game of phone tag going and I wasn't sure who's turn it was. The message he left gave me the tingles all over. We'd only recently admitted our feelings to one another and damn, did it felt good to hear him say it on his voicemail.

I smiled as I thought of the night Cole had finally said the words "I love you" out loud. White tablecloth, candles, and a surprise dinner on his boat at sunset. He'd pulled out all the stops—not that he needed it. While I wouldn't say it was love at first sight exactly, it was pretty damn close. Now, on the nights he wasn't around, I missed him in a way I hadn't felt for anyone else.

I'd texted him the moment I'd woken up but he hadn't responded, which caused my heart to clench a little. He'd never gone longer than a few hours without texting or calling and we were rounding twenty-four hours. Hopefully my stunt on the boat a few days ago hadn't pushed him away. I didn't always think before I acted, which I knew he didn't like.

As I caught up on some housework, I watched the news playing on TV. The newscaster on the screen wore a clear plastic raincoat and held onto the hood while trying to speak into a microphone. All the while, wind whipped his coat around and it billowed out, nearly obscuring the field behind him.

"Hurricane Luisa changed course overnight, bringing possible gale force winds and widespread flooding through-out the islands. Luisa is set to make land by nightfall on the East side of the Hawaiian Islands and is predicted to cause massive flooding and destruction to property we haven't seen since Hurricane Iniki in 1992. Stay tuned for the latest updates and tune into KHON 2 News for the latest weather alerts."

I texted Lani as I walked outside my condo. Myna birds squawked noisily at each other as mourning doves cooed, the cloudless blue sky and light breeze at odds with the forecast I'd just seen.

Lani texted back her cousin told her Hilo was getting hammered, but the mountains would probably block the worst of it before it reached our side of the island. She asked if I wanted to meet up at Seabird Coffee in Kawaihae and go over our notes on the case and see if we missed something.

You had me at coffee.

She sent a laughing face emoji back and I headed upstairs to grab my bag. I threw in a towel and bathing suit, just in case we had the opportunity to get in a quick dip. This time of year, I made it a point to get in the water whenever I could since conditions were reliably unpredictable.

Lani had beaten me to Seabird Coffee and had a little of-fice set up underneath the awning at the picnic table. Emma, the owner of Seabird Coffee, greeted me.

"You want your usual?" Emma asked. "Haupia Mocha with cold foam?"

I nodded and threw a look at Lani. She smirked back and held up her cold brew topped with foam.

With yummy drink in hand, I settled in next to Lani. Her laptop was open to the photos she'd taken from Otis's phone. His journal sat on the table, open to one of the tabbed pages.

She handed me the journal, and I studied it again but couldn't find anything new. My fingers danced along the forbidden pages, respect for Otis warring for the desire to find something, *anything* that might get us a step closer to finding his killer. I opened the journal to one of the unmarked pages. Lani cleared her throat.

"I know what Mack said," I told her. "But listen, if there's anything in here that might help us, I think we owe it to Otis to look. Here's what I propose. We look through the journal, but if the entries are of a personal nature we skip them and move on."

"I don't like it. You know what Dad said, and it feels wrong to read a dead man's journal."

I huffed out a breath. "I know. Emotionally I agree with you, but logically, it makes the most sense. And honestly—he's dead. He's beyond caring what we think."

"Fine. But you do it. If my dad asks me, you know I won't be able to lie."

I spent the next twenty minutes reading Otis's journal. Most pages were musings, poems, or just little anecdotes from his time in the military and here on the island. Despite what I'd told Lani, my body felt sticky with guilt and shame for reading his journal.

I tried not to sigh. Not only did I feel bad for intruding on the privacy of a dead man, but so far, I hadn't found anything

that would help us. I flipped to the last page right before the
list of registration numbers started—then sat up suddenly.

After a long and quite eloquent poem, Otis had scratched
in an entry. His penmanship up until this point was what
some might kindly call atrocious, worse even than a doctor's
illegible scrawl. But on the bottom of the page, he'd written
in block letters:

BIG GUMS 2200 HOURS. 3 LOADS.

"Lani, do you have any idea what this means?"

She looked over my shoulder to read the entry. She shook
her head. "No idea. If we knew who Big Gums was and had
a date or something, that would help tremendously. This
doesn't really give us much."

"Urgh. I feel like we're not getting anywhere. Any idea
what or who Big Gums is? It seems like a weird nickname, but
I'm sure I've heard something like that before." Frustration
rode like a wave over me.

Lani ran a hand over her ponytail and twirled the length
of dark silky hair around her hand as she thought. "Hmm.
In high school we used to call our senior class president Big
Gums because when he smiled his 'I bagged every cheerleader
on the island' smile he reminded me of a shark right before
it strikes prey. You know how they open their mouths and
the skin pulls back so all you see are their teeth and gums?
That's what he looked like. That's the only time I've heard
something like that before."

Her brows knitted in thought as she looked at me. We
both searched our memory banks, but nothing surfaced to
help us with the case.

After thinking about it for a while, Lani shrugged and re-sumed her search on Otis's phone. Paisley was the clear star of Otis's photo show. "She's just too cute for words," I commented. Lani kept flipping and stopped on one of her dad and Otis. It was a screenshot from an article in *Stars and Stripes*, a military newspaper that my dad also subscribed to, although he read his online.

In the photo, Mack and Otis, wearing desert fatigues, were shaking hands with a man I didn't recognize. He wore a smarmy politician smile and held up a plaque next to them with a coin centered in the middle.

"Oh, wow. This must be when they got their challenge coins. Remember when your dad told us about that mission that was basically labeled a death sentence? That's probably why they don't look very happy with that dude. I wonder what happened?"

Lani peered closer. "Yeah, I know Dad's pissed face, and I know his 'push me any further and someone's going to pay face,' and it's definitely the latter. There's a lot he won't tell me about his time over there. He has his coin with him everywhere we go, though."

"Didn't your dad say Otis wore his on a chain around his neck? I think I remember that now. There was gold at the edges and had a big eagle in the middle."

Lani nodded. "The other side had the words 'U.S. Army Counterintelligence Agent.'"

"Huh." A thought occurred to me. "Can you pull up the photos from the ME?"

Dutifully, she found and opened the file.

"Mack said Otis wore the chain everywhere, but he noticed in the ME photos he wasn't." I leaned away from the screen to look at Lani. "He's right—I don't see it on either set of photos. Do you think someone tried to rob him and that's why he was killed?"

She pursed her lips as she thought but then shook her head. "I doubt it. The coin in and of itself isn't worth any money. It's not made of gold or anything. It's only valuable to the wearer for pride and bragging rights."

"Hmm." I slumped. "Well, where's his chain then?"

She shrugged. "Good question."

The wind started to ruffle the pages of the journal and for the first time in a half hour I looked up, only to notice the sky had turned an angry shade of gray. Fat raindrops started to hit the pavement.

"Okay, I know the Dads want to be included in everything, but what about if we just take a quick look around the harbor, check those registration numbers again and see if we missed one. Most of the boats are posted up facing us, so it'll be easy enough to check without drawing attention." Boat registration numbers were a lot like license plates on a car—each one had a unique number that was posted on the side of any boat in order to make it visible.

Lani put her chin in her hand and thought about it, and I could almost see the waves of frustration rolling off her. Neither one of us were known for our patience on a good day, but hitting so many roadblocks with this case was beyond annoying.

"Sure, what can it hurt? Let's just send them a quick text. That way they know what we're doing and can't yell at us later."

I nodded in agreement and waved goodbye to Emma before driving to the harbor, the rain now coming down in earnest.

Turning the corner, we saw several staff from some of the commercial boats securing the decks and double-checking mooring lines. Jeff's boat stood empty, the mainsail furled up tightly to the mast.

The boats bobbed wildly up and down, and I saw Kevin's boat pillowed, his giant fenders flattening slightly in between the dock and the boat on the other side.

Driving rain pushed us back into the Rav.

Lani and I dripped little rivulets on the seats until I remembered my towel. Both of us took turns drying off as we watched the rain pelting the window in angry splotches.

"Yikes. This is a pretty intense storm. I didn't think it would do much over here on our side."

Lani hummed in agreement. "Yeah, usually the mountains block it." She shrugged and we sat, watching as people ran this way and that, fortifying lines. Mike was on *Moonshine*, his tall thin form barely visible through the sheets of rain on the windshield.

Something about the lighting triggered a memory of the pictures we found on Otis's phone. "Can you pull up Otis's photos? I want to check something."

Lani gave me a curious look but opened her computer, tapped on the Gallery icon, then handed it over to me. I scrolled through until I found the photo I was looking for.

I showed it to Lani. "From this angle, doesn't that look a lot like Jeff's boat?"

She lifted her head and looked first at his boat, then down to the photo and back up again. "Yeah, it kinda does." She scratched her head. "It's hard to tell for sure though. There's a fair number of catamarans in and out of here."

Resolve lit a fire in my belly. I turned toward Lani. "I think it's him. I think it's Jeff."

She was quiet for a beat. Then another. Eventually, she ventured, "What if you're wrong? Isn't that like one of Cole's closest friends?"

She had a point, but there was something off about that guy, I could just feel it. I shook my head. "No, you have a point, but I think he's up to something. He's super dodgy about what he does for work, and he's made some weird ominous comments."

By now, the rain was so loud I had to almost yell for Lani to hear me.

She looked at me with steady eyes. "Okay, I trust your gut and if your gut says something's off, then something's off. What do you want to do?"

Lani had been my ride or die since we were ten years old and her faith in me warmed my belly.

"We search his boat." I gestured to the rapidly emptying parking lot. "One of us can act as lookout while the other searches. What do you think?"

'I'm in."

Chapter Thirty Seven

COLE

AFTER STEWING IN MY truck for thirty minutes while staring blindly at the near-empty parking lot at my apartment complex, I decided to track Jeff down and confront him. Frustration with the way I'd botched things this morning set me on a warpath. Some might accuse me of displacing my anger, and those someone's could piss off.

Whatever Jeff was up to, I needed to know. I was sick and tired of this island being overrun with criminals, and I knew whatever Jeff was up to ran the edge of legal or else he would've been more forthright with me at the gym.

On my way I saw a missed text from Summer and responded that I'd try to call in an hour or two to plan our date for tonight.

Wind whipped salt spray onto my windshield, bringing the scent of the sea with it. The clouds had rolled in while I was getting my ass handed to me at Jack's, and one glance up at

Mauna Kea told me we were in for one hell of a storm. The news had been predicting Hurricane Luisa to pass a hundred miles to the south, but judging by the angry black and purple clouds, it had changed course.

One of Jack's complaints, and there were more than a few, with the way I'd handled my meeting with Takada, was my 'reckless disregard for standard protocol.' My neck itched as I thought about the look he'd given me. In the Seals I'd always been the steady one. Plan the work and work the plan. For some reason, with increasing regularity, I'd thrown that overboard and replaced it with spur of the moment decision-making based on what my gut was telling me.

Hmm.

I stopped at Foodland near Mauna Lani to grab a plate lunch and noticed Jeff's truck in the parking lot. Perfect. Two birds, one stone. When I reached into my pocket to ensure I'd grabbed my wallet, I felt the key fob Jack had outfitted me with for my meeting with Chief. My mouth dropped open and I felt like when I was a little kid and got caught stealing brownies out of the pan. A guilty smile spread on my face. I was going to have so much fun with this until Jack remembered and made me give it back. I'd cut my teeth on spy movies growing up; now I had real spy toys.

My gaze flicked back up at the lot where Jeff's truck was parked. He wasn't in his truck, so I trudged inside Foodland and searched the aisles for him. No luck, but they had Kalua pork, so the day was already looking up. On a hunch I left through the back exit and found Jeff sitting at one of the picnic tables, sipping on a smoothie and scrolling on his phone.

He was so engrossed in his screen he didn't hear me approach. When I clamped a hand on his shoulder, he immediately grabbed my hand and twisted.

"Dude."

Jeff, wearing a sheepish grin, released me. "Sorry about that man, force of habit."

I sat down across from him and studied him closely. His eyes were bloodshot, and his usual trademark charisma was absent. "Actually, that's exactly what I want to talk to you about."

He quirked a brow and narrowed his eyes. "Huh? What do you mean?"

"I'm pretty damn sure you're hiding something from me." I looked at him steadily.

He seemed to deflate right in front of me and blew out a breath. He shifted his gaze over my shoulder. "I never could put anything over on you, could I?"

"You're not here to help your buddy out, are you?"

He shook his head, his lips a thin line.

"Just tell me that whatever you're doing isn't illegal." I held my breath as I waited for his answer.

"Define 'illegal.'"

"Whatever you're into isn't going to involve a lengthy prison sentence."

He exhaled through pursed lips. "No man. I'm not doing anything that can lead to my best friend arresting me, okay?"

The tightness in my chest loosened. "Just level with me. It's me, man. Your brother from another mother."

This brought out the barest of grins. He scoffed. "Shit, my mama wouldn't make anyone as ugly as you."

The corner of my mouth lifted. "Yeah, yeah. You're just jealous I got the prettiest girl on the whole island."

This brought out a genuine smile. "Must've been a blind date. Did you tell her you had a stash of dough or something?"

I gave him a one finger salute and laughter rolled out of him. Balance felt restored somehow.

I lowered my voice. "If you tell me what you're up to maybe I can help."

He scrubbed his face with his hands then lowered his gaze to the table. "Remember at Taco's funeral when his little brother tried to take a swing at me?"

I nodded, wondering where this was going, but also deep down inside afraid I already knew the answer.

"He's been putting out a lot of hate online, swearing that we got Taco killed and promising payback. At first, I thought it was just noise, but then Johnson found a dead rat in his mailbox with a note telling him he'd be next. He didn't take it too seriously until his daughter was driving his car home from basketball practice and got ran off the road. He got another message asking him how it felt for his family to have a target on their backs, that Taco's death laid on all our shoulders. This was right after I returned from Bulgaria with Taco's knife. I reached out to his family about the knife but never heard a word in response. Shortly after that is when Johnson got the first note."

He took a drink from the cup in front of him before continuing. "The only reason I knew what happened to Johnson was because he reached out to check on me. Wanted to make sure the rest of the team was safe. I managed to trace Marquez's location online. By the time I got to the dump he'd been renting he was gone, but in his rush, he left behind a list of names."

He looked at me.

"Let me guess. My name's on that list."

He nodded. "Yours and mine both. Officially, I'm here to help a friend out while he's on vacation. But unofficially, I'm tracking Taco's little brother. I don't want to hurt Marquez, but someone needs to stop him. If I can catch him, maybe I can reason with him. Out of respect for Taco, I want to handle this peacefully if possible. But..." His eyes went flinty. "If he keeps going, I may not have a choice, because I'll be damned if I let him continue to go after my brothers."

My mind wandered back to the mission that our friend and teammate, Hernando Marquez, affectionately nicknamed Taco because he only ate tacos when on leave, was killed in. We'd been holed up in a little shithole town on the border between Somalia and Djibouti, waiting for intel about a hostage situation.

Per usual, Jeff wanted to storm the villa where two undercover operatives were being held. No one was supposed to know we were there. The operatives were working with a liberation faction that the U.S. was trying to put in power, but since relations weren't exactly friendly between the two countries, our presence was on a need-to-know basis.

Johnson was working coms and I was coordinating. After almost a week of pissing in bottles and sweating our balls off, we got word the rebels were on the move. We set out to intercept them in the desert...only it was a trap. They ambushed us ten miles outside of the city and unleashed hell.

SEALS are known for their stealth, and this was anything but. Johnson was calling in our location and screaming for an aerial weapons team and EXFIL, *now*. There were eight of us and close to two dozen of them.

While on the sat phone, Johnson took a round to the shoulder. Taco leapt up to cover him and some bastard nailed him right in the jugular.

The Apache laid down hate on the enemy's position so we could EXFIL, but it was too late. Taco bled out in the middle of a shithole desert in a shithole country.

Later, the U.S. denied the mission had ever happened and the operatives were never found.

Jeff's voice brought me back to the present. "Marquez is tracking us all down, one by one. The fact that I tracked him here means he's going after you next."

It took a minute to process, but something didn't add up. "If you tracked him here, why hasn't he made any contact yet?"

Jeff's grin was devoid of humor. "Dude, you hardly stay in one place long enough to take a dump, much less threaten. When was the last time you even checked your mailbox? I've been tracking you since the day before we met up and you are one unpredictable mofo."

I gave an amused snort. "You're not the first person to accuse me of that."

Sparrows and Myna birds were slowly starting to circle the table, looking for a handout. Obliging, I leaned over and put a few grains of rice near the Ohia tree next to the table.

Jeff cleared his throat. "Now that I've shared my deepest and darkest, I think it's your turn."

"What do you mean?" I cocked my head at him in confusion.

"The second you mentioned your chief, I could tell something was up."

I puffed out my cheeks as I thought how best to answer him. Going for complete honesty, I laid out the whole sordid mess after looking around and insuring there wasn't anyone else nearby.

After I finished, Jeff let out a low whistle. 'Damn, man. That's a crazy story." He shook his head and then added, "I'd like to help."

"For now, I'm letting Jack coordinate all ops, but I'll let you know. Actually, I was going to offer the same to you. Taco's death, that whole shitshow in the desert weighs on me. He shouldn't have died out there. I understand why his brother's pissed, but I thought maybe he'd cool down once he grew up a little. Shit, he was probably only sixteen or seventeen when it happened. Taco talked about him all the time—how smart he was, how good he was with technology. Taco said he hoped his son would turn out just like him." I shook my head, my heart aching for everyone involved, especially the defiant, angry young man who looked like a younger version of Taco. A young man who had confronted us at the funeral and accused of us murdering his brother.

A grim expression hardened his features, and I could tell Jeff was reliving Taco's funeral as well. With effort, he pulled himself back to the problem at hand. "If we can get a trace on the VPN he's using on the island, I have a buddy at NSA who can track his last location for us. The problem I'm running into is he keeps switching VPN's. By the time I get a bead on him, he's smoke in the wind."

I cupped my chin in my hand as I considered options. "Do you know the general location he's hanging out in? I can ask some of the patrol guys to keep an eye out in some of the smaller areas in case they noticed anyone new matching his description."

Jeff sighed and ran a hand through his hair. "I thought I had an idea, but it turned into another dead end." He blew out a frustrated breath.

"Hmm. Let me talk to some of the guys on the force. They might have some ideas."

Jeff nodded. He showed me the pinned spots where he'd gotten hits and I had him send me a screenshot so I could study it later, see if any sort of pattern popped up.

By then the wind had picked up, and heavy raindrops were starting to fall. Deciding to pick up the strategy session later, we stood just as Jeff's phone let out an ear-piercing beep. He frowned as he picked up his phone, then a wry grin split his face.

"Time for us to head to the harbor."

My forehead crinkled as I looked at him in confusion. He spun his phone around. Summer could be seen creeping around the cabin of his boat, poking her pretty little nose all over. When she got on her hands and knees to look under the bed, we both tilted our heads to get a better view of her very perky behind.

The sigh I let out would've impressed even my grandma. "Let's go get her."

Chapter Thirty Eight

SUMMER

TENSION COILED IN MY stomach as I stealthily crept over the bow of Jeff's boat, trying to time my movements with the frothy waves crashing against the bow. Lani stood just to the edge of my periphery and gave me a wan smile and thumbs up.

I wasn't sure if this was the right thing to do, but I'd never forgive myself if Jeff was here under false pretenses. Cole put a lot of weight in their friendship, and more than anything I didn't want him to be hurt.

My phone flashlight was the only illumination on board—the clouds were now charcoal gray, the light under the awning nearly non-existent. Nothing on deck caught my interest and I had the passing thought that any criminal worth his salt wouldn't leave evidence in plain sight. If Jeff *was* up to something he wasn't stupid on top of criminal.

My heart beat a rapid tempo as I tested the cabin door. Locked. *Drat.*

I reached up and pulled my hairclip from my head and set to work trying to pick the lock. Lani and I practiced lockpicking after watching a YouTube video a few weeks ago when we were bored and decided we needed to develop this particular skill, just in case.

Of course, when we practiced, I had all the time in the world and wasn't running off adrenaline and slimy hands from the harbor. Not to mention being pelted with sheets of rain. I was about to give up when I heard a click and the door swung open. Surprise that it worked caused a grin to spread across my face—I couldn't wait to crow about it to Lani.

Taking a deep breath, I stepped inside. It was even darker inside the cabin, and I was grateful I'd remembered to charge my phone.

The cabin didn't look any different than the last time I'd seen it. There were a full-sized bed, nightstand, and small desk in the corner crowding the small space. Along the back wall stood a tiny galley with a one-burner stove. A door at the back likely lead to the head, and a smaller door off to the right was a closet of some sort. It reminded me a little of the little camper Dad would take us camping in during the early summer in Arizona, before it got too hot to breathe.

Jeff's bed was made with precise military corners, and everything on his nightstand was lined up perfectly. This was a man who took care of his possessions.

Taking careful note of where everything was on his desk, I searched through a folder filled with documents. On the documents in a big, sloppy scrawl were dates and locations along with cryptic notes. The locations were worldwide, not just Hawaii. Along with the papers were four photos, faces of men I'd never seen and who seemed unaware their picture had been taken. My brow furrowed. I'm sure these were significant—but how?

After searching extensively, the only item of interest I found was a deadly-looking Beretta with a silencer on the end. Being careful not to actually touch it, I used my sleeve to shove it back under the overhang above the head of the bed.

Using the camera on my phone I took photos of the papers I'd found, the gun, as well as the men's pictures. Carefully arranging the papers back into the folder, I was so focused on my task I almost missed Lani's alert.

"Hoot, hoot, hoot." Her imitation of an owl was so close to the real thing I almost wouldn't have known the difference. The hooting began to increase in volume and tempo rapidly. *Shit*.

The only escape was back the way I'd come. I cracked the door and heard voices. Lani could be heard trying to stall whoever she was talking to, and I made a quick decision.

Slipping out the door, I crawled straight for the back and slid off the deck into the cold, frothy harbor water, brown and murky from the churning of the waves.

I did my best to keep my mouth shut and not swallow any water as I paddled blindly over to the boat next to Jeff's. My hands made contact with an outboard motor, and I felt around for some way to pull myself up on deck.

More luck than any kind of skill found me rolling like an ungraceful monk seal onto the flat deck. Shimmying like a worm to stay below the gunwale, I moved toward the front of the boat. An especially violent wave hit, rocking the boat so violently it rolled me on my back. In the shadowy light I could make out a dry table and farther forward a weight rack, the yellow coated lead a neon sign.

Yesss! I was on Kevin's boat. I knew this boat. Daring to stand up, I noticed the tension on his mooring lines, the creaking of the fenders as they flattened.

Ha! I could fix the lines and if anyone questioned why I was on the boat, I could say I'm crew, since technically I was, even if it was only for one day, and was just trying to fix the lines so they didn't snap.

The starboard side of the boat was cleated in so tightly I had trouble loosening the lines so they didn't snap. It was a fine balance to ensure they were loose enough for a little give in rough waves, but not so loose the boat could thrash around wildly.

After getting that side secured, I gingerly started to cross the deck to the port side, but I noticed the cabin door was open and a small slice of light could be seen. Concern for Kevin surfaced and I tapped lightly on the door. I waited, but he didn't answer the door.

I pushed the door with one finger, and it swung open. Treading carefully, I stepped inside. Kevin's boat was laid out similarly to Jeff's—I hadn't been in the cabin when I crewed for him earlier this week and I was surprised at the resemblance.

Unlike Jeff's boat, though, this cabin was a mess. Clothes and paraphernalia were strewn everywhere, the surface of his built-in desk barely visible underneath the papers and other items covering it. Something round with a slight sheen on the edges caught my attention and I moved over to the desk.

As I shuffled papers on it, I found a gold chain with a coin dangling from the end. The same coin I'd seen in the picture with Mack earlier. Frigid rivers of ice ran up and down my spine as I stared at the coin in my hand. The boat's rocking increased but I barely noticed. I was so focused on the challenge coin that I didn't realize I was hyperventilating until black dots started spinning around in my periphery.

"Whatcha got there?" A voice asked from close behind me. Too close.

I spun around and Kevin stood less than a foot away, his eyebrow quirked with a cold, calculated look on his face. Gone was the jovial newbie boat captain, in his place was something I was afraid to name. Merciless eyes crawled over my body, and despite myself I shivered, which only caused his grin to widen.

"Big Gums!" I slapped my forehead. "I get it now." Otis was talking about Kevin—his smile looked eerily similar to the logo of a smiling shark on the side of his boat. Looking back, I'm surprised I didn't make that connection sooner. And that's exactly what Kevin looked like right now—a shark already certain of his next meal.

He took a threatening step forward, and quick as a snake, grabbed the chain from me with one hand, the other grabbing my throat. Instinct kicked in, and I used one of the moves Lani showed me and twisted his arm up and out before slamming my foot into his knee and yanking his arm behind him. My heart was pounding in my ears and my whole body felt electrified with fear.

The tight quarters made it hard to get a firm grip though, and he managed to escape my hold, pouncing on me and attempting to choke me out. His face leered down at me, the smooth veneer gone. In its place was a monster with deadly intent as he wrapped his hands around my throat and squeezed. *Lani's going to be so pissed if I let this guy take me out,* I thought. A delirious giggle backed up in my throat.

Black dots were starting to swim in front of me as I bucked and kicked. I managed to wrap my hands around his and find the trigger point just below the web of his thumbs. I dug in and pinched with everything I had left, buzzing hope warring with stark fear.

His hands slackened their grip on me, and I drew in deep gulps of air. I cracked him upwards with a fist, driving my knuckles into his nose and watching with grim satisfaction as blood spurted immediately.

He howled and grabbed his nose, giving me the opportunity to jam my knee up and into his groin. My smile widened as he curled into the fetal position, one hand on his nose and one on his nuts. *Harley Quinn, eat your heart out.*

A sliver of light beamed down on me and then Lani stood over me, a halo of light behind her head, surveying the scene, a look of pride on her face.

"Good to see your training's working."

Oh man. I'd never live this down. She was going to remind me of this moment until I died.

Once I glimpsed another face behind her, I figured my death might be sooner rather than later.

"Jesus Christ, Summer." Cole shoved Lani out of the way and pulled me up and into his arms. He ran his hands over me, checking for injuries.

"Is that blood yours?"

I shook my head and looked down at Kevin, still moaning and rocking himself on the ground.

"Hmm. Great work."

If my eyebrows could've winged up off my face in shock, they would have. Clocking my surprise, Cole shrugged.

"I probably would've done the same thing." He blew out a breath. "In fact, today I realized I may be slightly impulsive and reckless myself." He gave me a lopsided grin.

"You don't say." I smirked up at him.

He wiped blood off my face with his T-shirt and then kissed me thoroughly. When he finally released me, I noticed Jeff had crowded into the cabin, and I stiffened, holding onto Cole more tightly.

Cole noticed and pulled me closer. "It's okay," he murmured in my ear. "He's one of the good guys, I promise."

Studying Cole's face intently for a moment, I nodded slightly and relaxed by slow degrees.

"What we gonna do with this guy?" Lani nudged him with her toe. Well, nudged probably isn't quite the right word. He groaned more loudly this time and rocked to his hands and knees, glaring up, murder plain in his eyes.

"How'd you do it?" Cole fiddled with his truck key before pocketing it and leaning forward toward Kevin.

"Do what?" Kevin replied, narrowing his eyes.

Lani reached down and pinched a spot just below his ear and his body went rigid, the whites of his eyes reminding me of a spooked horse. When he didn't speak fast enough, she gave him a little shake. "You don't start talking right now, I start peeling." She whipped a wicked looking blade out of her back pocket. While I was pretty certain it was a bluff, the look in her eyes gave me pause.

She pressed the blade to his neck, digging in just next to the bulging vein under his ear. Whatever she whispered in his ear must've convinced him. Kevin started singing like a coqui frog, his story so lurid I wished I'd had a bag of popcorn with me.

"I found one sucker on Maui, trying to work his way into a state senate seat. Made sure he got good and high before shooting photos of him with some trannies and hookers I hired just for the occasion. Told him if he didn't do what I told him, I'd release them to the press, his loving wife, and members of his wife's extended family with connections to Yakuza." He snorted. "He couldn't sign those papers fast enough. Got me a pretty boat along with a whole barrel of cash for my startup over here."

Meanwhile, he'd set up a network of drug runners from various gangs throughout the island, with the Bois being the predominant participants, and worked out a whole shipping schedule. Since the Coast Guard was monitoring the Big Island coastlines so closely after one of the boats sank, he had to diversify and procure more boats and more drivers.

"Those damn ice heads couldn't keep their hands off the merchandise and kept sinking my boats."

"Why the whole elaborate ruse that you're running charters here though?" My mind couldn't wrap around the sheer amount of effort that would've taken.

The look he sent me promised retribution, but one twist of the wrist and Lani dug the pointy end of the knife into the soft flesh of his jugular, and he screeched before reluctantly answering my question. "The boat was getting noticed running in and out of the harbor at night by that old homeless dude. Had to make it look legit."

"Wait—so you never really had another divemaster?" I'd fallen for his story hook, line, and sinker and felt like an idiot for not digging deeper first.

He gritted his teeth. "No. Just my guy running the coast and playing pickup when the one of boats sank."

"What were all the tanks for then?"

He shrugged, slumping back on his heels, the blood from his nose congealing a little on his upper lip. "Whenever I got sent the coordinates of the boats that sank, we'd dive around trying to recover the merchandise." He snorted. "That is, until he started liberating samples on the side."

A memory of him and Elias arguing in the Kohala Divers parking lot came to mind. "What did Elias have to do with any of this?"

He quirked a brow. "Who's Elias?" His genuine confusion sent a wave of relief for me—I hated to think Elias was involved with this guy in any way.

"The dark-haired guy at the dive shop you were arguing with."

He snorted. "Oh, that dude. What an uptight prick. Whenever I switched out tanks he'd rail on me for parking in front of the shop instead of a spot." He shook his head and spit out blood, the spatters landing on Lani's Converse. I winced a little as her eyes went flinty and the grip on his hair tightened to the point I was certain she'd come away with a handful by the time this was all done.

"That 'prick' is my friend, asshole," she said.

Lani pulled Otis's chain off the ground near Kevin and stared at it for a minute. "Why'd you kill him?" Her voice was soft, but I could tell she was on the knife's edge of losing control.

He spit again. "Bastard threatened to go to the cops if I came back." A sly smile crossed his face. "Wish he would've started there instead of the Coast Guard."

"So, in order to cover your tracks and silence Otis, you beat him over the head and dumped him in the harbor?" Angry tears were starting to fall when I thought what a loss it was to our community. Otis and Paisley brightened the day of everyone they came into contact with.

"That old dude was a lot stronger than he looked. Wilier, too. Had to tie him up just to make sure he didn't pull a Lazarus on me. Fisherman were starting to come in, so I just threw some weights in his pockets and called it good." His face was one of annoyance. "He should've just minded his own business."

Over the whine of wind, I thought I heard the faint sound of sirens in the distance. Soon enough I felt the boat sway and heard a voice call out, "Peterson—you in here?"

"Yep."

Pretty soon a young, good-looking guy roughly a few years older than me cracked open the cabin door, service pistol held at his waist and pointed down.

"This him?" The guy toed Kevin with a booted foot.

Uniformed officers crowded at the doorway, and Lani, Jeff, and I backed out to let them take care of business.

"That was pretty impressive," Jeff remarked to Lani and me, his tone full of admiration.

Lani raised an eyebrow. He gestured toward the cabin. "The way you two handled yourselves! I could use a few people like you on my team."

Team? What team?

"I'm guessing there's a lot more to you than meets the eye." Lani remarked.

He threw her a brilliant, charming smile and leaned in. "I'd love to show you sometime." He even did that subtle bicep flex move.

Cole stepped out onto the deck just then, and we both groaned. "Knock it off, Jeff!"

Lani's face had gone slack, and she leaned forward toward Jeff until I snapped my fingers in front of her face. "Kalani, remember?"

She shook her head like she was clearing cobwebs then smiled weakly at me. "Oh, yeah. Kalani."

Through gritted teeth, Cole ground out, "Don't feel bad—he seems to have that effect on a lot of women." With that he threw a glare my way, but there wasn't any real heat behind it.

"I think once we're done here, we need to have a nice long chat." Jeff looked less than thrilled at my statement, but Cole's dimple peeked out as he nodded.

"Absolutely."

Chapter Thirty Nine

SUMMER

AFTER HPD SHOWED UP, Kevin clammed up faster than a politician on the witness stand. The daggers he threw our way as they led him off the boat promised retribution.

Lani waved cheekily at him and called out, "I always keep my promises."

His face leeched of any color, and he gulped audibly before reaching down to cradle his groin. He made no protest as the officers led him away.

I raised an eyebrow in question.

She shrugged. "I told him I've been hunting all my life, and if he didn't talk I'd flay him open like a pig—starting with his nutsack."

Cole and Jeff instinctively winced and mirrored the same movements as Kevin. Lani grinned unrepentantly. I sure was glad we were on the same side.

After we all finished giving our statements, I saw Cole type something into the arresting officer's phone before they clapped each other on the shoulder and nodded. I made a mental note to grill Cole later about it.

Now, ensconced safely back at my condo with everyone, I listened with increasing trepidation about the man targeting Cole and his old Seal team members.

"So, this guy, Marquez, is on the island?" Fear gripped my heart, thinking Cole might be in danger.

Jeff nodded, his eyes grave. "Thankfully, Cole's so hard to pin down I don't think he's been able to get close."

That reassured me marginally, but that couldn't last forever. "So, what's the plan to catch him?"

He leaned back in the bar stool as I poured a bag of chips and a questionable canister of mac nuts in a bowl. I found the nuts shoved into the very back of the cabinet. Lights flickered, and I wasn't sure how long we'd have power—Waikoloa Village was notorious for losing power during big storms.

Lani and I had skipped lunch, and my stomach sounded like a ten-piece band. Stale nuts and a bag of chips were the best I had to offer. Since Elliot hadn't gotten groceries in a couple of days, our normally well-stocked refrigerator was pitifully bare.

Jeff made a face, then sighed. "Other than the sighting at Punaluu Bakery, I can't get a bead on him. Every time I think I've found him, it turns out to be a dead end." He shook his head. "He's getting better at covering his tracks. Cole, have you noticed any suspicious vehicles following you?"

Cole laughed. "Other than the Shrek Jack sent to shadow me, no."

Cole must've read the confused look on my face. "Shrek means someone who's pretty green, a newbie."

Jeff slumped and ran a hand through his hair. "Well, unless you've seen a grey Tacoma with rust on the front right fender, then I'm out of ideas."

I froze. Out of the corner of my eye, I saw Lani whip her head in my direction. Cole didn't miss a beat.

"Summer, is there something you'd like to share?"

I didn't appreciate his snippy tone. I debated answering, but then Lani cleared her throat in warning. Ugh. If I didn't tell, she would.

"There's been one that matches that description hanging out at the harbor. I've noticed it a few times. I'm pretty sure it's the same truck that rammed me and nearly ran me off the road the other day."

Cole exploded. "What?! Why am I just hearing about this now?"

I put my hand out to stop his tirade. "To be fair, you've been busy with your case, and you seemed really stressed and I didn't want to worry you. Besides, I didn't get a good enough look to give anything more than the barest details, and I didn't feel right bothering you with it."

A muscle in his cheek spasmed, and I could tell the effort to hold back his rant was painful. As I watched, he gradually relaxed, one muscle at a time.

"In the future, I would very much appreciate you informing me of something like this as soon as possible, no matter what."

Jeff's head bounced between Cole and I, an amused look on his face.

I tipped my head in agreement to Cole's request and his nostrils flared, but to his credit he remained silent.

Cole stood to grab a beer and groaned, rubbing a spot on his lower back.

"You okay, old man?" Jeff asked.

Cole wrinkled his nose and threw him the bird.

"Yeah, you had to lean in so close to hear Kevin I thought you'd fall into his lap at any moment." Lani chimed in.

Cole looked confused and then his face lit into a Christmas morning smile as he pulled his truck keys from his pocket. "After my meeting with Chief this morning, Jack was so pissed he forgot to take back his dope listening device."

Cole showed us the button on his collar that was actually a little Bluetooth receiver.

"Dude, that's so cool!"

Cole grinned like a little boy at Jeff. "It sends a recording straight to the app as soon as I activate it. James Bond ain't got nothing on me." He smirked.

Cole's obvious glee was cute. *Men and their gadgets,* I shook my head slightly and smiled to myself.

I reached across the counter and squeezed Cole's hand. "I'm so glad you showed up. Lani and I had things handled, but it sure was nice to have the backup."

"About that..." Jeff pulled out his phone and showed me a video. Of myself, snooping on his boat. Oops.

"Huh. Guess I didn't think about security cameras." I winced and rubbed the back of my neck.

Jeff waited for an explanation, his hands folded on the counter, the picture of patience. He and Cole looked at me with twin expressions of consternation. I shot a look over to Lani, and she lifted her hands palms up and shrugged. *Ugh.*

"Uh, well, here's the thing. You were pretty evasive about what you did for work, and you kept showing up places and making cryptic statements." I shrugged, hands out. "After looking at the pictures on Otis's iPhone, I figured you were a probable candidate for the role of villain."

Lani covered her mouth to keep from laughing outright, and Jeff's lips were twitching. "Villain, huh?" He looked almost...pleased. "My cover must've worked pretty well after all."

At one point during the evening the power went out and I suggested Jeff and Lani stay the night. It didn't take too much convincing on Jeff's part. I think he was glad to be around people after being alone so much.

Lani, on the other hand, wanted to go check on Mack in the worst way. He texted her at one point and ordered her to stay put, so she took Elliot's bed and Jeff took the fold-out couch.

Cole and I lay snuggled into each other, enjoying being together. "This feels nice," I remarked.

Cole pulled me deeper into the spoon of his body. As I wiggled my bottom to get closer, he chuffed out a laugh. "Yes, it does."

My lips twisted into a wry grin. "Not that." I reconsidered. "Okay, a little that. But what I meant was having everyone here. I know you've been busy with your case and Elliot's so wrapped in TJ, I haven't seen him much. It gets a little lonely."

I'd grown up an only child being shuffled between my mom and dad's houses every other week, and both of my parents worked full-time, so I was on my own a fair amount. Living with

Elliot was the first time I'd had a consistent friend around, and I liked it. Alot.

"I'm sorry I haven't been around as much lately." Something in Cole's tone caught my attention and I craned my neck around to look at him.

He kissed my nose and said, "This thing, with Chief." His warm breath came out in a gust and caused the little hairs on my forehead to dance. "It's not exactly over."

I turned in his arms to look at him more fully. "What does that mean?"

He searched my eyes and then lowered his gaze. "I'm going to have to do some stuff. Go deep." His eyes went hard. "I might have to be gone more than usual."

Regret unfurled between us. Whatever Cole had to do weighed heavily on him.

He pulled me in closer. "The HPD Officer's Ball is coming up, and I would love for you to come with me."

The sudden shift in topic startled me, but I responded, "Of course I'll go with you."

He blew out a breath. "It's black tie." The misery on his face as he said that caused me to smile.

"You'll look so dashing in your tux. We might have to play a little James Bond/Honey Rider afterwards."

His lips twitched as he replied, "Only if you're wearing a bikini. It doesn't have to be white though-that red one will do." He leered at me wolfishly, and I tickled him between the ribs, eliciting a grin and some wandering hands.

He snuggled my head against his shoulder. "I'm not sure how long the investigation will take." I heard in his voice how much he hated this whole business with the Chief, and how ready he was for it to be over.

I lifted both of my arms and cradled his face. "Then we're just going to have to make the most of the time we have together."

I kissed him deeply, and we made the night count in a way we'd never had to before.

Chapter Forty

COLE

Monday morning dawned clear and bright, the remnants of Hurricane Luisa only evident from the debris on the ground, the sky as far as the eye could see was a soft baby blue with not a cloud to be found.

Summer and I spent the weekend together and I treasured every second. Friday night we, along with Jeff, Lani, her boyfriend Kalani, and several other friends met at the Fairmont Orchid to cheer Elliot on in the cocktail contest.

He came in second; the winner wowed the judges with an ube coconut concoction with homemade syrup. Judging from the smile on Elliot's face as TJ hugged him openly, I don't think he cared much about coming in first anyhow.

The following day, we headed down to the harbor and had a memorial for Otis Hawaii-style. Cars were jammed into every available patch of ground and people milled around a memorial some of the fisherman had made for Otis.

Summer and I along with close to a hundred other people showed up on paddleboards and formed a flotilla out into the open water to scatter his ashes along with a mix of hibiscus and plumeria petals.

Mack led the charge, Paisley the goat sitting calmly on his board, her pink tiara glinting in the bright sun. She seemed to understand the solemnity of the moment and even bowed her head as we formed a giant circle and began chanting.

In the parking lot afterwards, people were tailgating and talking story about Otis and all the memories they had of him.

"Remember when Otis came over and helped us pull the boat onto the trailer after I forgot to put the plug in and flooded the bilge?" one man, his face like worn leather, asked.

A couple of men around him murmured in agreement.

"My favorite was watching him when the keiki would crowd around begging to pet Paisley. She stood there like a queen amongst her peasants. Otis never rushed any of them." The woman's voice was tinged with amusement.

"Uncle kept an eye out for us when we had to live in the car for a while," a girl who looked to be in her mid-twenties with long, black hair cascading down her back, said. "He brought us food and water sometimes and even watched Robby when I went on a job interview."

Something that struck me then was just how much the people here cared. Otis showed up with a love and respect for the land and the people, and the community embraced him.

That's what it's like living here, I mused. When you come with an open, helping heart and resolve to make a difference, the island responds in kind with aloha. There were very few dry eyes that I could see, and I hoped that someday my actions would have the same impact.

Now, as I stood in front of the entrance to HPD, I braced myself knowing I was becoming something I hated—a liar. I'd already kept too many secrets, skirted the edges of truth far more than I ever had before. A part of me worried this thing with Takada was turning me into the very thing I abhorred.

Pushing through the door, I took in a deep breath and smiled tightly at a uniformed officer as they passed me.

Before I'd even had a chance to set my bag down Chief's voice called out, "Peterson, my office."

I closed my eyes briefly, hoping to find the courage to pull off the deception awhile longer.

When I entered the office, Chief was sitting behind his desk, hands folded on top.

"Shut the door."

I complied and then sat in the chair across from him, mentally steeling myself.

Silence sat between us like a living thing. Finally, he spoke. "Do you have any idea what you've done?"

Stupidly I hadn't connected with Jack to figure out a long-term means of recording, and I realized belatedly I'd left my phone and key fob in the bag on my desk. None of this conversation would be recorded, and I could tell Takada had something big on his mind.

He leaned forward, keeping his voice pitched low. "You and your little girlfriend took down one of my main players." His eyes were hard and mean. "I'm beginning to think you're trying to sabotage my operation."

Surprise, real surprise washed over my face. I'd had no inkling Kevin had any connection to Chief, but now as I thought about it, it made perfect sense.

Takada studied me like a snake studies its prey.

"Chief, I honestly had no idea." I did my best to keep my voice steady. Frustration roared through me that I didn't have any way to record this conversation. Takada had just admitted to working in consort with a murderous drug runner.

Acid burned a hole in my gut, Takada's words echoing in my head.

"Silva was setting up to score big, but that old homeless guy caught him." Takada snorted. "Not like it was any loss to society when he got taken out." He sighed. "But Silva had a knack for choosing the most unreliable help to get the boats over here from the other islands." He tsked. "I warned him if he picked wrong, they'd eat up profits and blow the mission, but he wouldn't listen." He turned his cold, reptilian eyes back to me. "Because you already turned in evidence, there's nothing more I can do for him without risking my own neck."

His confession knocked me back on my heels, but I had to pretend to admire him for his cleverness and act contrite that I had any part in interfering with it.

A thought occurred to me. "What if he rolls on you?"

Takada's expression chilled me to the core as he replied, "Bad things happen to snitches. Especially in prison." He shook his head. "Silva's greedy, but not stupid."

By the time I left his office, the acid had worked its way up into my throat, coating it so thoroughly I didn't think I'd be able to speak.

"How ya doing, buddy?" Jonah grinned at me. "That back-side of yours sore?"

In no mood for his jokes, I spun my head and stared him down.

My cell phone buzzed, and I saw I had a voicemail from the realtor. She must've called while I was getting reamed by Chief.

"Mr. Peterson, I think I found the perfect home for you. It's not set to go on the market until next month, but the owner is an old friend and gave me the go-ahead to show it to a few select clients." Her voice was bright and overly sunny, like most realtors I'd ever talked to.

Summer's words came to mind about loving having a family of people around, and I admit a little ripple of anticipation went through me.

I called the realtor back and set up a time to do a walk-through. Despite my ongoing battle to get Takada off the force, I sensed something bigger and better on the horizon. In spite of everything, I smiled, then whistled my way out of the department to go get my girl and look at a house.

THE END

*Sign Up for My Newslet-
ter for More Barefoot
Cozy Mystery Fun!*

Acknowledgements

Writing any book requires focus, time, coffee (lots of coffee!), and support from friends and family. Well, I hit the lottery with the people in my circle—from my hubby who's my biggest cheerleader and tells perfect strangers about his "wife the writer," to my oldest daughter who's always down to beta read my trash pile of a first draft, to my youngest who is always waiting for the next book, to my middle who humors me when I blab on and on about my current work in progress.

Not to mention my amazing friends who cheer me on and support me through the messy middle and looming deadlines. Stacy Garrett, thank you for your relentless cheerleading, Jessica Belshe, thank you for being my book bestie and the best sidekick ever, and Shea McCloud, thank you for meeting me for coffee and putting up with my relentless questions!

To all of my fellow Ink and Aura Writers Group peeps-thank you so much for showing up each month and for all your love and support.

To my editor extraordinaire, Bryn Donovan, I'm so grateful for your advice, support, and little notes of encouragement before the big slash!

Finally, thank you so very much to you, dear reader, for picking up this book and spending your valuable time getting lost in my little world! Your support, encouragement, and kind words mean the world to me and keep me going on even the darkest days! I have so much fun creating these stories and I'm so grateful that you come along for the ride!

Ocean Cosmos Cocktail

This is the recipe Elliot entered in the cocktail contest. Sweet, creamy, and with a nutty finish you'll never even realize you've tipped over the edge into bad decision territory... :-)

2 oz. Blue Caracao

1 oz. Coconut Cream

1 oz. Macadamia Nut liquor

Splash of pineapple juice

Mix all ingredients and then pour into a cocktail shaker with ice. Strain into your favorite cocktail glass and maybe stab a few chunks of pineapple with a cocktail sword thingie and throw it in for vibes! Bonus points if you wear an eye patch while drinking and randomly insert a "Yarrrr!" into conversation every once in a while...

About the author

Christine Wellert is a writer, mother of three humans and several canines, wife to her high school sweetheart, Registered Nurse, and author of the Barefoot Sleuth Cozy Mysteries, set on the Big Island of Hawaii.

While Christine has spent most of her adult life working in the medical field, her true passion and love (aside from her family and friends) is reading, writing, and drinking coffee (and not always in that order...). Interested in all things metaphysical and woowoo, she weaves aspects of those into all her stories.

Christine studied creative writing in college and enjoys creating characters and stories that encourage and empower readers. She splits her time between the Pacific Northwest and Hawaii. When not chained to her keyboard, you can find Christine hiking, skiing, scuba diving, or traveling.

If you'd like to chat, you can find me on the links below or scan the QR code to go directly to my website:

Instagram- @christinewellertauthor
Facebook- christinewellertauthor
TikTok- @christinewellertauthor
Website- www.ChristineWellert.com

Your honest review will help future readers decide if they want to take a chance on a new-to-them author. If you loved the book and have a few minutes, I'd love for you to review my book.

You can also sign up for my monthly newsletter on my website, which is full of updates on works in progress, life, and pictures of cute animals and nature, as well as some occasional surprise goodies! And if you liked the book and really want to help a sister out, I would be so thankful (and maybe even send you homemade cookies) if you could write a review on Goodreads.com, Bookbub, Amazon, or wherever you typically leave reviews.

This really helps get my book in front of more people so they can share in the zany fun!

This book is dedicated to Hawaii and all of the beautiful friends and ohana I've made since moving there. Thank you for accepting me into your hearts- I hope I make you proud!

www.ingramcontent.com/pod-product-compliance
Lightning Source LLC
Chambersburg PA
CBHW031118160726
47991CB00004B/1445